Nightshade

REG GADNEY

HEINEMANN : LONDON

William Heinemann Ltd
10 Upper Grosvenor Street, London W1X 9PA

LONDON   MELBOURNE
JOHANNESBURG   AUCKLAND

First published 1987
Copyright © Passy International Limited 1987

British Library Cataloguing in Publication Data

Gadney, Reg
 Nightshade.
 I. Title
 823'.914 [F]   PR6057.A294
 ISBN 0 434 27789 4

Photoset by Deltatype, Ellesmere Port
Printed in Great Britain by
Billing & Sons Ltd.,
Worcester

For A.B.Z.G. and B.B-W., with love.

Secrecy is as indispensable to human beings as fire, and as greatly feared. Both enhance and protect life, yet both can stifle, lay waste, spread out of all control.

Sissela Bok
Secrets

1

On the last day of his life Richard Wigart kept an appointment he ought to have avoided.

The telephone woke him at sunrise in his apartment near the Parque del Retiro. The first chill air of Madrid's approaching winter had brought stiffness to the old bones of the secret agent. He took some time to walk into the living room. It would either be the Embassy or London. They were the only people who knew that you called early to get him at home. By day he'd be unobtainable somewhere in the city. At night the brandy meant he ignored the telephone altogether.

The man on the telephone said he was a 'friend'. He had an agreeable voice and spoke of 'routine matters'. He called Wigart 'Dickie' and proposed a rendezvous at the lakeside café in the Parque del Retiro. 'More convenient for you than the Embassy,' he added. 'I don't want to bother Smith. He's got enough on his plate already.' That was fine with Wigart who'd never taken to Smith anyway. The 'friend' said he'd be carrying Fodor's guide, *Madrid*. Wigart said he'd carry a copy of *Die Zeit*. There'd be no mistaken identities.

At first, it worried him that the friend had given no name. Yet it was the modern way to be careful what you said on the telephone even in the new Madrid of Juan Carlos. Nowadays, you could breach good manners and get away with mild discourtesies in the interest of security.

On the other hand, agents, like card-sharps, play their hands in many different ways. Just because a friend didn't give his name it didn't mean you panicked. Richard Wigart never flapped. He passed the morning in keen anticipation of the meeting. It was good to feel you were still wanted and that the friends still called him up. He assumed today's visitor would require what all the others had asked for recently: more, as

1

their jargon had it, 'follow-up detail' to the report he had written on the historical background to the Anglo-American intelligence alliance. Its renegotiation was in the air. 'Not before time,' he intended to tell his visitor as he'd told the others. He liked the chance to comment on the value of the past to the new people London sent. It was good to rake over old and not quite dead operations. They picked his brain for secrets and he picked theirs discreetly in return for London gossip. Some secrets, to the right people for reasons he considered to be right, he was prepared to pass on. Others, even to the right people, he never mentioned. Best to keep a few things up one's sleeve. He'd keep his own counsel, offering his young visitors the occasional irrelevant glimpse of his past as a diversion. Or, he'd make a charming apology: 'Loss of memory. Age. I dare say it's in Archives. Try the St Anne's Gate basement.' Then he'd be told once again that Archives were being weeded mercilessly and what was left from the old days was being unceremoniously carted out of London to some dismal warehouse somewhere in the light industrial wasteland near Heathrow. 'I'm better off over here,' he'd say.

That was his view of his existence in Madrid. He loved the city to the same degree he disliked the England of the late 1980s. He'd given England, or as he'd heard the Queen preferred it to be called, Great Britain, a try in the first days of his retirement. He very soon discovered it wasn't the sympathetic haven for elderly bachelors he'd hoped it would be. His London club had been amalgamated with another and was noisy in the evenings. The committee had even redesigned the tie. The cricket had turned violent. There were too many non-playing members of MCC. Old men in his beloved London parks were in danger of being confronted at knife-point by children demanding money. When he'd been a boy in London it was the old men you feared in the parks. Even old women were being advised to watch out for rapists. So he settled his affairs in London for the last time and came back to Madrid knowing he was home.

None the less, there were days when he felt the isolation. He supposed the new people in the Service had gradually given up on him. He'd always thought of himself as a secret servant. The new men thought of themselves as building-bricks in a career structure. They had to find a slot in the edifice before middle age. They'd be passed over unless they came back from the field to headquarters at Century House. But the very few remaining agents who'd joined during or shortly after the war had never wanted to leave the field for that. Some had left the Service altogether for one or other of the smaller City banks, for soft administrative jobs at Oxford or Cambridge, for obscure positions in even more obscure royal societies or charities. One or two even ended up in the Royal Household. Wigart was a dinosaur: sitting it out in the field in retirement, a creature of eccentricity with an unusually useful memory and little else. If that was what the new people thought – let them think it. He didn't care. He still had a secret tucked away that could surprise the pants off the new people; he still had a few people's skeletons in his cupboard. He could still take out the odd bone and change a bit of history. So they still came back to Madrid to search him out. Like the friend he set out to meet late that afternoon.

He took the usual precaution of turning up in the Retiro park fifteen minutes early with a view to spotting the man first.

Even at this stage in his life, there was the nasty chance an old score might be settled. A small flash of anxiety suggested he might have been wiser to have brought a hand-gun. After all, in many years of secret service he'd been responsible for more than thirty men's deaths. Revenge was taken when you least expected it. The wind rose sharply and filled his eyes with dust. For a moment he was blinded. When, at last he managed to focus his stinging eyes he saw the deadline had passed. It was a bad omen.

After an hour of waiting the wind was followed by the rain. It drove the *mamas, papas y ninos* scuttling homewards from the park.

Wigart dabbed his eyes with his handkerchief. Blowing his nose he saw a *nino* shriek with delight: a horse chestnut branch had fallen on *mama*'s head. She aimed a slap at the child and missed. Wigart smiled inwardly at the *mama*'s loss of face; authority eroded by embarrassment had more than once formed a part of his war too. His anxiety temporarily subsided. He found himself a table at the lakeside café.

The friend was very late.

Rain splashed into his coffee. He uncrossed his long thin legs, slowly got to his feet and tucked *Die Zeit* beneath his arm.

Limping painfully, he began to drag the metal chair and table to a drier spot beneath the trees. Almost there he saw a waitress, plump and motherly, swaying past the empty tables towards him, her arms outstretched with an offer of assistance.

'Muchas gracias.' The thanks were a gentle warning. His slow smile hid his irritation. He hated to think people felt he needed help and smiled at her with the defiance of the disabled. The waitress, like the others who'd left earlier, watched him with increasing curiosity. And he hadn't much liked that either. He supposed the women had been speculating about his nationality. Eventually they'd given up the game, defeated, as he'd hoped, by the appearance of the ordinariness he had cultivated all his life. Perhaps they were bored at the end of the long day with the few end-of-season customers.

The waitress flicked the rain from the table and walked back to the shelter of the kiosk.

There's the fail-safe, Wigart thought. The friend had mentioned the other place, the Florida beyond the park, where especially the Germans liked to eat, drink and dance. He'd agreed to the Florida with mild reluctance. It was a tourists' place and held no appeal. For him the face of tourism had long since turned old and ugly.

Regretfully he folded his *Die Zeit* and stuffed it into his coat pocket.

The motherly waitress followed his departure with a look of pity. Perhaps she should have suggested she buy him a glass of *horchata* on the Paseo de Recoltos. For when he refused her offer of help to move the table and chair she decided he was an English gentleman. He was charmingly obstinate and because he limped and carried no stick she reckoned he was also vain. Therefore English. And English gentlemen of his generation had a reputation for liking *horchata*. The milky drink made from tiger nuts was said to be an aphrodisiac.

She watched him limp away with the newspaper sticking out of his coat pocket. The vast blue coat engulfed him. Years ago he'd probably have filled it out. She could tell it must have cost him a lot of money.

She found he'd left her a sizeable tip on the table. Its generosity wasn't surprising. The lonely always made the best tippers. She set about closing up the café for the night. Perhaps

4

he'd be back tomorrow. If so, she decided, she'd definitely propose *horchata*. She peered after him one last time into the darkness. But he'd already vanished.

He walked stooping through the rain in the darkness towards the Florida. He'd have much preferred to be at home in the faded grubby elegance of his small apartment. For him the perfect evening meal was a brandy and a plate of scrambled eggs covered with a great deal of freshly ground pepper. Afterwards, a fresh peach, not quite ripe. Another brandy. The BBC World Service on his radio. Then to bed with the stories of Robert Louis Stevenson and another brandy. This was his idea of how the British exile could best deal with solitude. And, of course, the telephone unanswered.

He was alert to the misnomer, fail-safe: it usually meant danger. The flood-lit trees around the Florida, the garish dance floor, the lights beneath the canopy, all drew him like a moth. But he'd long since learned to live with all the vagaries and uncertainties of the secret life. They'd kept his love for it alight. There was no insurance to be taken out against the invisible assailant, against the untoward moments the Service cynics called acts of God. There was always comfort to be found in darkness and so he stood deep in the shadows of the trees looking for the signs of the friend. The old excitement came back. It was a heady drug offering relief for the pain that gnawed his spine and hips.

Heavy with the rain, the trees creaked above him. He peered at the dance floor and the Spanish couple in national costume strutting their exaggerated flamenco steps. It was a poor sort of show. The man was bald with a red face and dark glasses. His beer gut wobbled pathetically out of rhythm. His rat-faced partner compensated for her lack of artistry with grimaces. She had gold-filled teeth. The display ended and Wigart joined in the desultory applause. He watched Madrileños and a group of elderly Germans begin a samba. One of the huge women raised her fatty arms above her head and clapped violently. Wigart noticed the great rings of sweat stain beneath the armpits of her livid green silk blouse.

He turned away.

His eyes caught the glare of the flood-lights on the trees that shone down on the copy of Fodor's *Madrid*. The table was empty. A waiter had just removed an empty beer tumbler. He

5

was leafing through the empty guide book, looking about, wondering whether perhaps to pocket it for himself. He seemed about to lift it on to his small tray.

'Wigart?'

The calm voice came from behind. He recognised it at once.

But he kept on peering ahead at the book and the German samba dancers and the phoney awful grins of the men in the dance band. He didn't turn. Another sign of the veteran secret servant. Wait for the second time your name is spoken. Then turn.

'Wigart.'

'You're very late.'

He turned as he spoke. The movement sent a spasm of pain from the base of his spine all the way down his legs. The figure reached out from the darkness of the trees and pulled him close. The old Englishman's head was gripped with increasing ferocity. He could smell the nervous odour of the man's breath. He felt the gloved hands, the heavy black shoes. In the old days when he still had teeth he'd have sunk them into his attacker's flesh. Punctured the artery at the wrist. Wound up his lean frame and jerked a knee between the legs to crush the genitals. Savaged the shins with the metal heels of his shoes.

The samba rhythm beat out faster.

His body refused to follow the instructions for counter-attack. The strength had gone.

He fought to steady his feet on the slippery grass. Hopeless-ness engulfed him. He was sinking down and there was nothing he could do to resist the force of the attacker's pressure. He felt his face being squeezed from his skull.

His dentures fell out of his mouth.

The pain in his nerves and blood vessels behind his ears and in his neck was excruciating.

On the dance stage the band leader kissed the fat German in the green silk on both cheeks.

'*Zieh's aus*!' rose the cry. 'Take it off!'

'*Nimm's unter!*' 'Pull it down!'

The bandleader's hand clutched at the massive buttocks. '*Küss sie auf dem Mund*!' 'Kiss her on the mouth! Kiss her on the mouth!'

She bared her yellow teeth.

'*Mach's schön!*' 'Get on with it!' '*Get on with it!*' rose the chant.

The drummer slammed the cymbals. They clanged out to the dark and yellowish city night sky.

Three minutes later Richard Wigart died.

2

'Yobs.'

It was a cheap shot.

Delivered by Javier Guerra Salcedo in a second-floor office of the British Embassy at 16 Calle de Fernando el Santo, it was received with a shrug by the Visa Officer, Smith. The police officer, Salcedo, had arrived at the Embassy expecting to see the Ambassador. Geared up to be as awkward and as rude as possible – he had lost a cousin when the *Belgrano* went down off the Falklands – Salcedo had made it his business to bash the Brits at every opportunity.

'Is that a Spanish expression?' Smith asked languidly. 'Or do you mean "jobs"? I'm not sure I entirely follow you, Inspector.'

No matter Salcedo wasn't an inspector. Who cared about the niceties of rank in the Spanish police? What mattered was that the *Policia Judicial*, Madrid's version of the CID, that bitter and demoralised bunch of thicks, hadn't got a clue why Richard Wigart had been found dead in the Parque del Retiro. Salcedo, a police officer with pretensions towards expertise in sociological tendencies, told the Visa Officer his force was sick up to here with British thugs in Madrid and right across the nation. 'We say animals,' he said in passable English. 'You call them yobs.'

'What are you trying to tell me?' said Smith. 'Mr Wigart was a victim of British football hooligans, drunken tourists or something?'

Salcedo replied in Spanish: 'He was mugged. Beaten up. He was an old man.'

'Age has nothing to do with it. He was a British subject.'

Sod that, the police officer commented in silence. He turned the ugly gold ring on his finger. He said: 'We took the pains to identify him, Mister Smith. We found his dental plate, his *Spanish* dental plate, the work of a distinguished *Spanish* dental surgeon.'

'You're telling me you intend to close the investigation?'

'I am telling you we have already closed it, Mister Smith.' He produced the dirty remnants of a partially smoked cigarette from the top pocket of his jacket. 'Do you have a lighter?'

Smith pointed to the notice beside the photograph of the Queen. THANK YOU FOR NOT SMOKING. It infuriated Salcedo. 'There will be papers which require your signature.'

'Mail them to me here. Enclose a stamped addressed envelope for their return.'

'We do not provide free mailing services for foreign embassies.'

'In that case I can't promise you'll get them back, Officer. Sorry.'

'So am I,' Salcedo said, flouncing out.

After tea, Visa Officer Smith, in truth the Madrid Embassy's resident officer of SIS, signalled his headquarters at Century House in London. WIGART DEATH INVESTIGATION CLOSED. He asked his secretary if she'd mind disposing of the cigarette butt the Spanish police officer had dropped on the floor. She'd find a pack of Kleenex in the top drawer of his desk. 'Cigarette butts are deadly.'

When the new generation SIS officers in London tried to cancel Richard Wigart's memorial service it was a sign the old guard's day had gone for ever. The old boy's life had been a rare model of loyal, if not always conventional, duty to several Majesties' governments and their nominally United Kingdom. But the New Minds, as they enjoyed being called, had no time for what they saw as irrelevant gestures of remembrance. They hadn't even been able to write Dickie's obituary for *Intelligence Newsletter*, Century House's monthly journal, that is part in-house news-sheet, part old-school magazine. They finally persuaded old Geoffrey Hackett to write something. The two men had been recruited shortly after the outbreak of the Second War in the same year.

'*One was always dated by Dickie*,' Hackett wrote at the start of his piece. The remark raised a smirk on the faces of the New Minds who were sick to death of hearing about the donnish old spies in fact and fiction. Even Wigart's solicitor, Teyte, received a rough ride from the New Minds when he explained some of the deceased's specific instructions in the will. They were baffled by Wigart's request that SIS arrange the traditional memorial service, not in the usual church, St James's, Piccadilly, but rather in, of all places, the British Embassy Church of St George, in Madrid. Twenty years ago the SIS Executive would have followed Wigart's instructions without a murmur. In those days British spies, as they were fond of saying to each other, paid scant honour to the living but a very great deal to the dead. Those were the days when duty included doing things that were considered 'good form'. Even the phrase itself was no longer common currency in the Service. Some said it had fallen into disuse when headquarters went south of the river. Whatever the reason, the spirit of chivalry and good manners had withered. Dickie Wigart's request was thought to be a nuisance, a bore and as out of date at Century House as pin-striped suits. And God help anyone who turned up in a bowler.

It was at a Thursday morning executive meeting, under Any Other Business, that the Wigart memorial service came up. The Director, Chayter, asked his colleagues for their views. The main objection came from Ms Boden-Smith, Finance Director. She summoned the spectre of the Security and Intelligence Co-ordination Services Inspectorate who had already cut back on overseas travel (Welfare). Boden-Smith, a bull-dog woman, only daughter of a former lieutenant-colonel in the Coldstream, rarely snapped at the Director from her own kennel. She preferred to hint vaguely at a higher authority. Another member of the Executive, the Indian Mehta, a remote cousin of the Gandhis, collected up his papers, assuming Linda Boden-Smith had won the day.

'We are sending a delegation to Madrid,' Chayter told her quietly. 'That's what Wigart asked. My wife and I, the Newistons, Mahon and Geoffrey Hackett, who'll give the address. The Chaplain's taking the service. We're also inviting Lou Finucane and his wife plus some French, Spaniards, Germans. John Mahon will supervise the arrangements.'

'You'll have to clear a request for Finucane through their Embassy,' said Mehta. 'Or are the Yankees waiving their veto on getting in touch with retired officers?'

'Mahon will see to it,' said Chayter. 'With Smith in Madrid.'

'This is a frightful waste of time, Director,' said Boden-Smith. 'Even if the old boy's will covers expenses, what about the man-hours?'

'It'll be at a weekend,' said Chayter. Sensing he could now deliver his *coup de grâce* he smiled coldly into Boden-Smith's narrow eyes. 'Dickie Wigart died a very rich man. He's bequeathed a hundred and fifty thousand to the Family and Dependants Trust on condition, strictly on condition, the memorial service takes place as he described it. So suppose that the Trustees of the F and DT hear we haven't met the requirements of the will, that we've forfeited a hundred and fifty thousand pounds. . . ?' He paused. 'The Lord Chancellor is a Trustee. And so is the wife of the former Foreign Secretary. I dined with them both last Monday. They are rather pleased by the prospect of a windfall.'

'It's time we buried history,' Boden-Smith muttered to herself.

'Your time will come, Linda, I have no doubt,' said Chayter. 'I have said we'll take the money. And that is that.'

The morning meeting was at an end.

Chayter asked Henry Newiston to stay behind.

'What the hell's biting her?' Chayter asked him. Invariably it was H. Newiston, the ascetic Old Etonian, the Director turned to when Boden-Smith was at her most aggressive. He was a Chayter-man, equally devoted to the Service. Also he had a foot in the past. His father had served in the Service during the Second World War and survived its chaotic post-war years. Newiston's father had been an office and corridor man, an officer of compromise.

Newiston shrugged. 'Someone has to tie up the loose ends of Dickie's world. It'd better be you. After all, he was a friend of your father's. Go to Madrid. Speak to Smith. Then bring down the blinds on the whole bloody thing.'

Chayter had always read Boden-Smith's mind more successfully than he cared to admit. He knew she shared his dislike for the old days of SIS, its clubbable spirit, the air of quasi-masonic secrecy for its own sake, its familial squabbles. What she enjoyed, like Chayter, was power which wasn't publicly accountable. It galled her she could see the merit of Chayter grabbing funds whenever he could find them. SIS, like every

British institution, needed cash to keep up with the necessities of self-preservation.

Had she won her point that morning, had she succeeded in achieving the cancellation of Dickie Wigart's memorial service in Madrid she might, inadvertently, have prevented the catastrophe it generated.

Some people were surprised Newiston went to Madrid to 'tidy-up' after Wigart's death. Wasn't that Smith's job? Then it became clear that Smith had botched things up.

There was a chilling confrontation in the embassy on Calle de Fernando el Santo.

'Smith, why didn't you, personally, tidy up the old boy's files?'

'His secretary knew him much better than I did.'

'She's over eighty, isn't she?'

'I didn't ask her age.'

'What a pity,' Newiston said. 'Then perhaps you wouldn't have summoned a half-blind Spanish widow crippled with arthritis to sift through secret material.'

'She told me she'd been engaged on the task for years.'

'At her age, in her condition, I'd say that wasn't entirely astonishing, wouldn't you?'

Smith offered no comment.

'And the personal effects in his flat?' Newiston asked. 'What really happened?'

'She said a maid had gone in and tidied up. She was from a domestic agency Wigart sometimes used.'

'Why didn't you bother to find out whether anything's missing?'

'I don't know. There wasn't an inventory.'

'I'm not asking you whether there was a confounded inventory. Did you, Smith, enquire whether anyone, the maid, the secretary or anyone else might have found anything missing?'

'I didn't go to the flat.'

'Yes or no, Smith?'

'No.'

'Well, Smith, I did. It looked as though the maid had been unusually diligent. The whole place had been gone through with the greatest care. It was a professional job.'

'She was a professional maid.'

'You don't need to tell me how the bloody woman earned her living.'

Smith pulled out a drawer of his filing cabinet. 'Wigart's secretary told me she had been asked to crate everything up and send it to London. To his solicitors in Mayfair. I have their address.'

'Forget it, I know Teyte's address.'

'Ah,' said Smith. 'Well?'

' "Well?" – you ask. Well, you might. And you've got no proper report from the local police.'

'They're not very co-operative.'

'I don't suppose it'll surprise you to learn,' Newiston told him, 'that they say exactly the same thing about you.'

'I was trying to make contact with the few remaining agents Wigart knew.'

'London's already done so.'

Smith sucked his teeth: 'I'm sorry about all this. I did everything I thought best in the circumstances.'

'Your best isn't very good, is it?'

'One tries.'

'Try harder, Smith. There's always room for improvement even in a God-forsaken posting like Madrid. It's just as well Dickie didn't die in the line of duty. Never forget that even the Soviets use the odd mugger now and again. There's a lot of it about.'

Smith looked sheepish: 'Is there anything else you want me to do?'

'No. That's it. The matter's closed. The one thing I do congratulate you upon is the planning this end for the memorial service. I dare say, if all else fails for you, Lambeth Palace will find a cranny for you.'

Smith tried to laugh and failed completely. He offered to drive Newiston to the airport.

'I'll make my own way there,' Newiston said. 'If you'll see to my petty cash claims.'

'Of course,' said Smith. He checked Newiston's receipts scrupulously against the very neatly written claim sheet. He couldn't find a single fault.

He opened the safe and handed over the money.

'Don't take everything I've said too much to heart,' Newiston said, with an open grin.

'I won't.' Smith said. He could see why the majority of the Service said you couldn't help liking Henry.

Kirsty Newiston was bored with Henry. That, she felt, was the trouble. She no longer loved him, he just bored her. She was a reluctant party to the free-loading in Madrid and Henry's casual suggestion it would give them another chance to mend their marriage.

During the flight from London, Chayter asked her to go and sit with his wife so he could talk to Henry. They changed seats.

Lizzie Chayter talked loudly about examination results at Eton. 'The success rate has gone up over the last twelve months the same number of percentage points as the price of London property.'

Kirsty wasn't listening. She watched her husband huddled up with Chayter like a schoolboy conspirator on a jaunt. This invitation to Wigart's memorial service in Madrid was just another empty gesture of devotion to the Service. It had nothing to do with mending the marriage. She tried to remember when it was he'd said she had the sort of beauty that shone through even when she hadn't washed her hair. Typically, Henry had explained himself by listing what he described as her advantages: one, wide blue eyes with long lashes; two, generous lips; three, prominent cheek-bones; four, prominent breasts. 'Everything's prominent,' he said like a man from the counties admiring a horse. 'Basically, it's all there. The hair only needs a brush. You have a prominent sort of sex appeal.' She'd found his list a compliment. Too late, she discovered Henry only noticed her in terms of faults. Her resentment grew steadily more acute. She realised 'prominence' was, after all, an insult.

Lizzie Chayter had got on to her son's chances of getting into Oxford. 'If they don't take him we're thinking of Harvard or Yale. Granny'll stump up.'

'Yes,' Kirsty said with a look of wonder.

'She can't take it with her.'

'Quite right.'

'I wish we'd thought of asking Dickie to be godfather. He was loaded.'

It was insufferable.

Kirsty began to rehearse the opening moves for a terminal

row. She'd open fire when they got to the hotel room at the Ritz.

'The trouble about Madrid,' Lizzie prattled on, 'is the shopping. You can get everything you need in London or Paris. Except of course that terribly nice black soap.'

'Yes,' Kirsty said, shutting out the flow of useless information.

After midnight, alone in the hotel room, she waited for Henry to come to bed.

Terrible Spanish television programmes offered her no diversion. For want of anything better to do she unpacked the suitcases. Henry had bought a bottle of champagne at the Heathrow Duty Free. If he was boozing with Chayter and fatty Boden-Smith in the hotel bar then she'd drink the champagne alone. And he'd brought a present for her. So she opened that as well. It was a tacky nylon nightie. Henry had bought her a black one once before from the pages of a mail-order catalogue he'd seen advertised in the *Observer* small ads. This one was purple with a feathered hem. She was damned if she was going to dress up for him like a tart. If he'd bought it for his own pleasure then she'd tell him to wear it himself. If this was the pathetic reward for playing wifey to the man who might become the next Deputy Director she wasn't going to play.

She sat talking to herself in front of the bedroom mirror.

'If you'd face me. Show just a glimmer of passion. Your eyes are dead. It's everything that makes you so beloved of Chayter that bores me.'

She wished there was someone else: someone she could have an affair with, without calling down the full force of the Service's retribution. It came down heavily against those of its own kind who wandered from its paths of acceptable behaviour. She remembered what Henry had told her the night at the Savoy when he'd asked her to marry him. 'The Service is a marriage, a British institution. Leaving it is like divorce. There's a price to pay. The half-life of the socially excluded. The trouble is that it's the wives who come off worst.' She reckoned she'd been too much in love to heed the warning. She'd found it a turn-on to be engaged to a man at what he called 'the centre of things'. She thought it no bad thing to marry a man who was 'something in the Foreign Office'. The six diamond engagement ring seemed ample compensation in advance.

'Something in the Foreign *Service*,' he'd corrected her.

'If you're a servant that puts me one up on you,' she'd replied.

She switched off the lights and got into bed.

It wasn't long before Henry came into the room.

'Are you awake?' he whispered.

She pretended to be asleep.

3

Next morning in the sunshine, the unusual congregation assembled outside the British Embassy Church of Saint George on Calle de Nunez de Balboa.

The British arrived first.

They stood in silence on the pavement. The door in the red brick wall to the church's courtyard was locked. A small workman's canvas hut had been erected in the street. Stencilled on the canvas was COMPANIA TELEFONICA NACIONAL DE ESPANA.

A voice whispered behind Kirsty: 'Think they want to bug Geoffrey's eulogy?'

She turned to find herself staring into the face of John Robert Mahon with his untidy red hair and awkward charm, the most junior of the British delegation.

'If the church doesn't open up we'll have to hold the thing in the hut,' he said, his face grey with a hangover.

'Maybe they'll give us tea and buns,' she replied.

The others were watching the arrival of the French and Germans in their embassy limousines. The chief of Spain's intelligence service turned up in his own car, a large cream convertible Mercedes Benz. Its stereo blared out Gustav Mahler's *Greatest Hits*.

In the middle of the formal introductions the door in the brick wall was opened by the Assistant Chaplain. 'If you'd like to come in now. . .'

The spies and the British wives followed the Assistant Chaplain inside. In the courtyard, shielded from the sun by a large fig tree, Hackett began to stammer into Chayter's ear:

'The Americans aren't here.'

'We'll start without them.'

The procession continued into the church.

The congregation sat well apart as though seated by a head waiter of a once fashionable restaurant in an attempt to fill the place up. The Assistant Chaplain took the service efficiently and at high speed. He led the singing of Wigart's favourite hymn. Only the German sang, with a tuneless baritone voice. The British mouthed the words:

> 'Before us and beside us
> Still holden in thine hand,
> A cloud of unseen witness . . .'

The German raised his voice and looked accusingly at Chayter:

> 'Our elder comrades stand . . .'

At exactly this moment the American, Lou Finucane, arrived with his wife.

They slipped into a pew at the back of the church, beside a poster on an easel advertising the Embassy Wives Circle evening talk: *British Verse and the EEC Now*. The Finucanes stood for the rest of the hymn:

> 'One family unbroken,
> We join, with one acclaim
> One heart, one voice uplifting,
> To glorify Thy name. Amen.'

Geoffrey Hackett walked slowly to the front of the church and turned to face the congregation. He clenched his hands. His mouth stretched like a reflection in a fairground funny mirror. 'Please be seated . . . We have assembled here, my friends, to give thanks for the life of Dickie. It is appropriate we have just sung his favourite . . .' This was the only time the stammer interrupted. '. . . h-hymn. We are indeed "A cloud of unseen witness". Our family is unbroken in these days when most families are not and when we are, alas, bound to observe there is scant unity amongst the wider international family of nations. Of that great international family Dickie was a patriot. A man of the balanced view. The world democrat. The solitary man. The lover of the writing of Robert Louis

Stevenson much of whose verse he knew by heart. And I offer the word "heart" and the very phrase "by heart", in the fullest sense. For it was, indeed, with his heart that he loved those verses and his friends . . .'

Lou Finucane, the American, listened to Hackett's nonsense with his eyes closed. He was there at the request of the United States' London Embassy. His presence confirmed the opinion of the senior members of the European intelligence community that his new-found role in life was no more than a cover for his continuing service to the FBI. He was said to be trading as a London antiquarian book dealer. Could anyone seriously believe a veteran Special Federal Bureau of Investigation Agent had hung up his gun for the sake of books? It was, in fact, perfectly true. Just as it was true he had finally married his secretary, Lindsay Venn. He had made a decent woman out of the girl from Wisconsin twenty-five years younger than he was, with curly copper hair, white silk shirts, and the bleached-out jeans. Today she wore a black silk skirt instead of the jeans. As a couple they captured the imagination. And that was more than you could say for most things that went on in United States embassies anywhere in the world.

But Lou and books: Lanky Lou who forever seemed, as he'd been heard to say, to be approaching fifty from the wrong side? Was the antiquarian book trade really the post-retirement fate of a man now finished with more than thirty-five years of Bureau service from Newark, New Jersey; Washington through the capitals of Europe to London? It had to be a cover.

'We will now sing "Allelluia . . .".' With that Hackett jammed.

' "The strife is o'er, the battle done . . ." ' prompted the Assistant Chaplain.

The organist began his introduction. Hackett walked slowly back to his pew.

> 'Now is the Victor's triumph won;
> O let the song of praise be sung . . .'

No one remembered to announce the hymn number. Even the German was flummoxed. It was left to the Assistant Chaplain and Hackett to sing a raucous duet.

At the back of the church Lindsay Finucane asked her husband why he wasn't singing.

'I don't want to embarrass myself,' he whispered back with a straight face. 'And none of this is true. Lunch'll be the same. You see.'

The first-floor restaurant in the Cerrara de San Jeronimo had, according to Geoffrey Hackett, been 'chosen according to Dickie's wishes'.

'So has the menu,' he announced with false jollity. He unfolded a sheet of paper and recited the dishes like items from a shopping list. '*La sopa de ajo*, garlic soup; *cocido madrileño* in which we can expect chickpeas, beef, chicken; *chorizo* which is a sort of sausage confection. Don't want to bore you with details. But Dickie was a stickler for scoff. The *cocido* is also made up of blood pudding sausage, fresh bacon, the gamut of Spanish *cuisine*. There's something *louche* about people who bang on about food, don't you think?'

Everyone nodded appreciatively.

'There is, however, *rosqillas de San Isidro* which Dickie always had here. And the wine is a little thing from the *bodega* Marques de Murrieta if I recall correctly. All of which Dickie specified.'

'May I say grace,' the Assistant Chaplain broke in. 'No need to stand up.'

He moved his lighted cigarette beneath the table.

'For what we are about to receive may the Lord make us very truly thankful.'

'Amen,' Mahon said loudly.

It made Kirsty Newiston laugh and old Hackett pretended not to notice. He felt dejected and resentful. In the old days, the SIS career officers like himself and Dickie Wigart, would have held this sort of lunch with a kind of understated formality. They respected their dead with curiously oblique reminiscences and thus avoided any direct inner confrontation with grief. It was what wasn't said on such occasions that mattered; they had no need to mention names, places, cases or missions; theirs had been a kind of chivalric secrecy.

Hackett did make a vain attempt to steer the conversation in this direction but met with small success. His only listener was the Assistant Chaplain who chain-smoked throughout the meal. The priest shared Hackett's view of the Spanish Civil War. Hackett called it 'a dry run for all that followed'.

He gazed into his wine glass, watching the priest from the corner of his eye and the nervous puffing on the cigarette.

'The fascists against the democrats,' Hackett said. 'Communists, centralists and regionalists pitched against each other.'

He might just as well have been talking to himself.

'Christians?' coughed the Assistant Chaplain.

Pleased he had gained a reaction, Hackett tried a different line. 'It does seem to be a very long time since one's friends in the Service actually admitted to being practising Christians. We did have a number of Catholics in the war years. They were invariably rather eccentric, somewhat leftish. They weren't the same as the rest of us. Men apart.'

Chayter had picked up on the conversation and as if to confirm Hackett's private regret that the past was a closed book he said, 'Religion isn't an issue nowadays unless we're talking of Moslems.'

'A very different ball-game,' said Newiston.

Hackett was ignored. The conversation turned to the increased surveillance of the Soviet staff residences in Holland Park. Even the Assistant Chaplain seemed suddenly bored and began to read the menu to himself.

A feeling of inferiority overcame Hackett, the sense that his generation was of no more use was by no means strange to him. But the indifference to the memory of Dickie Wigart cut deeper. His memory had been dismissed. It had been wiped out and Hackett felt a sense of anger and distress.

He hid his feelings by watching the women: Kirsty Newiston, a Service wife who, outwardly at least, seemed not to fit the usual look, Hackett thought. There was a fullness in the mouth, some light in the blue eyes that spoke to him of wildness and none of the more conventional subservience. He watched her talking to Finucane's wife, Lindsay and then picked up Lizzie Chayter's description of the Rastro flea-market and enthusiasm for what she called 'the joys of black soap'. The women talked across Finucane and it struck Hackett that the American must have his ears open for the shop-talk about the surveillance of the Soviet residences. They were talking with little regard for security about the London Soviet officers. None of this lessened his resentment about the indifference towards Dickie.

His secret discomfiture was matched by Mahon's who was saying nothing at all. He didn't understand what the matter was with Mahon until the arrival of the *cocido madrileño*. This proved to be Mahon's undoing.

'I don't feel terribly well,' Mahon said to Kirsty and quickly left the table.

His departure prompted Henry Newiston to glare at his wife as if it was her fault. 'What's the matter with him?'

'Under the weather. He doesn't feel very well.'

His set jaw told her his mind had wandered into its secret labyrinths. She supposed their marriage had become the topic of gossip and speculation. Perhaps Henry had told his beloved chief the marriage was in tatters; how much she hated his career. Perhaps it had been Chayter who'd suggested they combine the memorialising in Madrid with a last bash at keeping the relationship alive. She could imagine Lizzie encouraging the scheme. There was nothing Lizzie enjoyed more than interfering in other people's unhappiness. She could imagine her saying 'Kirsty's burdened with such a strong imaginary life.' A long time ago she had been complimented on it; as a schoolgirl, and at the University of East Anglia. (Her father had wanted her to go up to Cambridge and used to ask her quite where East Anglia was. 'East Anglia isn't a *place*.') Marriage into Henry's world a year after graduation had crushed her imagination. She watched him agreeing with everything Chayter had to say. It was much easier than anyone had ever told her to hate her husband. She imagined the scene of an accident; finding Henry dead; where he'd have his memorial service. She'd have preferred to walk out calmly, for ever, and with no scenes. No scenes. She could hear her mother saying it on the sea front at Hove. 'You should be grateful,' the old bird insisted. 'You were an accident of middle age.'

'So were you,' her father had told her mother. 'My accident. My middle age.'

The *No Scenes* warning could have been swept out to sea years ago judging from the violence of that particular row. She was eight years old at the time and decided to marry a man who wouldn't quarrel.

Which was what she'd done and that was her bad luck.

She pushed back her chair and tossed her table-napkin into her untouched heap of *cocido madrileño*.

'Ladies,' she mouthed at her husband and left the room.

She decided to go back to the hotel, pack her things, get the next flight to London and bust free. Then she realised Henry had the air tickets, the travellers' cheques and the pesetas. Shoving past the coat racks she did not at first notice the man crouched on a chair in the gloomy passage. He was holding a glass of iced water in both hands.

It was Mahon. She wondered rather wildly whether to ask him for a loan to buy an air ticket.

'I don't feel myself,' he told her.

She saw Henry at the end of the passage.

'Can we have a word?' he said.

'I can't face it any more.'

'Flouncing out?'

'No. I only wanted some fresh air. A great deal of fresh air.' Henry backed away.

She called after him, 'I'm going to look after Mr Mahon.'

Henry didn't hear.

She took the glass from Mahon and handed it to a waiter. 'Try and stand up. I'll take you back to your hotel.'

They went downstairs to the restaurant's ground-floor delicatessen and forced their way through the press of customers into the street.

'Don't you think,' he began, 'you should go back? Couldn't it be awkward?'

'Maybe,' she said and waved at a taxi.

A man carrying a parcel of cakes wrapped in silver paper ducked beneath her raised arm and cursed the British.

By the time Finucane was left alone at the table with Chayter it was well past four o'clock.

'I'm very sorry about Wigart,' the American said. 'It was a terrible way for an old man to die. It's a shame they haven't caught the people who did it.'

'By all accounts the Spanish have done a fairly thorough job of investigation,' Chayter said, toying with his brandy glass. 'There's been a whole spate of violent muggings in that park. Dickie wasn't the first to be murdered. The police have come up with nothing. Odd, isn't it, how one doesn't really associate the Spanish with efficient criminal investigation?'

Finucane gave a weary smile. 'It had nothing to do with duty?'

23

'His work? No, no. We looked into it. No one came up with anything. The Spanish have closed the case.'

'Your embassy man wasn't at the service?' Finucane said. 'Smith?'

'He's on leave,' said Chayter.

'He came up with nothing extra?'

'No. I suppose that spares us any sort of public trial. That's all there is to be said for it. Dickie was the last of a long line. He knew everybody. Newiston's father. Mahon's father too. There's only Hackett left now and he should have retired years ago.' He glanced at Finucane, then away.

'I liked Wigart. He had quite a collection of books you know. He once told me he had a first edition, first impression of *A Christmas Carol* and another of *A Tale of Two Cities*.'

'Prized items?'

'Everything depends on condition. I never saw what shape they were in.'

The chief of the Secret Service gave the American a hollow smile. There was no place in his life for prizes like first editions of Dickens.

'It's been very good of you to turn out here,' he told Finucane. 'These things don't go unappreciated, believe you me.'

The American had learned long ago never to believe what such people said. He was glad he had an excuse to leave. Schad, the Austrian book-dealer with a figure like a garden bug, would be waiting with Lindsay for him. 'Thank you for your hospitality,' he said.

'Thank Dickie. We're only here because of Dickie, aren't we?'

And your feelings for him are about as dead as he is – Finucane managed not to say.

4

It fell to Lindsay Finucane to take brief pity on Hackett.

On the way to the book-dealer, Schad's place, she saw him smiling at her from a news-stand.

'So glad you were able to turn out,' he said with false brightness. 'So very glad. Thank you, thank you very much indeed.'

'You're welcome,' Lindsay said.

She could tell he was distressed. He folded his *Daily Telegraph* and tried to push it into his jacket pocket.

She saw his hands were shaking.

'I hope you felt it was a good show,' he said.

'It was neat.'

'Ah, yes. Neat. I suppose it was. What are you doing with the afternoon?'

'I'm meeting my husband at a book-dealer's. Herr Schad's. Like to come along too?'

Hackett appeared pleased and happy to be received warmly both by Schad and Lou Finucane who arrived soon after.

'I have few British clients nowadays,' said Schad, looking Hackett up and down. The Austrian's pale eyes were magnified by lenses of a modernistic design. The thin frames were bright red.

'I hope it may change for the better for you,' said Hackett, looking around Schad's drawing room. A portrait in oils of a middle-aged man in jeans with an El Greco face and droopy moustache glared down at the visitors. Beneath it was a harpsichord. There wasn't a book to be seen.

Schad announced the prizes in his stock like a radio commentator reading football results:

'Geoffrey Chaucer, *The Works*, 1561 edition. Sixteen hundred dollars. James Boswell, *The Life of Samuel Johnson*, two volumes, first edition, two thousand dollars.'

After each announcement he searched Finucane's eyes for a glimmer of excitement. He opened a drawer and took out the books separately placing them on a square of green baize spread across a small table next to the harpsichord.

'You said in your letter you had three copies of a Greene?' Finucane asked.

'*England Made Me*,' Schad said, quietly. 'First editions. Half-titles. First leaves blank, original cloth, dust-jackets, designed by Youngman Carter. The jackets all in fine state. 1935. The three together, an unusual bargain at three thousand three hundred dollars.'

'Two thousand five hundred.'

Schad's mouth twitched with pain. 'Pounds?'

'Dollars.'

'Three thousand.'

Schad spread out his palms like an image of Christ blessing the children in a Scripture Union pamphlet. 'Why not? We have too much to regret nowadays, don't we, Mr Hakluyt?'

'Hackett.'

'Ah pity. I can get hold of a fine edition of Hakluyt's revised edition of the *De Orbe Novo* of Peter Martyr of Anghiera. Hakluyt himself made a fine collection, didn't he?'

'I believe he did,' Hackett smiled. 'I am no relation.'

Schad wrapped the Greenes first in pale blue tissue paper and then in brown paper. He handed them to Finucane. 'If you can find a client for the Chaucer and the Boswell we can split the commission.'

'I'll do my best,' Finucane told him.

After drinking Turkish coffee in Schad's conservatory they left to find a bar. 'It's like the old days,' Hackett sighed. 'Dickie loved a bargain.'

'We paid over the odds,' Lindsay said.

'But you got the Graham Greenes. The little Austrian knew what you'd come for and bought your pleasure.'

'Schad's been loyal to us,' Lindsay said.

'Loyalty's always costly,' Hackett told her. 'So you paid over the odds. Loyalty costs far more than it did in my day. Look at that awful service and the luncheon. Poor old Dickie tried to buy a gesture of loyalty from the grave. What did he get? A mockery. A gesture of betrayal by new people treating the whole thing as a jolly. A swan-around. They don't *believe* in anything.'

'What did Wigart believe in?' Finucane asked.

Hackett wiped his eyes with a dark blue handkerchief. 'Loyalty to the Service. He used to say that loyalty was the best means of defence. And trust. I think that was something which made him exceptional. If he trusted in someone he believed in them. He trusted in the Service and so he believed in it. The new people believe only in themselves. Therefore, how can they put the Service first?'

Finucane was silent.

'I'll tell you,' Hackett said. 'They can't.' He stared at the barman who was fiddling with the hi-fi system. 'I'm not advocating a return to the old days. But I'll tell you what's true. We've lost the sense of England. That was also Dickie's view.'

His next remarks were drowned out by the barman's Madonna tape.

He raised his voice against the tinny music. 'Dickie believed the rot began when the British started clinging to the idea of *Great* Britain. Anywhere that's called *Great* isn't. Like British villages. *Great* this or that. They aren't. It doesn't wash. But he did, I suppose, believe in the Anglo-American intelligence alliance. He was realistic enough to know we can't survive at all without you people. That's a fact.'

The barman fought to control the sound system. He couldn't stop Madonna howling.

'I can't compete with this din,' Hackett said. 'I'll be off. Do forgive me. You've been so very kind.'

'I'm very sad about the loss of Dickie,' Finucane said. 'It was a terrible way to die.'

'It had the merit of suddenness.'

'You believe what they say about what happened to him?'

'I believe he's dead. He won't come back. The memorial service was a farce wasn't it?' He got up abruptly. 'Thank you for my brandy.'

He left the bar stooped and engulfed in melancholy.

Kirsty went with Mahon to his hotel room just off the Puerta del Sol.

'Why are you staying in a dump like this?' she asked.

'It's all right,' he said, slumped on his unmade bed.

'You look terrible.'

'I feel it.'

'Get undressed,' she told him. 'Where's the bathroom?'

'At the end of the passage.'

'What you need is a long cool bath.'

She left him alone and found the bathroom. She locked the door and turned on the taps. The water was cold and coloured with rust. She went back to his room.

Mahon had undressed and was standing wrapped in the bed sheet. 'Sit down,' she told him.

She sat on the bed.

'Next to me.'

He did as she told him.

'I very badly want,' she began, hesitantly. 'I very badly want to be your lover. It is something I have very suddenly decided. Maybe I've decided it for all the wrong reasons. But I have decided.'

'What are the wrong reasons?'

She kicked off her shoes.

'Boredom. Suffocating boredom. The alternative is for you and me to get very drunk. Well, it isn't really an alternative, is it? I mean, you look to have been pissed out of your head last night.'

'There's some truth in that.'

'You feel a bit better now?'

'A little,' he said touching the back of her neck.

She began to undress. 'Why don't you lock the door?'

He did as she said and stood by the door watching her sling her clothes on to the chest of drawers beneath the window. A pigeon cooed on the sill outside.

She left on her white camisole and lay back on the bed. 'I have a medical theory,' she said. 'The only completely reliable cure for a hangover is to make love.'

'Suppose it doesn't work?'

'Suck it and see.'

He unwrapped the sheet from around his waist and finished undressing her.

'Come on, do your best or your worst, Mr Mahon.'

'Would you terribly mind not calling me Mister Mahon?'

'I approve of formality.'

'In bed?'

'Particularly in bed. That's why the Japanese are such good lovers.'

28

'I've never known one.'

'If you had you'd know they follow the instructions. Anything Japanese always comes tightly wrapped with the instructions in several languages. So listen to mine carefully.'

Once again he did as he was told.

'I'll take things in my own hands,' she said. 'You won't be bored. I promise you.'

'There's no need to promise anything,' he said.

She kissed him slowly. She was a very skilled lover.

They agreed to leave separately. She asked him again why he stayed there. 'It's so sleazy.'

He explained that his father had stayed in exactly the same hotel many years before. 'Once upon a time he was our man in Madrid.'

'You're really rather sentimental, aren't you?'

'It's more legitimate to be sentimental about someone you've never met, don't you feel?'

'I don't know.'

'In this case it was my father.'

'And in mine?' she asked.

'It won't be quite so legitimate.'

'You mind?'

They were standing outside his room in the narrow corridor.

'Go on,' he told her. 'We can't be seen together.'

She laughed. 'Try not to look so guilty, Mr Mahon.'

5

Hackett proposed what he called 'a tour of the tat stalls', but Mahon soon realised the old boy had other things on his mind. They passed a stall offering bundles of girlie magazines. A boy in leather shorts flicked through *Clima*. The issue from last year boasted pictures of girls with breasts of huge proportions: 'EL "GUSTO" ES "MIO". "EL ZURDO".' Mahon watched the boy slit open the cellophane wrapper and blow a bubble with his chewing gum. An American woman said, 'It's tough to find a rarity nowadays.'

Hackett had found a barrow piled high with plastic Christ child dolls. They had metallic haloes wired to the backs of their heads like misplaced hearing-aids. He lifted up a lone black doll, boss-eyed and grinning, from the muddle of pudgy limbs.

'They seem to think of everything, don't they?' Hackett said. 'Isn't this extraordinary?'

Mahon said he thought it was.

'Of course it all used to be very different. The café life. Afternoon *tertulias*, a gaslight world. But the only place where you see donkeys carrying china plates, the *serenos* and *porteros* are in those beastly paintings the Germans like.'

A Tunisian, sitting cross-legged behind a box of disused *carnets infantiles* hissed, 'Souvenir?'

'No, thank you very much,' Hackett said courteously.

The Tunisian started to wave a plate decorated with the face of Robert Redford.

'Really, no. Thank you very much,' Hackett said more firmly. He gave the man a coin and steered Mahon away towards a tree-lined boulevard.

The old man's eyes looked tired. They flickered oddly so that from time to time as they walked he stood still and held his fingers to the bridge of his nose. 'Perhaps it's the result of the

Service appointing psychiatrists full-time. We only used the trick-cyclists when someone went barking mad.'

They headed for the Retiro Park drawn by Wigart's memory.

'I'm glad Dickie had no next of kin,' Hackett said. 'They'd have been hurt by that ghastly, hypocritical performance at the church. It'd have increased the pain. Lucky he didn't marry.'

Some uniformed sailors were shouting and laughing at a boat rowed by two young girls. The boats were on a collision course.

'Have you ever thought of marrying?' Hackett continued.

'No. Have you?'

The old man laughed. 'The right woman never came along.'

They walked through the trees.

'I knew your father,' Hackett said.

'What did he think of Spain?'

'His last posting.' The fingers went back to the eyelids. 'Like Dickie he was philosophical about it. It was Europe's dirty laundry basket. A sadistic broken place. Franco was like the Spanish duke who was asked when he was dying if he'd forgiven his enemies. "I have no enemies," the old bugger said. "I had them all executed." I once heard Dickie quote Lorca to the effect that one loves Spain because one doesn't like her. Very shrewd remark.'

'And my father would have shared that view?'

'Possibly. He came to Madrid because he was damned good. I'll tell you how good he was.' He sat down on a bench and gazed into the distance. Mahon sat down beside him.

'I'll tell you,' Hackett said, 'why he was so much better than all of your new people put together. He preserved the one secret that was going to change the whole future of the war.'

'What was that?'

The old man closed his eyes lost in his own thoughts. 'I have always thought it was so extremely odd he was killed in the way he was. He walked into a trap, you know. It was so unlike him. He knew Madrid was violent. Of all the people London might have sent he knew it as well as anyone.'

'It was a long time ago.'

'That doesn't alter the fact the truth was never found. Isn't it odd that we can say the same about Dickie Wigart. What do you suppose is the truth about it?'

'I don't know.'

'Which is the accepted view – no one knows. They're not troubling to investigate it further. His death has received about as much attention as some pet dog run down by a taxi-cab.'

The sun had turned the shadows a dark purple. Hackett set off towards the exit of the park. He walked with his face turned aside. They walked in silence and only when they reached the street did Mahon notice the tears in the old eyes.

'Establish the truth about your father's death,' Hackett said suddenly. 'It might set the record straight about so many things. I think the time has come.'

A cab pulled up.

Mahon wanted to press the issue but Hackett got into the cab and shut the door. He said something to the driver and as the cab drove off Mahon could see him holding his head in his hands, sobbing uncontrollably.

6

'It's all yours, mate.' said Hanratty, keeper of Nelson Unit, the depository of the Service archives. His large fingers scratched at the rim of the undervest Mahon could see beneath the grubby nylon shirt. Keeper Hanratty was possessed of the jovial solemnity of some guardian of a cemetery in a once fashionable suburb. He had a lively memory for the names of the dead and buried.

'That's your man,' he told Mahon, fiddling with the spectacles at the end of the metal chain around his neck. Perhaps he hoped Mahon would tell him why he was turning up his father's file. He stared enquiringly at the file on the table marked MAHON. But Mahon didn't say a word. He also stared at the file hoping that Hanratty would understand he wanted to be left alone. 'I think the time has come,' he remembered Hackett telling him. He couldn't blame Hanratty for being curious about the past lives he so dutifully kept hidden away at Nelson. But he didn't want to show the nervous excitement he felt about coming face to face with his father.

Hanratty knew better than to put a question. His miles of shelves kept the answers. Only the people back in London had the right to search. Out here, on the edge of Heathrow, he did as he was told. He was happy they hadn't got round to computerising his cemetery. He dreaded that day when he might no longer be of use and he would probably be sent to Norwich to train as a weeder or a shredder. Meanwhile, visits from the London lot delayed Hanratty's exile to East Anglia and he was grateful for them. 'How long will you be?' he asked.

'Give me an hour.'

'You can have as long as you like.'

Mahon was left alone. He heard Hanratty turn a key in the

door and he sat for a while and stared at the file. This was the closest he'd ever got to his father and he remembered, during his early foul days at boarding school, watching sons of Old Boys leaf through the bound copies of the school magazine for a mention of their fathers. For them, squatting on the holed carpet by the library shelves, their fathers were living heroes. His father had always been dead. His father belonged to other people's memories, like old Hackett's.

Mahon didn't believe memory could haunt you. He didn't believe in ghosts from the past or visions of the future. Yet here were his father's remains with his own name on the cover. The file lay on the table like a tomb-stone, dry and without an epitaph. He found he was reluctant to open it. The contents, whatever they might be, scared him. What was the line from Thomas Browne? 'Gravestones tell truth scarce forty years.' He didn't expect to find the whole truth in this particular family vault. Nor did he believe he'd discover nothing but the truth. He was realistic enough in outlook, others might have said wise enough, to have learned the currency of SIS depended rather more upon falsehood. The problem about returning to the past was not what you'd find recorded; on the contrary, it was what you'd find wasn't there. It would be a map without the place-names and the boundary lines. You couldn't be sure whether you were standing on dry land or floating lost somewhere in the ocean. He felt wholly unprepared to face the chart of his father's secret life.

The first shock was the sight of his own face staring at him from the scratched, cracked photograph: the frown, the thin nose, skin darkened a little possibly by the sun, the shirt open at the neck, and a large Adam's apple. The dark eyes mocked and challenged him. He had never before realised how great a resemblance he bore to his father and the confrontation made him anxious.

He leafed the whole way through the brownish typewritten pages. Purple carbons. Papers fixed together with rusted clips and pins. The headings shouted MOST SECRET. TOP SECRET. RESTRICTED. EYES ONLY RECIPIENT.

The papers had been stuffed together in a hurry. He turned to the end of the file to find the official verdict on his father's death. The final weeks before the death occurred in December 1941 made little sense to him. He leafed back and forth through a maze of cross-references to an operation named *Nightshade*; sometimes referred to as NS or N. The name meant nothing. Copies of coded signals mentioned Washington, Tokyo and Stockholm all stamped with the elaborate security gradings of wartime. As far as he could make out they described the arrival and departure times by air of what were described as 'ancillary staffs'. They yielded no picture of the purpose of travel or what connection it might have had with his father's duty other than that the intercontinental travel had a bearing upon *Nightshade*.

The *Iberian Peninsula* papers offered up a human touch. They told the story of two agents his father had run. There had been a woman called Vera Pineda and a man called only Ramon. Together, these two had blackmailed a Counsellor at the Japanese Embassy in Madrid.

Mahon read the report:

It would seem that the Japanese is a practising homosexual pervert who separated from his wife, a Belgian, sometime in July 1939. Pineda and Ramon were able to obtain photographs, 28 in all, of the Japanese in a hotel in Barcelona with a male prostitute. The photographs were purchased under Special Order 5 (d) for £500 (five hundred pounds sterling). Receipt attached.

Mahon searched the lists of agents his father had run for any further mention of Pineda or Ramon. There was no further material on the Japanese and no indication of what the man might have turned over to his father, if anything. The other small fry were mostly people who could prove reliable watchers of shipping passing Gibraltar. There was a chauffeur from Munich in the German Embassy, an electrician who worked for the Turks and a woman official in the Prado code-named Goya.

He turned to 'C' 's last Personal Report on his father:

Much of the Madrid material is first class. It has proved reliable. It is recommended the officer be kept in place for the foreseeable future depending upon the outcome of the theatre of the secret war in Europe. Given his particular abilities, it may be wise to consider him for posting to another neutral territory. Consideration may be given to either Geneva or Helsinki depending on the deployment of officers in the North Europe field.

There was no mention of exactly what his father had achieved. One paper guided the reader to *Statistics and Strategies*. MOST SECRET. There was no cross-reference. But the paper, no more than a note of three lines, advised the immediate dispatch of the material to the Prime Minister. 'Mr Richard Wigart's report to be attached.' It was signed G. Hackett.

On the next page there was the carbon copy of Wigart's report. Here was the official story of his father's death.

Mahon's body was discovered in the alley-way near the Rastro. He had been shot three times. Once in the chest, apparently from a distance of several feet; twice in the head from point blank range. It was generally considered the assassin was the man who had been the male prostitute photographed *in flagrante delicto* with Mahon's contact from the Japanese Embassy. But the male prostitute has not been traced and, as might be expected at any time, the criminal fraternity of Madrid has proved unwilling to co-operate in the circumstances.

Another report recorded, briefly, that the body of the male prostitute 'associated with this investigation has been re-trieved'. No time, no place and no identity was provided.

Two words brought it to an end: '*Investigation closed.*' Mahon closed the file.

A pigeon cooed outside the barred window. He remembered the pigeons outside the hotel room in Madrid and Kirsty. He remembered Hackett sobbing on the back seat of the taxi. What chaos of emotion had reduced the old man to tears? There and then, he told himself, he should have pursued Hackett when he was at his most vulnerable. He'd heard that the old men confessed more readily out of anger. Was it to encourage others to take the revenge they were too old to take themselves? He'd lost the chance in Madrid, but he could find another in London. He would definitely see Hackett again and as soon as possible.

Before then there was Kirsty.

Still facing the file with MAHON on it he began to ask himself why he had become so embroiled with her. It was too obvious to say it was her abandoned love-making. He told himself the excitement lay in the danger: clandestine moments brought a new spirit to his life.

He stood up, a grim and set expression on his face which belied the pulsing of his blood.

7

The Circle line train rumbled beneath Mahon's basement flat in Gordon Place.

'Didn't you realise you'd be living in a tube station?'

He feigned offence. 'The old girl before me never told me about the trains.'

They lay naked in his sheets; she holding one of his pillows to her breasts; he on his back.

'It's not the sort of thing you think of asking.'

'You mean, whether or not the tube runs through the house?' she said. 'My God, I'd have asked.'

'It only runs underneath.'

'It certainly does. She must have been completely deaf.'

'I think she was. But the art's in learning how to love the trains. Like an arranged marriage. It's not impossible. Some people learn to love mice they can't eradicate.'

Kirsty shivered. 'You have mice as well as trains?'

'They come out when the tubes stop.'

His bedroom looked out or, more precisely up, through a grille of vertical black bars outside the windows to the pavement. Passers-by could only be identified below the knees. This dog's eye view could be gained through the gap above the rotten curtains with their stained linings. His living-room, where they'd eaten lunch, was across a dark hallway taken up with a disused piano and derelict washing-machine. The living-room, also Mahon's kitchen, seemed occupied mainly by books and out-of-date magazines. He heated the place with gas-fires. Beneath the one sputtering in the bedroom was a pile of soot. He had explained that he kept the fires on all year round. It was as good a reason as any for them to get into bed together fast. His wardrobe leaned at an angle against the wall from which a leaf of wallpaper hung down. The wardrobe doors were attached by a knotted cord. His shirts lay on the floor still in the wrappers from the laundry.

'I don't spend much time here,' Mahon had told her.

'I can believe it. But I can't imagine where you found a place like this.'

He told her perfectly seriously he had seen it advertised on a noticeboard at the Commonwealth Institute. 'I was recruiting an African communist. The daughter of a general with blood on her hands. Abigail from Nigeria.'

'I'll bet you didn't bring Abigail here.'

'For a time.'

'You slept with her?'

'It was a long time ago.'

'Which means you still do?'

'No. Truthfully, I don't. For the very good reason I lost her.'

'Who to?'

'To the French. She died in a bomb attack in Neuilly just over a year ago.'

'I'm sorry,' she said, sitting up. 'I'm going to clean this place up.'

'Don't bother. I told you. I'm hardly ever here.'

'Unless it's with Abigails?'

'There aren't any more now.'

'Then you can go and make me some tea please. With lemon.'

Once he had left she got out of bed and looked at the table beneath the window. There were bills still in their envelopes and several copies of the *Guardian Weekly* still in their wrappers. Even the telephone was covered in a fine dust. No calls either to or from his bedroom. There was a portable typewriter at the edge of the desk. It stood at an angle, some of its keys raised in a tangle. It was balanced precariously at the desk's edge like a deserted house on a cliff eroded by the sea. There were paperbacks next to it: Natsume Soseki's *Light and Darkness* and Vonnegut's *Wampeters, Foma & Granfalloons*. Strange selections, she thought, for a secret servant. Neither of the books appeared to have been read. There was a single sheet of paper with names and letters scrawled on it: Hackett. 1941. NIGHTSHADE. Madrid. She opened the table drawer. There was a jumble of old cheque-book stubs, Barclaycard Visa accounts and some discarded packs of Italian cigarettes. Next to the cigarettes she saw the colour photographs of the black girl dressed in white with a thick silver chain around her neck. If this was Abigail, his girl had been very beautiful. Hair in ringlets, a teasing smile and large deep brown and purple lips.

She wondered what conclusions his black lover might have drawn about him from his flat. Had she felt safe with him when its mess and the conspicuous lack of care for the things showed he required nothing here to speak of home? She wondered what emotional contact Abigail had made with him. Or had she found that he really only lived in his head apparently isolated from the rest of the world? It was altogether too easy to say he lived only for his secret work. If that were the case the flat would probably reflect the Service: details might speak of the trained mind and ordered habits.

She found herself imagining that perhaps he needed her precisely because his secret life lacked any obvious centre. Perhaps he all too easily fell victim to women like Abigail and herself who offered him the sense of being himself.

She was disappointed by the squalor of the place. It far from coincided with her idea of him as a romantic lover. She closed the drawer so hard that the typewriter toppled to the floor with a clatter.

He was standing in the door with the tea and lemon.

'I saw the typewriter was about to fall off,' she said, lamely.

'No, you didn't. You were having a snoop. It's an occupational disease, isn't it?'

She tried to stop herself blushing.

'You won't find anything.'

She wanted to change the subject. 'Why don't we have a bath together?' she heard herself say. To her surprise he agreed. They took the tea with them to the bathroom.

'From now on,' she told him, 'I'd like to meet at my place.'

'No thanks. Keep Henry out of this.'

'I will. We'll go to my flat.'

'What flat?'

'The other side of Shepherd's Bush. In Frithville Gardens. It belonged to my aunt. She lived alone. Worked at the British Library. When she died she left it to me in her will. It's my place. A private island away from everything else.'

'A love nest?'

'Could be. No trains. No mice. And a very old rather

40

comfortable bed. Like one of those you used to find in French provincial hotels. It's very wide.'

They climbed awkwardly into the bath together.

'Do you,' she asked him again. 'sleep around a lot?'

'I've never known what people mean by that and it's one of those questions which you know as well as I do always gets a painful answer. It's always asked by people who have a vested interest and expect the worst.'

'Like me?'

'Perhaps,' he replied. 'Do you sleep around or do you just sleep with Henry?'

'I've just made love to you, haven't I.' She soaped his face and chest and moved the soap under water between his legs. 'I'm sorry I spied on your table in the bedroom. Try and understand. Haven't you done the same in someone's bedroom you're very fond of?'

'You mean someone you love?'

'No, I said fond. That's all. Abigail was attractive wasn't she?'

'Yes,' he said. And he had no expression on his face.

'Was she married?'

'Why do you ask?'

She avoided answering him and said instead, 'Had it ended before she died?'

'Yes, it had.'

'Why?'

'Because she was pregnant.'

Kirsty closed her eyes. 'It was yours.'

'So she told me. We had arranged an abortion. She miscarried. That was that.'

Suddenly she hated hearing him tell it all so coldly. Had he sat in this bath with Abigail as well?

'Didn't you feel anymore than "that was that" – not a twinge of regret, sadness?'

She wanted him to say he'd felt nothing, that he really hadn't loved Abigail. She also wanted him to say he had felt something, to show he was capable of some form of tenderness and therefore unlike Henry.

'I don't want to talk about it,' he replied.

She might have guessed: he was giving nothing away.

'Well, I'm sorry,' she said.

'Yes, thanks.' He smiled distantly. 'What else did your little search reveal, Kirsty?'

'Not a lot. Books. Notes. Mostly about Madrid during the war. Tell me.'

He got out of the bath.

'Tell me,' she said. 'What is this passion you've got for Madrid and the war. Is it your hobby? History?'

He began to dry himself on a large grubby towel with the name of a hotel in Copenhagen embroidered in its centre.

'If you want to know, I was looking into my father's past. When you get to past forty and you never knew your father a time comes, perfectly naturally, when you want to discover who he was, who you are yourself, it's all linked together. If there are links missing you're left with a feeling of incompleteness. That's all. I had a conversation with old Hackett in Madrid about my father and it's prompted me to look at what happened to him.'

Kirsty used his towel to dry herself. By now the towel was damp and cold. 'Was that all?'

'More or less,' he said. He didn't seem to want to talk about it.

They went back to his bedroom. Later Kirsty grew reflective:

'I loved Madrid. I didn't want it to stop in the end.'

'It's not going to,' he said. 'That French double bed'll help.'

She laughed.

'Those Americans were very nice. I like Lindsay Finucane, don't you? It's really weird to think she married that long streak who's converted from the FBI to bookselling. Lindsay said that a lot of the people they sell books to, those first editions and things, don't even read them. Can you believe it? If you've got a book that's unread it's even more valuable apparently. It ought to be the other way around, don't you think?'

'I would have thought so,' said Mahon, sitting on the unmade bed.

She kissed him and pushed him gently down across the sheet. 'I think you are sentimental after all,' she whispered. 'About your father.'

'You can't be sentimental about something or someone you never knew.'

'Oh yes, you can.'

'I'm not going to argue about it,' he said, turning around the small clock by his bedside lamp. 'It's time you left.'

'You want to get rid of me?'

'What do you think, Kirsty?'

She stood up from the bed and straightened her clothes. 'I want you to write to me.'

She went to his desk, picked up the typewriter. Very slowly she tapped out the address in Frithville Gardens. Under it, in capitals, she wrote, SAME TIME NEXT WEEK IF YOU WRITE FIRST.

He looked over her shoulder. 'It'll be dangerous to write.'

'Exactly,' she said, beaming at him.

8

A young man with the face of W.C. Fields shouted at two women in fur coats outside the London Coliseum: 'Murderers.' He pointed a spray paint can. One of the women hissed at him in French. Her companion struck out with an extendable umbrella which caught the ranter's cheek and drew blood.

Mahon stepped over the can on its way to the gutter. He turned into the high and narrow alley, Brydges Place, with the European conflict over fur and killings ringing in his ears. He wondered whether the French women would enjoy that evening's performance of *Madame Butterfly*.

The alley stank of rotting take-away food and wine. Mahon was pleased to escape up the stairs to the first-floor drinking club where Hackett was to be found on Mondays.

The old man was seated alone by the window with the view of an edge of Trafalgar Square. He seemed to be lost in concentration, his fingers tapping out a melancholy refrain of a song by Dinah Washington from the sound system behind the bar.

'I got here rather early,' he said to Mahon. 'One tends to be early when one's under the weather.'

Mahon ordered whisky for them both. He saw a Hackett who now looked more than his years with the air of a shabby preparatory schoolmaster. The collar of his cotton shirt was frayed beneath the white stubble of the jaw. The tie had not been straightened. He noticed one of Hackett's shoe-laces tied tightly in a knot. He had probably broken it that morning and Mahon wondered if the old man's fingers, blue and knobbly, would find the strength to undo the shoe-lace when later he returned to his lonely bedroom. Hackett's suit hung about him and Mahon realised, for the first time, just how ill the old man looked. The eyes seemed blurred, heavy and resigned to some unexplained sadness.

'Are you looking after yourself?' Mahon said quietly.

It stung Hackett and he pulled himself up very straight in the upright chair, shoulders back, bony chin out. It was the look of the military man stung to defiance. 'The doctors irritate me. What can possibly be the point of operating now?'

'You look fine.'

'Listen,' said Hackett. 'I've seen too many of my friends carted into hospital. Friends one never saw again. Carted out on the National Health. I have never understood why hospitals can't be made moderately happy places. After all, they're supposed to be dedicated to making people healthy.' He drank deeply from his whisky glass. His face grew flushed, feverish almost. 'I want to tell you how very nice it is of you to waste some time with an old man. Not, of course, that at my age one is actually lonely. One just gets fearful of being a nuisance.'

'You're not. You'll be pleased, I think, to know that I did as you suggested.'

'What did I suggest?'

'To look at my father's file.'

'I suggested that?'

'In so many words,' said Mahon, looking casually about the room to make sure the other members of the drinking club were out of earshot. He noticed Hackett's practised gaze do likewise. Yes, the old boy knew exactly what was being talked about. He might not admit as much. But he knew all right. 'I went out to Records.'

'High Wycombe?'

'No, they've moved the dead files to just near Heathrow.'

'Yes, I'd forgotten. How appropriate.'

'I turned up my father's file. It was an odd experience. Rather like looking at some family album. If you can imagine it.'

'I can,' said Hackett. 'Certainly. And so you don't need to know any more.'

'On the contrary,' Mahon argued. 'I rather surprised myself by not having been prepared to discover so very little.'

'Isn't it all there still?'

'Everything and nothing.'

Hackett's eyes seemed to declare something remembered from a distant past. 'So like your father,' he said. 'The habit of speaking in riddles. Comes so easily in our world, don't you think?'

'Perhaps,' said Mahon, wanting to agree. 'Perhaps it was because you people, including my father, needed to disguise the truth for its own sake. The reports don't tell the whole story.'

'They never did,' said Hackett. 'All you seem to do nowadays is make reports, isn't it? So much is committed to paper I often wonder what will come of it all. I personally was never a paper man. I think Dickie wouldn't have minded me saying that he was. But then he was something of a bibliophile, like that curious American and his awfully young wife. An odd pair. Odder still for being bibliophiles. But I'm sure your father's file told enough of his story. In its way it was heroic. Not a word you hear generally now, "heroic", but I am sure you know exactly what I mean.'

'I think so.'

'Then you want something more from me?'

'If I knew the questions to ask it would all be so much easier.'

Mahon paused with that same expressionless look he gave when an issue of feeling was about to be raised and might require to be confronted. Hackett must have sensed what the younger man was thinking. At any rate, he guessed.

'I never knew him,' Mahon said.

'Dead relations are always more interesting than living ones. That's why genealogy enjoys so great a popularity. Our world isn't far removed from that science if science it be.' He laughed to himself. 'One can, of course, invent the past with genealogy just as one can the future with astrology. Do you believe in astrology?'

Mahon said he didn't.

'I knew your father rather in the manner you perhaps hope to discover him. Through the reports he sent back to London. On paper. The memoranda. The files. The advisory notes and recommendations. What we called the school reports.'

'We still do.'

'I'm not surprised.'

'I'll tell you what I want you to tell me,' said Mahon. 'Why was Wigart's report on my father's death so completely inadequate?'

'Was it?' said Hackett.

'You were the London man,' Mahon searched the weary old eyes angrily. 'Yes. Inadequate.'

Again Hackett seemed lost in far-off recollection. 'As I recall Dickie was a new boy at the time. Madrid he'd known as a tourist not as a serving officer. Not that I recall he was, for one minute, happy with his own report. Not so. You can imagine the situation there as it was then. The Japanese was invaluable to us. But by the time the Jap died he had effectively dried up as a source of much consequence. That cannot, I imagine, have been the reason why his lover was supposed to have murdered your father. The Germans, as well as Franco's people, regarded the matter as something of a scandal. There was no alternative. We wound up the investigation.'

By now Mahon realised Hackett was closing up. How should he redirect his approach? The appeal to nostalgia for the old Service and the halcyon days? Hackett's obvious dislike of all the modern generation had done to his Service? Or just plug on and ease the way with booze? He elected to combine all three tacks. He called for more whisky.

'So where exactly did the Jap's material land up?'

'London.'

'Of course. But where?'

'You mean with whom?'

'You tell me, Geoffrey, if you can. I'll understand if you don't want to. Nothing will go any further.'

Again Hackett laughed. Some of his whisky dribbled from the side of his mouth. 'Nothing *always* goes further.'

'Then tell me.' Mahon's voice, for the first time, was sharp and insistent.

'We had our fair share of paper men in London. Not hard to see why. Most of them had been academics. Some of them pretty washed out by now I imagine. One sees their saggy faces in *The Times*. The great and the good. The wise and reliable. Trustees of this and that. When I read that this country's future may be guided by their so-called wisdom I despair for the future I'll never live to see. The country would be better off in the hands of astrologers. Like the old girls who used to ply a trade in the first-floor rooms off Oxford Street before the war.

Madame This-and-that.. Half a crown for the future. You could buy it like sex.'

'Tell me, Geoffrey.'

The bony fingers set the glass down on the folded copy of the *Standard*. Hackett had been doing the crossword.

'Tell me,' Mahon attacked.

'Order and method. Aim, purpose, situation. All the old army solutions to help a man seek an empty victory. The Jap's stuff ended up in the pigeon-holes of tidy minds. The hard bastards. It didn't fall to my lot to provide an assessment of it.'

'But you'd have liked to, Geoffrey. That's what you'd have liked. Maybe you'd have got an OBE. God knows, might even have been appointed to the wise and good with a house in Bloomsbury, Hampstead, Richmond or wherever the old jerks live. Big pension. Money in the bank. Everything for a rainy day. But – instead – what happened? You're sitting here. With me. We're both a little the worse for wear.'

'Pissed?'

'You say so, Geoffrey.'

'I do. But not pissed enough not to know you're insulting me.'

'Only with the truth, Geoffrey. You're hiding something. You don't mind me knowing it. You don't mind because I know you *want* to open up to me. You want to talk and I know why.'

Hackett's eyes had tightened. They were very cold.

'Out of guilt?'

'No.'

'Out of what then?'

'Hate, Geoffrey. You know, like I do, how to hate. Otherwise you wouldn't have spent your whole life in the Service. Just like me now. You know, I know – that the best servants work out of hate. It's so terribly close to loyalty. You're just like all the rest, Geoffrey. All of us, countless hundreds, aren't there – waltzing around the UK some still serving, others retired. A great reservoir of manpower and intelligence preserved in brine.'

'Pickled?'

'I'm not being funny. Brine, I mean. Hate. You can see it. Like vinegar in a bottle. When you take the cork off you can smell it. Drink it and you can change everything. For the worse.'

'I don't entirely follow you,' Hackett said.

They faced each other. The young man and the old man no longer tied as friends of dead men but bonded as adversaries. Hackett, veteran of such confrontations, resorted, albeit briefly, to a kind of wit. 'The reason I turned down the OBE was because I refused to accept any Order from an Empire which, perfectly properly and in my lifetime, was wound up with due ceremony. I believe, modestly, but firmly, that anyone who accepts an honour to do with a defunct system of empire, or from any body connected with it, is either a pathetic hypocrite or a certifiable lunatic.'

'Geoffrey,' said Mahon, his face almost showing he was prepared to hear anything, touched Hackett's fingers where they lay on the table. '*Tell me.*'

'I was removed from the case not because of anything I had done.'

'Then why *were* you removed?'

'Because another man took it on.'

'Who did?'

'Old Newiston took it on. Henry's father. I told you, "Order. Method." The technician. We had the poets and the technicians. Both arrived at falsehood from different and opposite points of the solar system. I was your poet. Newiston was the technician.'

'Then just what were the last few weeks of my father's life about? What was *Nightshade*? Why was Wigart's report so pathetic?'

The old wet mouth contorted into a stammer. 'It was all beyond my control. Believe me, do not misunderstand, it was not, emphatically not, my responsibility. Your father was a heroic officer. I can't think of a greater compliment.'

'Then what the fuck were you saying in Madrid?'

Hackett winced. He pursed his lips into a rose-bud shape. 'The story ended. There's no point now retelling it.'

'But you talked of some great secret, Geoffrey. You mentioned that. Those were your words, weren't they? You're the cynic. The man who doesn't like the pantomime. Honours. All that trash. So what do you mean by a *great* secret?'

'You can interpret it how you wish.'

'I do not, repeat *not*, know what you're trying, what you're so desperately wanting to tell me.' Mahon paused briefly. 'Let me tell you this, Geoffrey. There's no going back now.'

49

To Mahon's astonishment the old man stood up perfectly steadily. Very clearly, and without a pause, he said, 'I've achieved what I set out to. Oh, I have no doubt of that, James.'

With that Hackett nodded, almost coyly, turned and left.

James?

It was his father's name.

Mahon watched him leave. The stoop increased visibly as the bony hand clutched the door handle. Then he was gone.

This time there had been no tears. Those, Hackett had let out in Madrid. For his father? For himself? For Wigart? The old man was worn out, a husk. All that remained was the dry and ancient kernel that drove him on, to the end that most likely would be bitter and alone, a secret servant to the last. Only now he could see that Geoffrey Hackett wanted to pass the secret on, obliquely, manipulatively, like some dreadful old seducer persuading a little girl to share a clandestine act.

Hurriedly, he left the club, hoping he would find Hackett ambling along the alley-way. He was seized by a wish to literally knock it out of the old man. It was his secret. His father belonged to him and not to Hackett's alcoholic fantasies.

The alley-way was deserted except for pigeons rootling in the upturned take-away packs. He turned into St Martin's Lane to lose himself among tourists with their sad faces and their complaining voices.

A bloated woman with her feet in vivid plastic shopping bags howled at him for money.

There was no sign of Hackett in the night crowd. At the entrance to the London Coliseum an umbrella leaned against the hoardings for *Madame Butterfly*. It was collapsed and broken. The pool of liquid on the pavement looked like blood.

9

'It's so nice to have someone to talk to,' Kirsty told Lindsay Finucane in the first-floor flat in Frithville Gardens. She made her confession to Lindsay with her back turned and staring down into the street. Outside stood a yellow skip loaded with broken floorboards, split bricks and crumbling plaster chunks. The iron gate lay propped against the garden wall.

Earlier they had met for a swim at a fitness club in the basement of a hotel off Kensington High Street. The swimming had made Kirsty's eyes reddish and it looked now as if she had been weeping. Along with Lindsay, naked in the sauna, she had suggested they visit the flat in Frithville Gardens. 'It's my private island,' said Kirsty. 'I used not to want anyone else on it. But I suddenly feel I'd like more people to know I have it.'

Out had come the theory about the aunt who had worked at the British Library and a story about her being progressive, a comment that Lindsay took to mean the old dear had enjoyed a succession of lovers in Frithville Gardens. It sounded an appropriate place for a girl to take her men.

Kirsty turned away from the window and said, sadly, 'It's a bit of luck having a place like this, isn't it?'

Lindsay thought it was. Yes. A bit of luck.

'I mean, I know it could do with a lick of paint. Maybe it doesn't quite feel lived in. But that's why I like it. A strange place I can come to and be a stranger. A secret place.'

'What about Henry?'

'Oh, Henry. I don't love him. I don't believe you can ever love a husband. The very word – husband – puts me off. It sounds like market-gardening or something to do with a suitcase. You know what I mean?'

Lindsay said she did. But actually she couldn't make the

connection at all. It didn't seem worth labouring her in-comprehension.

'Don't you like the plants?' Kirsty asked with melancholy breeziness. She began to point to the shelves of plants like a guide in a museum. '*Cissus antarctica, Hedera, Philodendron scandens, Saxifraga sarmentosa, Zebrina.* I can forgive *Zebrina* anything because she's got such a sweet name. They all have one thing in common. They don't need heat in winter. At least, that's what I've discovered. Maybe I should write a book about plants. The only trouble is my life consists entirely of living with hothouse plants. Would people like a book about ones that don't like the heat?'

'I guess they might,' said Lindsay with faint encouragement. 'I really like the way you keep the plants here.'

'I have a theory they keep the air fresh,' Kirsty said. 'Let me show you around.'

It was a normal routine. *This is the bathroom. Lav. Kitchen. My bedroom.*

'You sleep here?'

'Not at night,' Kirsty said, truthfully.

They sat down on the bed side by side.

'And you want someone to talk to?' Lindsay asked.

Kirsty bit her lip and shook a shoe from her foot. 'Maybe you don't find it with Lou. But I get so incredibly lonely in my marriage. What's it for? The only time we're close is when Henry's being foul. At least he gets worked up. It's better to have him bawling about the place like a fat child who's wet his trousers rather than slumped in a chair with papers all over the bloody place. And the more he says it's important the more I think he's unimportant. Who, finally, gives a fuck for what the Secret Service does? I'll tell you. No one. Why? Because no one knows about it in the first place except those pale-faced twitching miseries who work in it. If people in this country really knew what went on the whole God-damn thing would be closed down overnight. They think it's like a TV soap opera about spies. All dark walks on Hampstead Heath and plush houses, trips to lonely coastlines. That's fantasy. It's no more or less than petty rivalry of the kind you'd find in a domestic science college or a store in Oxford Street. Finally, trivial, disposable and above all, cheap.'

'Why not suggest Henry quit?'

'Because his whole world would fall about. He'd break up. It'd make a change. But it wouldn't help.'

'Maybe you should concentrate on doing this place up. Take up art, or something. Get a knitting-machine.'

Kirsty broke into laughter.

'Churn out jumpers for Henry? He'd love it. That's what the man wants. A Mummy. Some smiling old dumpy listening to women's programmes on the BB bloody C in the afternoons. He can stuff that.'

'I'm talking about you,' Lindsay said.

'Same thing.'

'You and Henry – the same thing?'

'That's what's so foul about it. I can't escape.'

'Then what's this place for?'

'Just an island.'

Lindsay looked at the bright blue eyes and was sure they told her Kirsty had a secret. She got up from the bed. 'It's the sort of place I wouldn't mind,' she said.

'What would you do with it?'

'I'd buy some new bed-linen. All white. Big pillows. Get a rug for the floor. Some new curtains.'

'Then what would you do?' Kirsty asked.

'Don't know,' said Lindsay.

'Bring Lou here?' Kirsty asked.

'No need. But what about you? Henry?'

'No,' Kirsty said. 'That's what I wanted to talk to you about.'

'I'm not much good at marriage guidance or therapy or whatever.'

'What would you say if you knew I was bringing someone else here apart from Henry?'

'Not for me to say. It might depend on who you were bringing here. I'd hope to hell it wasn't Lou.'

'It isn't.'

'You are bringing someone here? A lover?'

Kirsty took a deep breath. 'Please don't think the less of me. But I was dying, literally dying slowly. I could feel it creeping up my legs to here.' She tapped her stomach. 'All the way to my head. Can you understand?'

'I can understand a little of what you feel. Maybe, even of why you feel it. And I don't want to sound mean. But no one's the winner in those things.'

'I know that,' Kirsty said with renewed confidence. 'Meanwhile I'm a loser anyway. I've nothing to lose.'

'Unless you're found out. That wouldn't matter except that it obviously matters to you. You're scared, Kirsty. Scared, excited.'

'No. Relieved and happy.'

'Really? I'm pleased for you.'

'You know why I want it?'

'I think so.'

'So this,' said Kirsty, 'is what I want to ask you. It's very simple. Just for a short time. I'd be happier if I could say to Henry I'm having lunch, or going to some art gallery or something with you, Lindsay.'

'So that you can get into bed with Mr X here?'

'Sort of, yes.' Kirsty took her hand. 'Please, Lindsay. It's incredibly important to me. I'll do the same for you.'

'No thanks. No need.'

'Please?'

Lindsay felt trapped and heard herself telling Kirsty that she could indeed say she was spending time with her if that was really what she wanted. The feeling of being trapped was eased a little by Kirsty's outburst of delight. She said she'd make them both tea and lemon.

Lindsay supposed that was probably what she drank with her lover. She hated tea and lemon. She hoped she wouldn't live to regret what she'd just agreed to do.

Kirsty handed her the lemon tea. 'You haven't asked me who he is.'

'I don't think I need to know, do you?'

'Actually, yes. Yes, I do. For my sake, I'd like you to know. Just in case there's some awful emergency.'

'You think there may be?' Lindsay asked.

She followed Kirsty's gaze to the grubby panes of the window. It had started to rain heavily. The noise from the street was deadened.

'You don't want to know?' Kirsty said.

Lindsay looked aside.

'I'd like to tell you.'

'I know you would,' Lindsay said, more coolly than she intended. 'But I think. . .'

'Go on.'

'I think it would make me feel too involved in your deception. I don't like to feel trapped.'

'Don't take it so seriously,' Kirsty said. 'It's my affair. You've met him. You know who he is anyway.'

'I don't think so.'

'Well, he's John Mahon, so you needn't worry about it. He's trained to keep secrets.'

By the time Lindsay left the rain had stopped and a grey mist hung over the streets. She headed on foot in the direction of home wishing Kirsty had not unburdened Mahon's identity.

She found herself heading only in the vague direction of the Kensington flat from Shepherd's Bush to Notting Hill Gate. She hurried down into the pedestrian tunnels towards Holland Park Avenue. A Chinese girl violinist busked Mozart accompanied by a portable hi-fi. She was dressed like a boy and her tweed cap lay at her feet. Lindsay dropped a fifty-pence piece into it and the Chinese girl bowed her head gravely.

She walked, growing breathless, on her circuitous route the whole way to Kensington. She thought perhaps she'd buy something outrageous to change her mood, and went into Kensington Market. It was packed with freaks: thin people in soiled T-shirts ripped at the armpits. She saw pierced ears, teeth stained yellow, white flesh, shaved heads. Spiky hair the artificial colours of children's painting blocks. Livid. She breathed in the air smelling of wet blankets. Desperately she fought her way out and crossed the street the way she had already come. She bought a newspaper and sat on the low wall by the war memorial outside St Mary Abbott's Church. The paper read like a litany of violence. She caught a headline: DEATH IN GAS BLAST. FOUR DEAD. Reading on about the mystery explosion in north London she was aware a man and a woman had sat down either side of her. A voice said, 'You selling?'

She stared at the woman's bruised fore-arms, punctured, her patchwork of filthy elastoplasts. The addict's companion stank of almonds like dry rot. The eyes were sunken. She could smell the fear on his breath. 'Smack.'

'No, thanks,' she said, folding her newspaper, and the pusher gave her a sharp leer of contempt.

This wasn't the London she loved. The whole place was For

Sale, up for grabs, and if you didn't join the game you were resented even by the drug dealers. There had been a slight tone of resentment in what Kirsty had said to her also. But she understood and sympathised. Wasn't Kirsty doing what half the married women were doing anyway? Hadn't they always cheated on their husbands? Marriage was nowadays a matter for the statisticians: the more the wives cheated the more it had become acceptable. And there was no denying that Kirsty looked happier on it. Like they said of her husband, you couldn't help liking her. Hers seemed to be about the only human face in a society of cheats. It was hard to blame her for it.

10

Lou Finucane assumed he had said his last goodbye to the Federal Bureau of Investigation. He was perfectly happy to think the worlds of undercover criminal investigation and secret intelligence now considered him, if they considered him at all, merely as a minor figure of recent history. He had been far less comfortable with the view of the United States Ambassador who had called him 'a legend in his own lifetime'. At the farewell party when the Ambassador made his little speech about Lou's departure a new precedent was created when the Ambassador's wife was asked to make a presentation. 'I am honoured to present Mr Louis Finucane, on behalf of the Government of the United States, with his office desk.' It was a heavyweight nineteenth-century monster and neither Lou nor Lindsay wanted it. When, a month later, they were married, the Embassy sent no present. Perhaps it was felt the gift of the desk had been enough; or, maybe, the new staff were relieved to see him go. There was, they said, something mildly eccentric about Finucane.

He had, after all, told a succession of his superiors that CIA Headquarters was the only place in the United States where the garbage trucks delivered and never collected. He had even once explained to J. Edgar Hoover, no less, that an agent's life was spent mopping up the past so new generations of politicians could find yet another novel way of making a mess of the future. They said that Finucane was one of the few agents who had puzzled Mr Hoover. Maybe, Lou said, it was because Hoover was so sick in his last years that he had singled Lou out as a fine fellow. Lou said that was the kiss of death.

He sold his prized collection of rifles he had stored in a Houston bank vault. True, he'd no intention of going back to Houston anyway and hadn't added to the collection for over ten years. The main reason for selling them was to raise a capital sum to launch his career with Lindsay as L. & L. Finucane, Booksellers, from their top-floor flat in Kensington Court.

The idea of a former FBI agent, with a new wife so much younger than he was, buying books from the British, selling books to the British, also seemed, to some, a little odd. It was like an old prize-fighter signing on as a child-minder to the nobility: possible, but weird. Some people said it had to be a cover; the old fox couldn't stand life beyond the Bureau and was operating freelance, still on call to Washington.

It wasn't true.

Mr and Mrs Finucane became specialists and chose their specialities with care. Twentieth-century first editions of women's fiction was one: Bowen, Compton-Burnett, Woolf, Bainbridge, Spark, Drabble. They gambled on some newer writers. Finucane especially liked Anita Brookner's first novel and invested in six copies on publication day. Lindsay handled Ann Beattie, Spark and Iris Murdoch; even, Miss Barbara Cartland whose early fiction fetches a surprisingly good price if you know the name of the Nagasaki honey manufacturer who's a Cartland addict.

This stock in trade filled the floor-to-ceiling shelves in their flat. They stacked old cardboard shoe-boxes packed with coloured reference cards on top of the dreadful mahogany desk. Filing cabinets contained the catalogues from Christie's, Sotheby's, Maggs Bros and Rota's. In the midst of the papers stood Lou's old Remington typewriter.

His new identity yielded few signs that he had organised and administered cunning and irregular violence on behalf of the Free World for three and a half decades of the century. With Lindsay and his books he found a new and simple happiness.

For a long time before, things had been different. He had left his first wife because she was an alcoholic. It'd been bad when she drank and equally intolerable when she dried out to become an evangelical teetotaller. He had concentrated all his energies on his job and had cultivated a powerful and somewhat forbidding shield of solitude. He had never considered marrying again and had successfully resisted the advances of several divorcees who reckoned he might make a fine replacement husband. When Lindsay came along everything changed.

L. & L. Finucane became characters in the London trade. The dealers warmed to Lou's new world politeness, his economy of speech and manner. They appreciated the formidable memory and his delight in a bargain. He charmed the sniffier of the London dealers who variously described him as 'good news', 'a breath of fresh air' and 'one of us'. It was rumoured he had been asked to provide a memoir for *The New Yorker*. Had the offer really been made Lou would have turned it down, declining to write anything of a personal nature. The book dealers who liked women understandably appreciated the American bibliophile's sexy young wife. One or two had been heard to admit to envying his nights with her. There were some arcane in-jokes about her 'contemporary mottled calf', 'original wrappers' and 'small floral tool'.

After she'd been at Kirsty's place Lindsay went home to try and lose herself in work on the books. She carefully noted the tears in dust-jackets, numbered stains and blotches, copied out scribbled annotations in the margins. The less a book showed signs of actually having been opened let alone read, the greater its value to the prospective collector. Sometimes she stopped work to think of Kirsty, finding herself still affected by what she'd heard of her emotional chaos. She felt she had blundered into a mess. Kirsty's considerable unease was infectious.

It was Lindsay's job to type the book-lists they offered on their limited mailing-list to the specialist collectors and dealers. She enjoyed ordering the chaos. One of the collectors, a man at Christie's, was devoted to first editions in the espionage category. Two of the spy books were proof copies destined for him. He had some years ago been a student of Anthony Blunt's at the Courtauld. He had a small collection of Blunt's letters. The old traitor had corresponded with a friend at Oxford about Poussin. The man from Christie's was building up a collection of books on espionage to supplement the letters, and he had commissioned the Finucanes to assemble it. They had a fairly rare item for him, a proof copy of Kim Philby's *My Silent War*, his autobiography. The first edition had been withdrawn by the publishers before publication for it had offered a mild threat to state security. This vague sense of illegality was made additionally attractive by the book's introduction by Graham Greene.

Kirsty came to mind as she wrote to the collector of espionage material.

She went on to type up the entries in the Twentieth-century Fine Printing section:

Gervasi, Esther M. *A Week in Como*; poems. Drawings and an afterword by Nadia Gagliardini. 1984. Of 60 numbered copies, signed by the author and the artist, this one is one of 20 on Indian handmade paper. Printed in blue, brown and yellow in Dante. Folio, quarter red morocco, pictorial boards, morocco tips. New Copy. £650.

This vigorous collaboration brings together eight figure drawings of the poet and a self-portrait, with four poems especially written to accompany them. The duotone process used to print the drawings gives them the quality of hand-pulled lithographs.

Nadia Gagliardini's delicate drawings of the Israeli poet reminded Lindsay of Kirsty. Bright worried eyes. Same slim hips. They showed an edgy and nervous woman of considerable vulnerability.

She set aside a complete set of Patricia Highsmith and reckoned she was on the up. She typed out an entry for John Fowles's *The Collector,* a snip from the War on Want shop she had bought for a pound. Perfect dust jacket. Fabulous find. Signed by Fowles in his minute scratchy handwriting. She offered it for sale at £400.

In another room in the mansion flat off Kensington Square she could just make out snatches of Lou's conversation with a client.

'*Murderers' Cottages* by Glynn Boyde Harte from Jonathan and Phillida Gili's Warren Editions. One signed by both the artist and Mrs Gili.'

The client, a man from the Prisons Department of the Home Office, bought the lot. Lindsay listened to his departure. He oozed the pride and gratitude of an addict who has found his safe supplier. It had crossed Lindsay's mind that book dealing was not entirely different from dealing in illicit drugs. The clients were hooked in both cases. It also occurred to her that Kirsty might be addicted in her own way to her illicit love affair.

Lindsay decided to keep the identity of Kirsty's lover a secret from Lou. To have told him would represent a challenge to the safety of their own world. Moreover, she had had a straightforward rule of thumb about secrets: namely, it's easier to keep them if you put them out of mind altogether. She had, of course, been greatly tempted to tell Lou. When she imagined what his reaction might be she decided with even greater determination against telling him. She was sure that to involve him in it would increase the deception and tighten the trap she felt was gripping her.

Lou came in and leaned over his old Remington to read the blurb about the Gervasi-Gagliardini collaboration.

'If anyone calls for me,' she said, 'say I'm out.'

'Out where?'

'With Kirsty Newiston.'

He sat beside her opening the day's mail and saying they might do well to follow Rota's terms of description, '*Good copy* is used to denote reasonable second-hand condition. . .' when he broke off:

'Why?'

She hesitated before replying. She'd have to tell him a part of it.

She told him about the flat in Frithville Gardens, about Kirsty wanting to preserve her sanity, to regain her self-respect and identity by taking a lover. She heard herself saying it almost tentatively, offering up the reasons like a list of excuses. The longer the list the less the conviction.

He listened blankly whilst she explained the nature of the mild deception she was entering into for the sake, as she put it, 'of discretion'.

She could not at once tell what he was thinking.

'I didn't want to draw you into it,' she said, reaching for his hand. 'I haven't mentioned it before because it didn't seem to matter.'

'It matters a hell of a lot,' he said. 'For some women a bit of screwing about can be beneficial. For Newiston's wife it's different. For a start her husband's main skill in life is dealing with deception. It's his whole life. Keep out of it, Lindsay.'

'I can't.'

'Why not?'

'She needs a friend.'

'You?'

'Me. If that's who she's chosen.'

'And what's your role? Confidante, dead letter-box, go-between?'

'I don't like it, Lou.'

'But you like Kirsty, that it?'

'Sure.'

'Then let me tell you, Lindsay, Henry won't be one of those husbands who're the last ones to know.'

'It's his fault, Lou. He's the one who's driven her to it.'

'How do you know?'

'Because he pays her no attention.'

'And what evidence do you have for that?'

'They don't make love in any meaningful sense. In fact I'd say she's keeping things going by taking a lover.'

'What we used to call a mid-flight refueller?'

'I'm being serious, Lou. You know, everyone knows it's happened a thousand times before. It'll happen again.'

'Sounds to me,' he said, 'slightly pathetic. If it stops there.'

'What makes you think it won't?'

'Has anyone told you a story like that which does end there? All I'm saying is that a man like Newiston is addicted to his work. It's the secrecy that gives him his power. It's his life. It's precisely that addition which'll draw him to find out his wife's cheating on him. Kirsty's an amateur. She probably told you underneath she's scared.'

'Maybe. But I'm not sure how scared she really is.'

'Depends on the man.'

She hoped Lou wouldn't ask. Inevitably, he did.

'You know him,' she said.

'What's his name?'

'Perhaps it's better if I don't say. If you're involved in the whole thing it'll be better if I don't say.'

'If you're involved in the whole thing it'll be best if you tell me.'

'It's John Mahon.'

'You're not serious?'

'I am.'

'Holy shit.'

11

The clock on the wall of Mahon's office said just after three o'clock when he returned from lunch. He found Henry Newiston waiting for him.

'I think we'd better close the door, John.'

Mahon did as he was told.

'I wanted you to hear the news before anybody else,' Newiston said.

Mahon's first thought was for Kirsty.

The telephone rang and Newiston answered. 'I'm afraid he's in a meeting,' he said. 'Perhaps you'll call back.' He replaced the receiver with studied care. 'The Poles, Dziendzina and Kuzminski,' Newiston said.

'What's happened?'

'They're dead.'

'I don't believe it.'

'I'm afraid it's true. We heard an hour ago. They were shot during the night in Gdansk. It looks as if the East Germans got to them. Terrible bad luck, isn't it? But I doubt they said anything, do you?'

There was a silence.

'I don't know,' Mahon said.

'Precisely. One can never be sure. I'm sorry. Chayter thinks we should wind the whole thing up. Unless you have any other ideas? He's asked me to pick your brains. Of course, if you want to press on, find some replacements, I suppose we could start again. But we'd be open to so much more risk, don't you think?'

Mahon stared at the clock. It was old government issue and gave off a low continuous hum. He thought of the two young Poles and the promises he'd made them of a new life at the University of Leicester and wondered if they'd been interrogated before they'd been shot. 'I feel responsible,' Mahon said. 'It was going almost too well.'

'It happens,' Newiston said. 'It'll probably happen again.'

'One had got to know them.'

'I know how you feel. Personally involved. One always is.' Newiston examined his fingernails. 'John Chayter and I wonder if you'd like some leave. A short break from the desk, as it were. A rest?'

'I'd prefer to pick up the pieces.'

'There's no need. We'll let the whole thing lie down for a time. I've spoken to Warsaw. Everyone thinks it'll be for the best to keep a low profile for the time being.'

'What about the students Kuzminski was running?'

'They can be spoken to. They don't rate getting out, do they? Suppose they did run?'

'We'd be shown up.'

'Exactly. Let sleeping dogs lie, don't you think? Perhaps our East German friends had put two and two together. Perhaps not.'

Mahon remembered his last meeting with the two young Poles in Stockholm. He wondered whether even then the East Germans had watched him. It had been his personal recommendation they take the Poles on. Now it was all over. 'You're quite sure they're dead?'

'There's not a shred of doubt.' Newiston hesitated. 'Chayter wonders whether you've lost some of your spark, whether there's been a dimming, as it were, of your love for the hunt.'

'That's why he thinks I need a rest?'

'Just a change of locale. A posting, perhaps. How would you react?'

'I'd rather stay in London for the time being.'

'For personal reasons?'

Mahon again thought of Kirsty. And when he looked up at Newiston he fancied he saw something in his eyes. 'No,' he said. 'Nothing personal.'

'You don't have any private problems, do you?' Newiston asked. 'You can always talk things over with me. Please do.'

'I'm very grateful for the offer.'

'Bear it in mind.'

Suddenly he saw Newiston as Kirsty's husband, the man who shared her bed at night. He felt a sudden sense of pity for him.

64

Newiston was saying: 'I can understand everything you'll be feeling about the Poles. A pang of mourning, perhaps. It's no exaggeration to say the loss of an agent's like the end of a love affair. But always remember nobody ever actually dies of a broken heart. They went into it with their eyes open didn't they?' He was by the door. 'It was a bold try. Don't let it upset you.'

Two days after the failure of Mahon's Polish operation Kirsty made dinner for him. A get-together with some old school friends was the alibi she gave Henry. She tried to pretend to Mahon the evening was a spontaneous event and proposed they shop for food together. She made him carry her large string bag and bought a jumble of almonds, onions, garlic, green chillies, ginger and yogurt for them to prepare a leg of lamb. She was trying hard to make it pleasant; the meal was Indian and she burned a patchouli incense stick. The scent was overpowering. She wanted each encounter to be separate and novel. She knew that one day her lover might be bored, or that sooner or later, the issue of Henry might intrude and destroy what she believed had renewed her life. She prepared herself to say that Henry no longer loved her. What she least expected was the direction from which the intrusion now came.

'How much does Henry tell you about his work?' Mahon asked her over dinner.

'Virtually nothing at all,' she replied. 'He may say that he'd be interested to know what I thought about such-and-such an attaché at some embassy thing. What's his wife like? That sort of thing. He usually asks when he thinks a wife may have confided some unhappiness in me. Of course, they rarely do.'

'Has he ever talked about me?'

'Only to say that the Chayters found you amusing.'

'Amusing?'

'They were discussing the eligibility of service bachelors. They reckoned you were eligible. It was a perfectly innocent comment as I recall. No more or no less than a little gossip.'

'Nothing else?'

'Why should he?' she asked. 'Unless, of course, he knows you're my lover. If he knew that it'd be different, wouldn't it? Why should he ask me about you?' Her mood had shifted. She looked at him with worried curiosity. 'Is something wrong?'

'Only that for the first time I am responsible, indirectly responsible, for two people being shot, murdered. There was nothing I could do to prevent it.'

'Who were they?'

'Two people in the field. Same age as us, maybe a little younger.'

'Was it your fault?'

'I'm not sure it was my fault although you could say I was to blame.'

'Do you want to tell me about it?' she said almost maternally.

He smiled at her. 'It won't help either of us if you know.'

'Is Henry involved too?'

'Only in so far as I'm answerable to him. We're all involved. But they were expendable in their way.'

'Then you've nothing to worry about.'

'Henry's attitude towards me was fairly odd. He seemed to be sounding me out. Chayter apparently thinks I may have lost my enthusiasm for the whole business. Henry asked if I ought to take some leave, have a rest.'

'That's perfectly understandable, isn't it?'

'Perhaps. Except that he was showing an overweening interest in my welfare.'

'He likes to father people. He's not much good at the real business of being a father or, for that matter, at being a husband. But when it comes to work it's all different. It's just about the only outlet he has for his feelings. At least I assume that's the outlet. He certainly doesn't find one in his family.' She hesitated and looked sadly at Mahon. 'Don't let's discuss him.'

After dinner they went to bed and made love. Afterwards Kirsty held him in her arms. 'What is it you're so unhappy about?'

'Henry told me there's some talk of a posting.'

She sat bolt upright in the bed.

'Don't worry,' Mahon told her. 'I won't accept it. I just wondered if there might be another reason for them wanting me to go abroad again.'

'Such as what?'

'You perhaps.'

She laughed at him and his surprise must have showed.

'You think it has nothing to do with us?' he asked.

'I know it hasn't.'

'What makes you so sure?'

'Because I know Henry's style. If he thinks he has an enemy he sails in close.'

'That's exactly the point I'm making.'

'But he doesn't show his hand like that. You feel the responsibility for the two field agents you lost. They probably think you'd like a change of scene. All you have to say is that you don't want it. You don't, do you?'

Instead of replying he kissed her deeply and after they had lain still for some time in silence he fell asleep.

When he awoke he saw Kirsty had already dressed.

She looked at him from the end of the bed. 'It's time to go,' she told him. 'Sad, isn't it?'

He left alone, some minutes before Kirsty, and headed down the Uxbridge Road searching for a cab. The rain glistened on the pavements. Dirty water from a bus splashed his trousers. Ahead of him he saw the figure of a man turn and stare at him. The glare of a streetlight hid the features. He was certain the man was watching him. He looked around quickly. Sure enough, as his instinct had already warned him, there was another figure. A cab came towards him and Mahon waved it down. He gave the driver his address in Gordon Place. When the cab passed the second figure, he saw the man move into the shadows of a shop entrance and he couldn't see the features.

He had to confess to himself his fear had begun to stalk him. He hoped it was only a passing sense of guilt to do with Kirsty.

12

It was his modest gesture of hospitality to Hanratty that brought Mahon's breakthrough at Nelson Unit.

Hanratty was delighted to be invited to lunch at the Hounslow Raj.

'You can always tell a good restaurant by the quality of its table linen,' he declared. 'I'll tell you what my mother used to do,' he added, with the air of a man imparting a compromising personal secret. 'Whenever we dined together in the fifties off the Finchley Road she was always most careful to examine the serviettes. Never paper serviettes mind.' He fingered the garish red paper table napkins. 'She'd have died at the sight of these. Bad for trade. She was in the laundry business.' He fingered the edge of the table cloth. 'Slightly starched. A good sign.'

Mahon said he supposed it was. After all Hanratty must know what he was banging on about. He was the guardian of dirty linen. It seemed appropriate his mother had spent her life in the laundry business.

Soon enough his patient listening to Hanratty's curious reminiscences was rewarded.

'Speaking for myself,' the archivist told him, 'I think of myself as the family solicitors' senior clerk.' He tapped his forehead. 'It's all in here. Sometimes, you know, I think I have a better picture of history than anyone else. And other times the thought scares me. You see, I never set out to be a cog of any consequence in the machine. It's been visited upon me. The Fates decreed it.'

'You obviously have the right instincts.'

'You develop an instinct for visitors like yourself, Mr Mahon.'

'About what especially?'

'About what you're looking for. I'll show you what I mean

after lunch. Meantime, I'll have the tandoori chicken if you don't think that's an extravagance.'

Mahon's continuing search confirmed that Henry Newiston's father had been assigned to liaison duties in Washington sometime in 1941. Newiston Snr had been given this job before the main flow of intelligence that might have been connected with *Nightshade* had begun. And yet still there was nothing of consequence about the *Nightshade* intelligence and his father's last operation. He remained convinced his father had in some degree finally been similarly connected with an American operation. The clues were all there in the records of small expenses. You could rely on the accountants to leave their mark behind. But it took Hanratty's instinct to make the point.

He produced a mug of Earl Grey tea and the *Nightshade* file. He brought it in with ceremony and with gratitude for his lunch. 'It's never a question of knowing everything,' he announced. 'It's a question of knowing where to look, isn't it?'

Mahon agreed.

'I'm nipping out for a *Standard*,' Hanratty said. 'For my stars. I'm a Gemini. The *Standard's* the best for Geminis.'

Mahon now saw his father's past staring him in the face. At last, he was on the way.

He was still reading when Hanratty returned.

'It's bad news,' said the archivist.

'I'm sorry.'

'Maybe they'll be better tomorrow. Want to know yours?'

'I don't believe in all that,' Mahon said.

He had no need of astrology now. At last he felt he was facing certainty. He'd seen one picture of history he believed and he could see why such pictures of history sometimes scared Hanratty. Unlike the astrologer's charts it spoke more grandly of death and truth.

Lizzie Chayter first noticed Kirsty's new bloom at dinner with the Newistons.

Once a month the senior wives gave dinner at home. Tonight it was Kirsty's turn to play hostess. Lizzie had long since realised that Kirsty normally 'bought in' dinner ready-made from Lidgate's, a butcher's across London in Holland

Park Avenue: pâtés, cold meats, chocolate mousse. It was an agreeable deception for the food was always good. But on this occasion Kirsty had gone to considerable trouble to prepare dinner herself: watercress soup, poached saddle of lamb, terrine of oranges with raspberry sauce. And one of Lizzie Chayter's sillier theories about womankind was that the cook who bothers is the one who's satisfied in love. She looked, in vain, at Henry for signs that he was the source of his wife's new-found satisfaction. She watched Kirsty, Henry opposite her; Dilip Mehta and his wife, Karuna; Geoffrey Hackett and Linda Boden-Smith. Kirsty had perceptibly changed. After all, one thing about the regular dinners never changed: their relentless sameness. Now there was a different Kirsty. Her hair shone, her eyes were altogether livelier; she was wearing some new perfume unfamiliar to Lizzie. Indeed, Lizzie noticed, Kirsty was the only woman there wearing an outfit that hadn't been brought out for a previous dinner. She observed Kirsty's transformation with a fascination bordering on the suspicious. For a start, she thought, Kirsty's the only one here who isn't watching everyone else. When the saddle of lamb arrived she began to wonder whether Kirsty might not be in love. If so, it certainly wasn't with Henry. Lizzie Chayter had long ago concluded, rightly, that the Newistons' was a loveless marriage. In so far as that was no exception to the general service rule she felt no great sympathy or pity. It was just another fact of service life in which love had no place. Everything that Henry was saying confirmed her view. As usual he was bent on giving a good account of himself. It was Chayter's mild criticism of the Soviet infiltration of the United Nations which prompted Henry Newiston's self-righteous outburst:

'The Service is a national asset. It resides at the moral centre of the nation. There are only two institutions this country has given the world – everyone knows the one.' He looked around the table, jaw jutted: 'Parliament. And the other?'

It fell to Hackett to give the answer:

'The Service.'

'Yes,' said Henry Newiston. 'Exactly. And the UN has never grasped the virtues of our systems of debate just as no other nation has properly followed the example of our Service.'

Lizzie noticed her husband watching Dilip Mehta. It was to

her a familiar duel of words invariably fought out across the Service dinner tables. It was a duel fought for the benefit of her husband by those who thought themselves the most suitable candidates for the Deputy Directorship. It was, of course, not strictly on to appear too keen, too up-front, too obviously ambitious. Henry Newiston used all the apparent force of his hollow piety to present himself in the best of lights. It was a slightly repulsive show. But it sounded right enough to Geoffrey Hackett:

'Wouldn't you agree with me that your generation might be in danger of too much single-mindedness?'

'What do you think is wrong with that?' Dilip Mehta asked.

'Pursued,' Hackett stammered, feeling himself under gentle attack, 'as it usually is at the expense of fellow officers – it can be a real danger to the Service fabric.'

'I agree,' Henry interrupted.

'Let him finish,' Dilip Mehta protested gently.

'What matters is the paramount importance of the Service. It's been my life. I think there are some younger people who'd share my view.'

'Such as?' Chayter asked

'Mahon?' Hackett offered.

Henry Newiston smiled: 'Without being critical in his absence I'd say it's that precisely, his absence no less, which pretty well shows up his lack of commitment. Look at the Polish débâcle.'

Hackett came to Mahon's defence. 'We've all lost people at one time or another. Is there anyone who hasn't?'

'Me,' said Linda Boden-Smith.

'Your time'll come,' said Chayter.

Boden-Smith looked crushed. 'I hope not,' she said, lamely.

It was Hackett who came to her defence and Mahon's too: 'I don't imply such misfortune is a *sine qua non* for the recognition of loyalty.' He tapped the table with his finger. 'His idealism, if that's what one may be allowed to call it, is not misplaced. He's his father's son. Just as you too are, Henry.'

Kirsty, who had finished eating ahead of the others, looked around the table at her guests' plates. She did not dare to look into anyone's face in case she caught a watching eye. She badly wanted the others to hurry up and finish so she could leave the dining room and bring in the terrine of oranges with the raspberry sauce. She was trying to appear interested but the mention of Mahon's name had made her shiver. Well enough, she knew that, even in your own home, you could never feel safe if you'd married into the Service.

'Kirsty,' she heard Lizzie Chayter say. And she looked up, trying to hide the sudden agitation she felt at the mention of her name, straight into Lizzie's face and saw her all too pleasant expression. She felt a sharp sense of *déjà vu*. It seemed as though Lizzie had been watching her like this for the whole evening.

'Can I help you at all?' Lizzie asked. 'Pudding?'

'I can manage perfectly. Thanks.'

Lizzie Chayter was already on her feet holding out her hand to Dilip Mehta for his plate.

'We haven't quite finished,' Henry said, quietly.

Kirsty felt everyone's eyes burning into her head.

'I'm sorry,' she said.

'But it was so very good,' said Dilip Mehta.

His wife agreed with him.

Kirsty heard Hackett asking Henry about Eton and her son, Hal. For a moment she greatly envied Hal for not being there. She envied Mahon his absence too. She wished she was in bed with him, that she'd made him dinner, that they were sharing it together, naked, laughing.

Lizzie was carrying a plate in each hand, holding them out for Kirsty to take them. 'Do let me help.'

'It's fine, Lizzie, thanks, really. Here.'

Kirsty took the plates and turned her back on her guests. She wanted to get out, go, anywhere. Above all she wanted to be alone. She heard the conversation start up again behind her and hurried out of the room to the kitchen.

A dog moaned in the darkened street outside Mahon's basement. He could just hear the cries above the dull repetitive thuds from a hi-fi beating out somewhere else in the house. In the early hours both the dog and the hi-fi stopped. The only sound was of Mahon's fingers turning the pages of the *Nightshade* story that he read with a dreadful fascination.

He sat slouched over the desk with his left hand clenched and his right at the top of the page ready to turn it over fast and he felt as if he were reading the story of someone else's clandestine love affair. He had the sense that the participants, known to him at one remove, had been drawn to duplicity almost unwillingly, that they hadn't been able to help themselves. Above all his father's powerlessness unfolded. He knew he was going to die but the horror ahead would be the circumstances of death though he knew the drab file would not describe the pain or squalor of the final moments. The official record unwittingly would spare the personal details.

The dull officialese recorded Churchill's efforts to befriend the United States; it described the pattern of the old man's tenacious befriending of Roosevelt. All that time his predecessors in the wartime Service insisted the Japanese would not assault Russia with the Germans. Instead, the Japanese would strike southwards. The most likely date was thought to be the weekend of 29 November 1941. No one was prepared to say quite when.

Then he found the summaries of his father's radio signals from Madrid. His father was living on the brink. He felt the agony of his father's waiting days; he shared the fear of the secret meetings snatched in the bars, alley-ways, and decrepit Madrid hotels.

His father had seen Pearl Harbor coming and had told London. His own people, the Service, the old generation had known ahead of time. It was plain to see. They had decided the Americans must not be warned. They would let it happen. They wanted the ally they had courted so assiduously to take the full force of the Japanese attack. As the duplicity became clearer his mind leapt forward, full of self-doubt, confusion and anger. This was why Hackett had shed his tears. The old boy must be suffering the confused emotions of the senile. Masterfully, Hackett had managed to engineer the discovery. It was the classic move: give someone else the motive, means and will to commit the crime. He felt a new and greater rage against Hackett and his kind. Could Hackett also have been a party to Wigart's murder? Was he shedding tears of guilt as well?

Perhaps Wigart had himself been about to talk, to make some final confession of the truth knowing, in spite of everything, he would smash the one relationship upon which the success of the Service was now founded – with the Americans, irretrievably change the Service, his own life, and –for that matter – everybody else's.

He thought he could still hear the moaning dog in the street outside and walked to the window. He drew aside the curtain. Dawn had broken yellowish across the London sky. He felt very cold.

His bedside clock said 05.50.

It seemed appropriate to have opened up the tomb at dawn, in the cold, and quite alone. Before closing it again for the last time he promised himself he would pursue the truth about his father's death to the end.

13

That Friday afternoon he didn't turn up at Kirsty's flat.

She waited two hours for him to telephone. She imagined he was ill, the victim of the unseasonal cold. There must, of course, be some entirely legitimate reason. Again and again she looked at the clock, told herself not to lift up the telephone, to pretend it did not hurt her. Above all she hoped there was a reason and not some false excuse showing up indifference. Was he tired of her? Had he simply forgotten? It could wait no longer. It was time to return to Henry. She telephoned expecting there to be no reply. But when there wasn't she feared the restoration of her life had ended.

In the evening she resolutely refused to talk to Henry. She told him to make his own dinner. It was about time he learned to take care of himself. She felt like telling him that Hal ought to learn how to cook too. Why should Etonians be exempted from learning the housewife's skills? She recognised her unreasonable responses and took herself to bed seeking solitude.

When Henry joined her she pretended to be asleep. She heard him say 'Good night.' Heard him fall asleep and begin his dreadful heavy breathing. Eventually she fell into a restless sleep.

Next Friday he didn't come either. Again there was the waiting, the watching of the clock, the telephone call to his flat unanswered. She had written to him angrily the week before. There had been no reply, she left for home weeping.

She stood before Constable's *Haywain* in the National Gallery waiting for Lindsay. A woman with thinning silver hair was lecturing a group of Japanese. Kirsty stood to the edge of the group: 'The one permanent fact of England is the impermanence of English weather,' the lecturer droned. 'It is the abiding greatness of John Constable, born over two hundred years ago, that he managed to paint weather. And if you will now be so good as to look at the foreground you will see Constable's great gift for the painting of mud.'

'Lud?' interrupted a Japanese with pained astonishment.

'Mud,' the lecturer continued with a false smile, 'watery soil.'

Kirsty saw one of the Japanese eyeing her breasts and turned away willing Lindsay to arrive.

She had left home after breakfasting on coffee secretly laced with brandy and a blazing row with Henry about the telephone bill. She couldn't understand why Henry made such a fuss. The Service paid for it anyway. He answered her with silence once more. Now she wondered whether their telephone was bugged. Perhaps someone had tipped Henry off that she had been trying to telephone Mahon and had failed. She wondered what conclusion the eavesdroppers might have reached; whether they could discover who you were calling even before you were connected. She felt a hand touch her on the shoulder and turned abruptly, thinking the Japanese had crept up in silence with a sullen proposition.

It was Lindsay.

'Let's find an empty room,' Kirsty said. She glanced at the shrilling lecturer. 'I can't stand any more.'

They moved to a corridor where the light was dimmer. Except for a uniformed attendant at the far end, it was empty.

'You look very tired,' Lindsay said.

'Yes. I am.' She said she wanted Lindsay's advice.

It tumbled out. 'I could get out of the marriage. He hasn't touched me in God knows how long. Do you know what I feel for him?'

Lindsay was watching the attendant on his chair, trying to calculate whether he could hear what Kirsty was saying.

Impatient, Kirsty continued, answering her own question: 'It's like living with a brother you don't like. Can you imagine it? I've been through the whole lot. Lover, mother, friend, sister. And now.' She paused, looking at a painting without seeing it. 'Now I'm an enemy.'

'Let time take its course,' Lindsay said.

'What? Days, months, years? Waste the rest of my life? No thanks.'

'You've got to give it more time.'

' "It"? You mean Henry? Why should I? He's taking mine, my time. It's running out.' She looked around and Lindsay could see she was full of a wild anger. 'I want to get out of here,' she shouted.

They walked through the midday traffic to Trafalgar Square and sat by the edge of the fountains.

'I think you should get some help,' Lindsay said.

Kirsty ignored her. 'There's only one person who can help me, you know.'

'Kirsty, what's happened?'

'He's stood me up two weeks running. He's not answering my telephone calls. I assume he's there and just not answering. I can't ring him at his office. Well, I suppose I could. But you never know who's listening in. I can't leave a message for him to call me. It's all so unfair.' She picked up a discarded newspaper and tossed it at the strutting pigeons. Some of them flew up to settle further away. 'What would you do?'

'I'd get some help. Talk to your doctor.'

'What could he do? Prescribe some valium. Tell me to see a shrink. Take Henry to see some pious marriage counsellor. That's the last thing on earth Henry would do. We've said all there is to say. It's dead, completely dead. And I'm in love with someone else. I suppose I could tell the doctor that. What would he say? "Go away for a holiday, Mrs Newiston." Okay, so where to? Who with? Who else could I talk to?' She twined her fingers together. Her knuckles whitened.

'You can always talk to me,' Lindsay said. 'Any time you like.'

Kirsty shook her head slowly. 'I don't deserve all this. I really don't. I just feel so utterly trapped. If only . . . ' She gave a bitter laugh.

Lindsay waited for her to continue.

'If only he'd say he loved me.'

'Henry?' Lindsay said.

'Oh, no. I don't ever want to hear that from him again. No. I mean John Mahon. If only he'd tell me what he felt. If only he'd say this isn't just some trivial game.'

'Are you sure that's what he thinks?'

'I don't know what he thinks.'

'Then ask him.'

'I would if only he'd see me again.'

'Give him time. He will. I'm sure.'

Again Kirsty gave her small sad laugh. 'Come and see me to say goodbye. That he can't go on. That he's compromised. Isn't everyone in their way?'

Lindsay smiled at her. 'He'll come back to see you. I'm sure.'

'I wish I was,' Kirsty said. 'I do so wish I was.' After a pause she added, 'It isn't as though I've been unkind to him. I haven't hurt him. So why is he hurting me?'

'I don't think he's hurting you intentionally,' Lindsay said. 'I think you're hurting yourself, Kirsty. And you deserve better than that. If he doesn't come back you call me. Call me either way.'

Kirsty was on the verge of tears.

'It's okay,' said Lindsay, putting her arm around her. But she knew it wasn't and wished secretly Kirsty had never drawn her into the hopeless muddle of her life.

14

Mahon drove across Richmond Park through the evening mist. He was held up at the back of a line of traffic. The cars had stopped to let deer cross the road. A child leaned out of the car in front, taking photographs. The deer ambled away swallowed up by the mist and the cars moved on again.

He knew he was missing Kirsty. He wondered whether his silence might cool her obsession; briefly, he hoped it might. The more he thought about it he hoped it wouldn't kill the flame.

Geoffrey Hackett's house stood at the end of a small private estate off Kingston Vale. It was one of those houses that had been daringly modern in the thirties and now seemed wholly out of place, like a villa transplanted from a south coast resort. The concrete path to the door was flanked by several plant troughs full of weeds.

He opened the door to Mahon with a look of mischief.

'Everyone always has frightful difficulty finding me out here,' he stammered. 'Come in. I bought some hot-cross buns for tea. They make them all the year nowadays, you know. Every day's Good Friday.'

He couldn't disguise the frailty. He was more stooped than ever and the voice had an uncomfortable rasp to it which made Mahon want to clear his own throat.

Mahon followed the old boy into the gloomy hallway past a stand packed with walking-sticks. A coat rack stood at a tilt weighed down with overcoats. Two dusty bowler hats lay on an oak chest. The dark interior smelled curiously of camphor and stale tobacco. It was the chill and damp retreat of an old schoolmaster, friendless and solitary.

The living-room windows looked out over a wide lawn bordered by roses, tangled and overgrown. A long and low bench had been fitted beneath the window. It was covered with cushions in worn corduroy. Three bars of an electric fire glowed in the fireplace beneath the mantelpiece. On the walls were nineteenth-century English primitive paintings of prize Sussex and Hereford bulls by Whitford and Davis.

'My sister collected them,' Hackett said. 'They came with the house. She gave the lot to me. One should be grateful. Though I'm bound to say I've never shared her liking for paintings of agricultural stock. Father was a farmer. He liked to be reminded of his commercial successes. Hence the paintings.' He laughed bleakly, an announcement he was about to make a wry joke. 'My sister is a vegetarian. You'd have thought she'd disapprove of pictures of cattle, wouldn't you? Will you have tea with the buns? Or do you prefer coffee? I have some Java beans.'

Mahon opted for the coffee and went with Hackett into the kitchen. He watched the stiff hands struggle with the coffee grinder. He noticed the familiar frayed shirt collar and cuffs and wondered whether Hackett had any different clothes. Even the shoe-lace was still tied in a knot. He wore decrepitude like a uniform. It seemed like he hadn't undressed at all since the last encounter in the drinking club.

'There's some milk in the fridge,' Hackett said. 'If you wouldn't mind.'

When Mahon opened the refrigerator he saw its contents added up to no more than a small milk carton, a pack of carrots and a jar of Cooper's Oxford marmalade.

Hackett fiddled with his coffee-maker. 'I was at lunch two days ago at the Athenaeum. A friend was saying how difficult it's proving to upset the Poles. Wasn't that one of your little schemes?'

'Eastern Europe's scheme,' Mahon said. 'You win a few, you lose a few.'

'*Tant pis*. The Poles always were so emotional. Mind you, they've had a lot to be emotional about down the years. The only man I lost was a Yugoslavian. He'd upset Tito. It never paid to upset Tito. Shall we have tea in the drawing room? You can carry the tray.'

The hot-cross buns were stale and glutinous and the raisins hard.

Mahon began: 'You told me my father was heroic.'

'Yes.'

'But *Nightshade* was hardly heroic. His file doesn't have an end. It simply peters out. How do you expect me to interpret what's left in it?'

Very slowly Hackett crossed his legs. The bird-like fingers stroked the arm of his chair. 'There was a memorandum written by Newiston which objected powerfully to anyone passing the Pearl Harbor material to Washington. Of course, at the time, it was completely understandable. You can understand the dilemma that faced the executive. To tell the Americans within less than a week of the Japanese attack might have in some way deflected the Japanese. They were on the way, yes. But they might have turned back if they'd found their surprise blown. They might have turned on us somewhere out there instead.'

'What did you think?'

'At the time? About the decision?'

'Yes.'

'I thought the policy was correct. After all, at the end of the day, the point was to make perfectly sure that sooner or later the Americans came in on our side. Obviously, we couldn't have insisted on it. It was up to them to decide for themselves. They weren't necessarily showing any signs of doing so. Roosevelt was in a cleft stick. The whole point was to let them persuade *themselves* to come in. If that needed the Japs then so be it. If it required loss of life, the destruction of the United States Pacific Fleet then, well, so be it. There was virtually nothing else it seemed, that was about to bring them in. So it was decided to keep the whole thing completely secret.'

'You went along with it?'

'I've already told you.'

'Then what was my father's role?'

Hackett grew more fluent and the croaking subsided: 'Don't believe for a minute that one hasn't given some careful consideration to the history of it all. One has.'

He fell silent, lost in thought and Mahon said nothing.

Hackett continued: 'One never knows the whole story. I'm sure you appreciate that. The fact is there were objections to the whole thing. There was a view it was an act of considerable inhumanity towards the Americans not to issue the warning. But against that, it would not be wrong to speculate on what might have happened had we told them.'

Mahon began to see something of what Hackett wanted to tell him. Should he wait, let the old man come out with it; should he pursue, bully, insist, perhaps say his time was running out anyway, that he spill his story before it was too late altogether, for the sake of honour? He elected to appeal to sentiment.

'It matters a great deal to me, Geoffrey, to know exactly where my father fitted. You said he was heroic.'

'That was my view.'

'And now?'

'I don't think there's anything that would alter my view. Not that I am aware of.'

'But you don't want to reveal the whole story? Not now, not even after over forty-five odd years or so? Why not, Geoffrey?'

'That's my privilege. Yours, on the other hand, might be to find it out for yourself.'

Mahon was about to interrupt but Hackett raised his hand. 'All right,' he continued. 'Your father signalled an objection to London.'

'About what?'

Hackett stared at him with accusation: 'Think for yourself. Put yourself in his shoes. God knows, you're his son. Of all people, you ought to be able to achieve that. What do you think? Can't you see it?'

'I can guess.'

'Then guess.'

'My father objected to the policy of not warning the Americans. Always assuming, of course, that he knew of the policy.'

'Yes,' Hackett said very softly. 'Yes. He knew. He was the only man who objected. It took a considerable degree of courage at that time, to speak out against something everyone from Churchill down desperately wanted. Your father spoke out.'

'But there's no record of it,' Mahon insisted.

'Of course there isn't. Do you honestly believe people care to keep a record of what really matters when a degree of deception so great, so venal, is involved? The prudent course is caution. The wisest course is to say nothing at all. Wipe the record, as they say, clean.'

Mahon stared at him. By now Hackett sat hunched up and it

82

had turned dark. He could see the whites of the old man's eyes and fancied he could hear the faint clack of dentures when he spoke.

'Disillusionment isn't the exclusive province of your generation,' Hackett said at length. 'It can fasten its grip at any age.'

There was no point continuing now. Mahon felt he had outstayed his welcome. He would come back again another day. Now he needed some time to consider what the old man had told him. Perhaps his thoughts had been read, for Hackett said: 'Visit me again if you want to. It's really up to you now.' But the manipulation hadn't left him. He added: 'I can only tell you which strings to pull. I may have one or two more. But you really must go now. The doctor's paying me a visit in half an hour. It spares me the difficulties of getting to his surgery. One can't drive any more.'

15

' "There are things I can't talk about," ' said Kirsty, mimicking Henry. ' "Even to you." '

'You know that isn't fair,' Mahon said, knowing that it was.

Up till then the reunion had been ecstatic. He had turned up early at Frithville Gardens with a large bunch of red tulips. She had answered the door. Saying nothing at all she led him to the bedroom. They undressed and made love. She didn't even bother to draw the curtains.

Afterwards he told her she should put the tulips in some water.

'I don't care about them,' she said, oddly.

'You told me you liked tulips.'

'I like being given them. There's a difference. They're still tulips whether they're in a vase or by the bed. It's the fact they came with you that matters.'

'I still think you should put them in water. Someone once told me when you stop caring about flowers it's the end of love.'

She squeezed the end of his nose with her fingers and laughed. 'That proves it. You are sentimental.'

'Now you know,' he said, grateful that she seemed to bear no resentment towards him for having neglected her. But he wasn't off the hook yet.

'I'm not sure I'll forgive you,' she warned him. 'You could have telephoned. Why didn't you?'

'There are things I can't talk about.'

Here Kirsty delivered the impersonation of Henry.

'It's unfair to tell me you can't explain why you didn't even bother to telephone. My God, that's what I've put up with from Henry for as long as I care to remember.'

'It just happens to be true,' he said.

'You're frightened?'

'Of what?'

'That someone will find out we're lovers.'

He looked at her sharply. 'You think someone has found out?'

She got out of bed and put on her dressing-gown. 'Well, you can't be sure of anything. Once two people know a secret it ceases to be a secret doesn't it? You ought to know. You're the expert.'

He climbed off the bed and drew on his shirt. 'You're as much part of the "family" as I am.'

'The difference being that I want to leave it and you don't,' she said.

There was no apparent hostility in how she was talking to him. She was hiding whatever bitterness she felt by her playfulness. 'I've made you a really good lunch. Get dressed, come on.'

Whilst they were eating Kirsty said, 'You needn't worry that your job's being threatened by being my lover. I promise you. I'm making sure no one knows. Not even Henry.'

'What do you think he'd do if he found out?' he asked.

'No idea.'

'Wouldn't he get violent? I would.'

'No, you wouldn't. Suppose he did. He'd only make a fool of himself.'

'Suppose,' Mahon said, 'it was the other way around. Suppose he was, as it were, taking advantage of a colleague's wife. Imagine yourself in the position of her husband. Wouldn't you charge into Chayter and object?'

'Chayter would be relieved it was all in the family. I dare say it happens all the time. It always happens with the people you know closest. It's like incest. Far more common than you'd think. You'd be astonished at the statistics. You should find time to read them.'

They laughed.

'You see,' she said. 'I think you need me. I think – '

'What do you think?'

'I think you'll never get bored with me. Never.'

'I don't know whether that's a compliment or an insult.'

'Treat it as a compliment. Just as long as you never use work as an excuse for not seeing me. And don't talk to me about duty and all that stuff, vocation, the centre of things. That's Henry-speak. It hasn't a thread of authenticity about it.'

'I think it has.'

That was the spark which fired her desperation. 'Listen to me. Don't you know how lonely it is? Can't you imagine? Try. Try to think all I felt when you, the one person in the whole world I really care about, went silent. Completely silent. When you cut me off. Can you possibly imagine what that's like?'

'Yes.'

'Prove it.'

'Will you let me?'

'I'm asking you to.'

'I'm telling you it's impossible to avoid the self-obsession that overtakes you in the Service. It's an inevitable condition and you have to learn to live with it.'

'And that's what's biting you?'

'More. It's the one overriding and powerful reason for my being in the Service in the first place.'

'Which is what?'

'My father. Someone I never knew at all. It helped the process of recruitment. They knew the background. But, you see, I didn't. I accepted all along that he was murdered by the Nazis in Madrid. Just another casualty. Maybe no more than a name on the lists of the War Graves Commission. One of the few who died on neutral soil. That was that. But it isn't enough. Come to think of it, it never has been enough. And it never will be. So why shouldn't I be entitled to know what happened? I'm his god-damn son. I am entitled to know precisely how and why and when he died.'

'I thought you did.'

'What makes you so sure?'

'Well, he's your father. He was in the Service. So are you. Surely, you knew. I just thought maybe you didn't want to talk about it.'

'I didn't know the story.'

'Then tell me it. Go on. Tell me.'

For a moment he was silent. Then the story tumbled out. He spoke very fast, quietly, his eyes full of anger, wider than she'd ever seen them before.

He told her of what he had read in the files in Nelson Unit. Of how Hackett had led him to his father's history and how he felt the story was now his own. That he had reached a point of no return. That he was going on to the end of it. It was, he told her, as much a part of a search for himself as it was for his father. 'The official record is always as much a compilation of lies as it is of truth. Like official histories. They need writing because someone's said they need writing. You only learn anything when you can see where the gaps exist. My father's a gap. I'm entitled to see what's missing. The reason for his death exists somewhere. It's been buried a long time. I mean to unearth it. That's the main reason I didn't turn up to see you. You'll just have to understand. Try and trust me, that's all.'

He told her details of what he'd read. She didn't follow all of them but she was grateful he'd explained away his absences and certain he wasn't indifferent to her at all. That was what mattered most. Kirsty felt renewed elation and a new sense of hope. Here was someone trusting in her and she loved him for it.

The next morning she went to Lindsay to apologise for what she described as 'the awful outburst in the National Gallery'. They talked at length in the Finucanes' flat in Kensington Court. Lou was out 'scouting' as he called searching for books. Kirsty tried to explain that her lover really did care for her after all. That was the reality of the matter. She had merely imagined the worst. She had panicked. She was sorry to have burdened Lindsay with the whole thing.

When the justifications were over and Kirsty seemed wholly confident in herself once more, Lindsay began to edge towards a warning. 'Things change so very suddenly.'

'I know,' Kirsty said, confidently. 'At least, perhaps I didn't before. But now I think I do know.'

'And that's the best time to let things cool down a little.'

'Believe me,' Kirsty said. 'I won't let it get out of control again. You can be quite sure of that. Really.'

'What makes you quite so sure?'

'Because I can see the exact difference between my husband and my lover,' Kirsty announced solemnly.

'What's that?'

'My husband doesn't see what keeps him away from me. He's self-centred. Hugging only himself. Probably, deep down he's hopelessly insecure because his mother didn't love him enough. The usual Englishman's complaint. It's reached rather epidemic proportions. His life is his beloved Service. It's hermetic. I have no place at all in it. Never have had, never will.'

'And you think your Mr Mahon is one bit different?'

'I know he is.'

'You'd better be completely sure of yourself.'

'I am.'

'Why?'

'Because, for the first time in my life, I completely trust someone. I trust him. And, perhaps even more important, he trusts me.'

'Aren't you betraying him by telling me?'

Kirsty stared wildly: 'No one knows.'

'Not even Mr Mahon?'

'God, no. I wouldn't dream of telling him I've spoken to you about it. It's strictly between you and me.'

Kirsty spilled it out:

The story of Mahon's search for his father's life and for the details of his death. She was convinced he'd find everything he was looking for. She said it was the search of a man possessed of what she called 'an unusual nobility'.

'What about the threat to his career, to security, all that?'

'He's prepared to jeopardise his career,' Kirsty said, 'by loving me. At the same time he's discovering himself. That's what I meant by "nobility".'

Lindsay was stunned by the account.

She listened to everything Kirsty said with scrupulous attention, memorising the details:

Nightshade.

Hackett's involvement.

Mahon's father's brief career.

The whole conspiracy of silence surrounding the British decision not to warn the United States Government of the attack on Pearl.

She listened, disguising her anger, wishing Lou had been there to hear it. After all this was her government Kirsty was talking about. It was her country.

She waited until Kirsty had finished talking.

'I'm not sure I believe a word of it,' Lindsay said. 'Do you?'

'Yes. I do.'

'Well, I'd just keep it to yourself now, if I were you.'

'Naturally. The same goes for you, doesn't it,' Kirsty insisted.

'Yes,' Lindsay said with conviction. 'It does.'

But Lindsay knew it didn't.

She told Lou the same night after dinner.

At first Lou Finucane thought it was absurd.

It was one of the nights they took a walk to a pub in Kensington Church Street near Albert's, the dealer in cigarette cards. They stood peering into the window at the small portraits of Randolph Scott, Ann Dvorak, Elizabeth Bergner, Barbara Stanwyck and Dolores Del Rio. 'I saw Ann Dvorak with Richard Dix in *Massacre*,' Lou said absently.

Lindsay corrected him. 'It was with Richard Barthelmess.'

'Yes, yes. Maybe you're right,' he said, his mind far away. 'Let's not go to the pub. We'll walk.'

They headed through the back streets of Notting Hill.

He made her go over everything Kirsty had said.

'You don't think Mahon had been searching before Madrid?'

'I don't know. She only said that it was Hackett who set him on the track. That was in Madrid. After that Mahon found some pretext to turn up his father's file in their archives. No one knows he did. His rank allows him to give himself the necessary permission. It didn't need a second signature. He'd confronted Hackett, saying he reckoned his father's past had been buried. I didn't exactly follow all Kirsty said about that. Maybe Hackett was the one who wanted to tell all. Maybe he still does.'

'You think so?'

'I don't know, Lou.'

Through the windows of the houses they could see the evening news on the televisions.

'We could leave the whole thing there. Maybe in the telling it's all got distorted. Maybe Mahon's got a pretty wild imagination. Maybe he thought the whole thing up to persuade Kirsty he had good reason to stand her up. If he dumped her she might go completely wild. Her husband might hear of the whole thing and hit Mahon with it. It could wreck his career. Indirectly. He'd make Newiston his enemy for life and Newiston could play dirty against him.'

'I don't think Mahon was inventing it.'

'You don't?'

'No.'

'We'll see,' said Lou. 'I'll check it out for myself. If it's true, half-way true, I think all hell could let loose.'

The duty officer at the Legal Aid Office of the United States Embassy took Finucane's call. In answer to his request Finucane was told an address in Kingston-upon-Thames and given a telephone number.

There was no reply that night. But in the morning, shortly after ten o'clock, a woman's voice said that Mr Hackett had left yesterday by car.

The woman said she was Mr Hackett's cleaner. She was most obliging.

'He was taken away by car.'

'When's he coming back?'

'I don't know. Mr Hackett is very ill.'

'I'm an old friend of his,' Finucane said.

'There is a forwarding address. If you'd wait a minute. It's by the other telephone. Would you hold the line?'

Finucane waited and when the woman came on the line again she gave an address in Suffolk. 'He's gone away to Suffolk. Sea air. He wanted to look at the sea.' The woman's voice was breaking down. 'He's very ill, you know. Who shall I say called?'

Finucane put the receiver down.

16

The address was at Orford on the east coast, some two and a half hours drive from London if you were lucky with the traffic. He had left London in the cold dawn. The roads were clear enough. Beyond Ipswich the wind buffeted his small black Volkswagen. It was blowing a gale when he reached Orford.

The few shops in the village were closed. A single figure in a vast overcoat struggled against the wind in front of the hotel; the wind slung pages of a newspaper against a caravan, and a disconnected TV aerial wire whipped the side of a house from which a clump of ivy had detached itself. He asked the figure, a woman with a college scarf wrapped around her face, where he could find the address Hackett's cleaning woman had given him. She looked at him with suspicion as though she considered him a burglar. Or was it the address she considered doubtful?

'Beyond the church and the castle,' she said, lowering the scarf. 'You'll find a track. It's at the end of it. Dr Grochal's place, isn't it?'

Finucane's thanks were lost on the wind.

On the gatepost at the end of the rough and holed track was a copper plaque green from lack of polish. It said GROCHAL.

He left the car to one side of the gatepost and leaning against the savage wind, he walked up to the house.

He pressed the bell and waited. It seemed an odd place to convalesce: perishingly cold and so bleak it made you tired just looking at the weary landscape.

There was no reply.

He squinted at the marshlands. Birds he couldn't identify fought a losing struggle to fly against the wind.

A voice said: 'Yes.'

When he turned he found himself looking down at a woman in a heavily knitted white sweater hanging low over blue baggy workman's trousers. She wore a silk scarf tied loosely around the neck.

'Can I help you?'

'I'm a friend of Geoffrey Hackett's.'

'Who?'

'Geoffrey Hackett.' It occurred to Finucane that she might be the owner of an address used by SIS as a decoy. A person and an owner used to throw the curious off the scent of someone they wanted to hide away. He said, 'I believe he's staying here for a while.'

With that she closed the door in his face.

He stayed put a few feet away from the entrance. For some minutes he stood still. Let her make the next move. Somewhere inside she'd be reacting, perhaps telephoning the police or whomsoever were her masters. The thought crossed his mind that he'd gone out alone, looking for someone in hiding, without having told anyone where he was going.

He walked a few feet further away from the house and looked up at the windows. They were double-glazed. All the rooms on the upper floor had their curtains closed.

The rain on the wind lashed his face.

The door of a garden shed banged open and shut with a crazy thudding.

He was staring at the shed door when the woman called out: 'What name is it?'

'Mr Finucane.'

'You have the wrong house.'

'I'm an old friend of his. I need his help.'

Again she closed the door.

After the time she must have taken to call out his name inside the house, she opened it once more. 'Would you come in.'

She led the way into the house. In the hall there was the smell of floor-polish and all the staleness of a public institution's welcome. The woman went back to the front door to double-lock it and slip a guard-chain back into its slot on the wall. She whispered, 'Please understand, Geoffrey is very seriously ill.'

'I'm sorry.'

'Yes. So we all are. He's very tired. Sleep isn't easy without the drugs. He'll see you for a few minutes. Please, for his sake, do stick to a few minutes.'

'I will.'

'Where have you come from?'

'London.'

'It's no weather for driving, is it,' she said.

She walked ahead of him slowly.

The figure of Hackett sat dishevelled in an upright chair at the end of the living-room. His face was unshaven, dusted with white stubble.

Hackett said: 'Eleanor. This is Mr Finucane.'

Finucane took her hand. The fingers were bent and arthritic.

'My sister, Eleanor Grochal.'

'Time for elevenses,' she said.

'Find yourself a chair,' Hackett said. 'This is something of a surprise.'

'I hope not too unpleasant,' said Finucane.

'No, no. Not at all. One likes a visitor. Though I'm bound to say I didn't expect to receive one here quite so soon after my arrival. I haven't been myself recently. The doctors believe it will be wise for me to be looked after for a while. But one can't run, alas, to the provision of a nurse. One depends on relations. Eleanor is the only surviving one. My youngest sister. We are, as it were, the last of the line.'

'I apologise for not telephoning before coming out here,' Finucane said. 'I wanted to make quite sure of seeing you.'

'How did you discover my retreat?'

'Your cleaning woman gave me the address.'

Hackett's eyes opened wider. 'When did you speak to her?'

'Yesterday. She spoke to me.'

'She did?'

'I asked her where you were.'

'How very odd. Today is Tuesday. She never comes in on a Monday. How very odd. You're quite sure it was my cleaning woman, Mrs Hamnet?'

'She didn't tell me her name. She said she was your cleaner.'

Hackett clutched the arms of his chair. 'She is indeed. But she never comes on Mondays. Or does she? It's a trifle confusing. Perhaps you'd explain why you've come to see me. It's not, I imagine, in the nature of a welfare visit, is it?'

'Not exactly.'

'So what can I do for you?'

Finucane was cut short by the return of Hackett's sister carrying a tray with two large cups of milky coffee and a plate of biscuits. She handed a cup to Hackett and left the tray next to Finucane on a nest of tables. 'I'll be in the kitchen, Geoffrey.'

Finucane waited until she'd left and began:

'I want you to help me lay a rumour which could cause maybe a minor, maybe a major ruction.'

'Whatever I can do to help. What do you want to know?'

'I assume it's safe enough to talk here,' said Finucane, glancing in the direction Hackett's sister had left.

'Entirely,' Hackett said. 'My sister worked for the Service in Bonn for many years. One, as it were, of the family too.'

'She wasn't with you in the early days of the war?'

'No, she wasn't,' Hackett said with mild curiosity.

'Does she or anyone else know what work you did during the war that was connected with the United States?'

'Nothing at all. What makes you ask that?'

Finucane hesitated. You could never be sure of the subject of interrogation. It was always helpful to begin, rather than end, with a question about anyone else who might throw light into the shadows of an initial search. But Hackett, however sick he might be, would also know something of the techniques. He was a fox facing a fox. Both of them had lived their lives in the shadows.

Hackett smiled. He was an old man remembering. 'It was my privilege to play a very small part in wartime operations which involved the United States at an early stage. I like to think what was achieved was, in essence, the conception of our special relationship. Not to coin too grand a phrase, I'd say it was the bedrock of our alliance. Even today. Wouldn't you?'

'I'd say so.'

'I doubt anything will change it,' said Hackett.

Finucane watched the old man's eyes. They were very clear and penetrating. The interrogation was pumping adrenalin through the sick body.

Again Hackett gave a smile. This time it was slightly mischievous: 'What is it you want from me?'

Lou confronted him straight out:

'Your judgement on the supposition that your people knew before anyone else the details of the Japanese strategic and tactical planning throughout 1941 the whole way to Pearl Harbor?'

94

'My judgement?'

'That's what I've come for.'

'The answer is emphatically that we did not know.'

'You didn't?'

'That's what I said.' He paused. 'It's perfectly true we wanted you as allies. Churchill wanted your active participation in the struggle for the Atlantic. He didn't seek trouble with Japan. After all, the Japanese might sever our supply routes across the Indian Ocean. None of us wanted a war in the Far East. I recall Churchill turned to Roosevelt as early as May 1940 with a request that FDR keep the Japanese dog quiet in the Pacific. Those were, I believe, his very words. Two months or so later, he asked if FDR could send a squadron to Singapore as a signal warning to the Japanese. He didn't want a war with Japan.'

The old man was wriggling. All this was a smoke-screen.

'But he felt that our entry into the war would overcome all the evils put together.'

'I'm not sure he said it in so many words.'

'He did. Those were his words.'

'I bow to your memory of the thing,' Hackett said with pointed courtesy. 'But there were some things he was not prepared to do.'

'Such as?'

'Conniving to arrange the Japanese attack on Pearl Harbor. Listen, Mr Finucane, we heard the suggestion that Roosevelt entered into some secret pact with Churchill to the effect that if the Japanese launched an attack on British territory then the United States would declare war. It was nonsense. There's plenty of evidence to show it's nonsense. What are you trying to tell me?'

'I want *you* to tell me what you remember.'

'Churchill made a promise to the Foreign Secretary, Anthony Eden. It's a matter for the record, "If the United States declares war on Japan, we follow within the hour." '

'And if the United States didn't come in?'

'We'd have made common cause with the Dutch. Those were Churchill's words, more or less exactly, as I recall, to Eden.'

'What would have happened had the Japanese not attacked – if you'd made common cause with the Dutch?'

'Who can tell? Roosevelt declared his support for us in the Far East at the start of December 1941. Two days later he promised armed support. The Japanese were already on a war alert.'

'You knew that?'

'I didn't say that, Mr Finucane. No one knew where the Japanese would strike. One nation alone, Japan, took the decision to destroy the United States Pacific Fleet. Are you, an American, pursuing again this old evil idea that Roosevelt knew of the Japanese plans?'

'I am not pursuing Roosevelt.'

'Churchill?'

'No.'

'Then what are you asking me?'

'Whether or not your secret intelligence system *knew*.' Finucane leaned forward in his chair. 'Has your Service been functioning for so long on the basis of a deception?'

Hackett remained silent a while. He seemed to be reflecting on the incongruity of the confrontation. At least, that was Finucane's impression.

'This is so unexpected,' Hackett said. 'One would imagine, in any event, I could suppose, to be forgiven for imagining at this stage in my life that such matters belong to history. That they remain a matter for public scrutiny and the exercise of historians. One hardly expected to find such an issue raised at this juncture.'

'Why not?' Finucane said with sudden anger. 'What's at issue here is the special relationship; the Anglo-American relationship is built upon – deceit. That its very bedrock is eaten up with deception and the British reluctance to come clean. If that's the case then what's the price of trust? Your country is eaten up with deceit. How else do you explain your decline? That this is a third-rate nation.'

With a great effort Hackett got to his feet and walked to the window. Without turning round he said, 'Is history that important? The great majority like the impression of history. The trappings. The pageantry. Ceremony. Monarchy. The sense of royalty. They just like to think it's there. If all you're saying were true, would it matter? As to sleeping dogs . . . isn't it better, as the maxim has it, to let them lie? Our job is to protect the realm. That's not the same as discovering truth. If it were there would be no need for the likes of me in the first place, wouldn't you say?'

Finucane was on his feet.

'There are a few of you alive who were involved. As long as you live you're answerable. Like the Nazi war criminals.'

The door to the living room was open.

Hackett's sister was standing there with a look of horror in her eyes.

Very quietly, she said, 'Would you go now, Mr Finucane. Please, won't you leave us alone?'

Finucane looked back at Hackett and when he caught his eyes he saw a look of satisfaction.

Going back he was less fortunate with the traffic. The wind, rain and roadworks defeated his attempt to make it to London as soon as possible.

The delay allowed his mind to wander from the details of Hackett's history lesson. Why couldn't he have just come out with it and said, yes, there's the man Mahon, the man you've met, who's turning over the pages of the past to find his father and has dug up a whole army of corpses?

He regretted he hadn't properly enquired about Hackett's obviously deteriorating state of health. But then he'd long since found the English expected Americans, sooner or later, to breach those codes of manners. Why that look of satisfaction in the old man's eyes? It was mysterious, he decided in a traffic snarl near Chelmsford, that a man like Hackett should set Mahon searching in these directions. Was Hackett trying to protect himself, make some late atonement? Who was being manipulated?

The old experience of the streets was telling him to follow the procedure: when in doubt pass it upwards. It was a condition of retirement and the continuation of the pension that you passed back unfinished business. This was unfinished business. By the time he was in London he'd made up his mind. He'd tell Lindsay to sail in close to Kirsty and he would make a trip to Washington. There was always a time in life, usually near the end, when the wisest thing was to pass the buck.

17

'Hi, Lou.'
  'Lindsay?'
  'I can hear your echo.'
  ' 'S the satellite.'
  'Yeah. I miss you.'
  'Me, too.'
  'What are you doing?'
  'Waiting. Same old place. Same room even. Same rats in the trash around Columbus.'
  'Lou, I saw Kirsty. She's still seeing him. He's still on the tracks. Have you spoken to Yoram?'
  'I left a message with his office.'
  'Send him my love.'
  'I will. Take care.'
  'You too.'

Yoram Katz was given Finucane's message during dinner with a senior partner in his law firm in a Park Avenue apartment. The conversation over coffee turned to Cuomo's chances as presidential material. He disentangled himself from it with a story about a wartime intelligence operation in Geneva. The Italians had come out of it in a surprisingly good light. He told his friends in Park Avenue a short joke and during the laughter he excused himself and left discreetly. He had a knack of getting away without anyone minding. He went on to the street and found a cab to take him the short journey to the hotel near Columbus Circle to answer the summons from his friend.

  Finucane was lying on his bed after the call from Lindsay, marking up a new catalogue from Rota. Lionel Ritchie sang 'Say you, Say me', over a TV through the wall. He'd nearly finished the catalogue as Katz arrived.

He was a much smaller man than Finucane. The square face like a pug-dog's had a charming ugliness. The nose was noticeably off-centre. It had been broken in a flying accident during the war. Ostensibly, his working life was taken up with Law. In fact, it provided cover for his links with government intelligence. Every President since Kennedy had regularly called him to the White House. On the few occasions Finucane had been telephoned personally from the White House, it was because Yoram Katz had told the President he had an old friend whose brain he'd like to pick.

More recently he'd been a witness at Lou's marriage to Lindsay. He had more godchildren than any man Finucane had known. He'd never married. He was, in many respects, something of an odd man out. A friend to many, guardian to some, intimate to none.

For many years he had been a friend of SIS. A limited friendship he would say. He was one of the few Americans who'd seen the full extent of the unholy mess SIS had fallen into during the post-war years. With some of your friends it sometimes paid off not to get too close.

The two men talked long into the night.

Back and forth through names in Washington during the forties and fifties.

Finucane slowly unfolded the details of what he'd learned of *Nightshade*.

Katz chain-smoked.

He couldn't believe the British had worked their way to the core of the Japanese strategic and tactical planning during the last weeks before Pearl.

'I need to be convinced by the evidence. Directly. You show it to me, Lou. Then I'll give you an opinion. I never did believe any of the arguments that FDR was in any way responsible. I knew people who were by his side. People who knew his mind. It was tough enough to do that at the best of times. And tough enough too for FDR to know his own mind much of the time. We all knew something was up. We were deciphering intercepts between Tokyo and their Washington Embassy prior to Pearl.'

'And from Tokyo to where else?'

'Take your pick. Moscow. Lima. Berlin. Beunos Aires. Rome. Batavia.'

'London, Madrid?'

'Sure. Everyone knew the Japs were preparing for war.'

'But everyone *didn't* know about Pearl being the Jap target.'

'Not everyone. There was so much communications *noise*. It was hard to get to the centre. I cannot believe the British succeeded in doing it.'

Finucane filled Katz's whisky glass. 'I've been told that an officer in the British Secret Intelligence Service has evidence, cast-iron evidence, that the British did know the Japanese war plan and that they deliberately withheld it. So that the Pacific Fleet would be destroyed. So that beyond any question, any shadow of doubt, the United States would come into the European War.'

'I don't believe it.'

'Why not?'

'It would have come out before now,' Katz said. 'We lost *Arizona* and *Oklahoma*, two destroyers and a target ship. We lost over two thousand four hundred men. You can't seriously tell me that the British would have tolerated that.'

'Only a very few people had to tolerate it.'

'You know, Lou, I lost my eldest brother, Alex, at Pearl.'

'I know.'

'What evidence have you got?'

'Only what I've been told. The contact's very good.'

'You don't think it could be a Soviet plant? They might have faked up the thing.'

Finucane shook his head. 'It's one thing to fake up the record to manufacture the evidence, and another to plant the phoney evidence in the British secret intelligence archives. They have other less chancey ways of breaking the alliance. Okay, fine, they'd score some points if it got out. But I've thought it through. It does not smell like that to me.'

'If the evidence is good,' Katz asked, 'what then?'

'You tell me, Yoram. Consider your own reaction. You lost your brother. A lot of people lost fathers, brothers and the rest. It suggests the British are prepared to cheat on anyone, anywhere at any time.'

'They were losing a war at the time, I suppose.'

It was an uncharacteristic observation on Katz's part. He added: 'But you can't tell me they were cheating on the one ally they needed more than any other at that stage in the war. It would be taking one hell of a risk.'

'If it got out now,' Finucane asked. 'What would be the reaction?'

'Certainly shatter a few myths. Even destroy the special relationship. It'd upset the British more than us.' Katz paused. 'Maybe even the fact they've hidden the thing for so long. I imagine it'd make a lot of people wonder what the hell else they're holding back.' Again he paused. 'I don't think there's anyone around who could substantiate even whether Washington was suspicious at the time. I'm pretty damn sure it'd be hard to prove this end.' He lit another cigarette. 'Have you thought of confronting the British with it?'

'Yes,' Finucane said.

'Why haven't you?'

'Because if they suspect I know anything about it they'll destroy the evidence before you can take breath. I can't get into their archives in any way that's legitimate.'

'Illegitimate?'

'Too late.' He reflected a moment. 'What would you do? Keep quiet? Forget it?'

Katz was silent. At length he said: 'I'd speak to someone. Go back to someone in the system.'

'Who?'

'I don't know right now.'

'It'd have to be someone who won't press the panic button. Someone who can work their way into things.'

'You want me to find a name?'

'If you can.'

'I'll talk to someone,' Katz said. He drank the rest of his coffee. 'I'll have someone from my office leave you a name and address. It'll probably be the one on East 85th and 3rd. The person you'll see will be a woman. I'll be there too.' Katz looked at his watch. 'In about two hours from now.'

He stood silently looking down at Finucane's hunched figure. Then he said, 'The last time you were here was when, six, eight years ago? And I do believe it was the British we were trying to sort out then, wasn't it?'

'I think it was.'

'And now you're a Londoner.'

'Right.'

'I'll tell you this. I don't think you're going to be any too popular in your adopted country if there's any truth in what you've discovered in their past.'

18

Finucane's shoes clattered on the marble floor.

I don't feel too popular in my own country either, he reflected, entering the apartment block on East 85th Street. The doorman gave him a surly nod and told him to see the man at the desk at the far end of the entrance hall.

The eyes glanced up from some television screens. Most of the black and white flickering pictures seemed to be of the bit of the interior that the man could have seen for himself. Perhaps the television gave him a heightened sense of reality.

'I have an appointment with Steven Ranft.'

'Who are you?'

'My name's Finucane.'

'Identification.'

Finucane produced his passport and handed it across the desk.

The man licked his fingers and riffled through the pages. 'You're quite a traveller.' He opened a small file and checked the names under F. Then he handed back the passport. 'All right, Mr Finucane. You take the elevator on the right to the fifteenth floor. Mr Ranft's expecting you.'

Once more Finucane's feet clattered across the marble.

He took the elevator to the fifteenth floor and when the door opened there was a small man standing in the corridor peering through thick glasses which magnified the eyes. 'Steven Ranft.'

Finucane shook the man's hand. It was cold and slightly damp. He reminded Finucane of a tropical fish in an illuminated tank.

The apartment was at the end of the corridor at the corner of the building. Finucane noticed its two entrances. It was a typical CIA selection. Their visitors could come and go without seeing each other. It was like the sort of apartment run by an expensive medical consultant whose patients wanted their identities kept secret. He saw the elaborate video security system in the ceiling of the corridor. He wondered whether the man on the desk below could see his arrival and who else knew what the apartment was used for.

The woman who answered the door nodded at Ranft and Lou watched the tropical fish look-alike vanish along the corridor. She introduced herself to Finucane as Kate Linger. He put her in her early thirties. She was tall and calm. In her black jacket and skirt, white cotton shirt with its thin black ribbons tied neatly in a bow, you'd have guessed she worked for a Wall Street bank or a law firm like Yoram Katz's.

She nodded at Finucane to sit down by a table covered with green baize.

Yoram Katz got to his feet.

She turned to Finucane without ceremony. 'We're interested in what you've told Yoram.'

'It's only the bare bones,' Finucane said. 'I was putting some flesh on it on the way here. If the intelligence collaboration between Washington and London began before Pearl Harbor, wouldn't you say that makes the whole thing the more unbelievable?'

'How important is the material itself?' Katz asked.

'I think it matters. Anything that damages whatever good-will's left after allowing the military their bases in the UK has a potential danger element. There's plenty of material none of us want released. The British kept Ultra secret for more than thirty years. We never said anything about Ultra. Suppose this comes out? The British would be under further pressure to discuss intelligence publicly. They'd probably have to surrender power in intelligence matters to a wider sphere beyond the executive. It'd finally show up that the Prime Minister's Steering Committee on Intelligence doesn't receive all it asks for.'

'We're talking about something that happened *forty-five* years ago,' Katz argued.

'There are still plenty of people who'll feel raw about it,' Linger said. 'From the President down. There'll be a full-scale outcry for a complete exposé. That means revealing far more than just the British action over Pearl. Far more. I mean it. Here and in Britain. It'll become the subject for discussion by the select committees on intelligence in the Senate and the House of Representatives. The Congressional committees debating an issue at the root of the Anglo-American intelligence alliance would be something no one wants. The British would object for a start.'

'Who'd listen?' Finucane asked.

'I think a lot of people would,' Linger said. 'Don't you?'

Until now she had delivered her assessments like a teacher conducting a private seminar. She was almost impassive. Finucane found her curiously lacking in inquisitiveness. She had hardly asked any questions. It struck him that she had already discussed the matter with her seniors in the hierarchy.

When she began to talk about the British SIS it was with a kind of weary resignation as if she were discussing some anti-social neighbours whose presence was lowering the value of the surrounding real estate. 'There's a struggle in London for the post of Deputy Director. It isn't open conflict. But the candidates are presenting themselves. It's a tight-knit executive. Chayter, the Director, who wants his knighthood. Newiston who knows the Service inside and out. Mehta, objective, diplomatic, a compromiser. Boden-Smith, the one woman, careerist, hard, very intelligent. And your man with the file, Mahon, whom Chayter uses to counter Newiston's influence, to keep it in check.'

She turned to Finucane: 'How much do you know about him?'

'Very little beyond what I've already told you two.'

She shrugged. 'Like you and me, Yoram, he's Jewish. His mother was. He never knew his father. Didn't know his mother. Unmarried. Or, if you like, married to his work. He's had charge of an East Europe operation in Poland. It went wrong. They lost some agents. But they've managed to prevent too much damage.' She hesitated. 'We've come in at a time when we're boxed in. We can't ask to see the file. They'll deny its existence. Probably destroy it.'

'What about Lou's man Mahon?' Katz asked.

'We think it'll be advisable to keep a twenty-four hour surveillance on Mahon for an indefinite period. Maybe we can get something on him. Something that may persuade him to co-operate.'

For the first time Finucane saw hard determination in her

face. She said finally: 'We don't want the file leaked. We don't want it destroyed. So it's knight's move. We move away from the file. We sit next to Mahon.'

She gave the two men the knowing look of someone who knows she's taken charge of the game. She looked at Finucane: 'There are people who're grateful to you. Put in for repayment of your fares and subsistence. Yoram'll see to it.'

'When does this operation start?' Finucane asked her.

'It already has.'

Earlier that day the doctor at Orford had made arrangements for Geoffrey Hackett to be moved to a hospital at Ipswich. His elderly patient offered a strong protest. His sister made a milder one. In the end, the doctor won the day and an ambulance was called. By now Geoffrey Hackett was in great pain.

Eleanor Grochal drove her small Ford saloon behind the ambulance into Ipswich.

She stayed for some time with her brother until a nurse told her it was time for his injections. Eleanor went home alone to Orford.

There were four people at the hospital reception desk: an elderly woman with *Country Life* sticking out of a fruiterer's carrier bag. She told the clerk she had come to see her sister.

'You know which way to go,' said the clerk.

'Oh, yes,' said the elderly woman and put a twenty-pence bit into the Oxfam box on the desk.

Now it was the turn of the man in a long tweed overcoat.

'I've come to see a Mr Geoffrey Hackett,' he told the clerk. In one hand he carried a worn brown leather brief-case; in the other he held half a dozen white roses wrapped in white paper. The clerk seemed to be familiar with the name.

'Yes,' she said. 'I'll see where you can find him.'

'My name's Freedman,' the man said with a tone of authority that prompted the clerk to call him 'sir'. Mr Freedman's accent suggested he was a professional man; perhaps a doctor, an army officer or lawyer.

'I'm an old friend,' he said.

The clerk looked up into the man's eyes. She gave him a quizzical look as if to say I know your face. But the man was staring along the corridor in the direction of the old woman carrying the bag with *Country Life.*

'If you'll go to the first floor,' the clerk was saying, 'you'll find Mr Hackett's room at the end on the left.'

'How is he?'

'If you'll speak to Sister.'

'Ah, yes,' he replied. 'Of course. Thank you very much.'

He paused a moment, turning to face the blind Indian behind him who had his arm tucked through his wife's and he smiled with an air of grace into the solemn unseeing eyes.

'And what can I do to help you?' the clerk asked the Indian couple. As the Indian woman began to explain the man with the brief-case and white roses walked away to the stairs to the first floor. A nurse passed him and gave him a gentle look. It was that sort of hospital: informal, friendly and quiet with the communal atmosphere.

He met the sister a few doors down the corridor from Hackett's room. He was the model of courtesy with good manners that were not especially memorable.

He held up the bunch of flowers.

'I've brought these for Mr Hackett,' the man said. 'I'm an old friend of his.'

'They're lovely,' the sister said. 'You'll find a vase on the table by his bed. But I'm afraid he's sleeping.'

'How is Geoffrey?'

'He's sleeping. In less pain than earlier.'

'Ah, that's good,' the man said sympathetically.

'I'm afraid you won't be able to have a chat with him though,' the sister said.

'If I might leave the roses.'

'Of course.' She directed him to Hackett's room. 'If you'll forgive me I have another duty to attend to.'

With that the sister left him to go to Hackett's room.

Alone in the corridor, the man took in his surroundings.

It was a fortunate coincidence that the patient's room was at the end of the corridor. The door to the room was ajar. Opposite was a swing door. And it was the swing door the man pushed open first. He was in a small brightly lit service area painted white with a sink on one wall, two metal trolleys loaded with small trays and white paper cartons.

He stood still and listened. There was no sound from the

corridor. What he wanted above all else was facing him in the small service area: the locked white cupboard above the sink.

Setting the brief case and roses down on the sink he drew out a small leather fold-over case of keys from the pocket of his tweed coat. He squinted at the lock on the cupboard door and touched it with his gloved hand.

The first key turned the lock.

Carefully he opened the door and eyed the phials and disposable syringes. It only took him a few seconds to load the syringe, slip it into the brief-case, relock the cupboard door and collect the roses. Satisfied he'd left the place exactly as he'd found it he pushed through the swing doors and made his way across the corridor to the room opposite.

Geoffrey Hackett lay asleep in the dim light of the small room. The curtains were drawn. There was a bell switch a few inches from Hackett's head.

Once more the man waited, quite still, listening for any sounds from the corridor. Then he gently closed the door behind him.

Crouching over the bed the man quickly drew back the sheet and single blanket. He drew out the syringe, laid Hackett's forearm on the sheet and searched amongst the bruises and veins for a place to inject the dose. The needle punctured the skin at an angle and the injection began. It took longer than he had anticipated and he had very nearly finished when he heard, clearly, the sound of the footsteps in the corridor.

He was just in time.

The door opened.

'You gave me a fright,' whispered the black nurse carrying a vase. 'We keep the door open.'

'I do apologise,' the man told her. 'I thought my friend wanted to say something. You know, a whisper. But it was nothing comprehensible.'

'Let's put the roses in the vase,' the nurse said.

'Do be careful,' the man warned her softly. 'The briars are terribly sharp.'

'It's all right,' the nurse said. 'Let's get them into the water. We wouldn't want them to die, would we?'

Geoffrey Hackett's visitor nodded gravely and gave her a sideways smile.

107

19

For a few days word spread through Century House that East Europe had made an old fashioned British cock-up in Poland. Little excited people more than someone else's misery. There was talk of an in-house inquiry; even an *ad hoc* commission. A few of the Wise and the Good had been seen arriving on a Saturday morning. That inevitably meant trouble. Someone from Satellites in the restaurant at Monday lunchtime said Washington was especially irritated. It had put back the Polish efforts for at least five years. Moscow would be laughing its head off. What price Western inroads in the last days of Kadar's regime? Hungary would have been a prize. Everyone had offered good odds on the seduction of the Magyars. Now, after Poland, it looked as though we were losing the initiative in Hungary just as we'd done in Romania and Yugoslavia. It was the British disease. We thought ahead, worked out the plan, produced the prototype and then, at the last minute, ballsed it up. Others in the know said that Mahon had botched Newiston's chances of the Deputy Directorship. He was tarnished by the Polish fiasco. It now looked like Mehta. Except that he was Indian and the thought of his being Number Two was as unlikely as Boden-Smith who was actually a woman and, though it couldn't strictly be admitted, therefore disqualified. The appointment of Deputy Director was up for grabs. The Prime Minister was said to be thinking of bringing in someone altogether fresh from M15, a new technology man who'd finally replace the seasoned bureaucrat with machines. It had happened before. The Prime Minister was a stickler for precedent.

Traditionally, in the lull after a major cock-up, the officers considered to have been responsible were said to be 'in interval'; that's to say a period of days or even weeks whilst new intelligence initiatives were haggled over in committee, budgets fought for and new sub-committees appointed, they remained in the shadows. If leave was suggested to you it was as well to treat it as a warning sign. The suggestions were therefore not always taken up. Everyone involved in a failure went on to alert to the possibility of unseen examination of their lives. Could the mistake be put down to personal weakness or private crisis: booze, depression, womanising?

Mahon, 'in interval', was perfectly well aware of the system of checks and counter-checks which lumbered into operation following a cock-up. Two agents were dead. They'd been his men.

Even so, his mood was buoyant. He drafted a satisfactory report on the failure in Poland. When he asked for more time than usual to be absent from Latchmere, it was granted to him. Once the Polish report was out of the way he could pay more attention to *Nightshade* and also, on Fridays, in Frithville Gardens, to Kirsty.

It was a Monday, just past five in the afternoon, that he first noticed the two watchers in the Mercedes at the corner of Gordon Place and Pitt Street. To park in the nearby streets you needed a resident's parking permit issued by the Royal Borough of Kensington and Chelsea from the Town Hall in Hornton Street. The Mercedes didn't have one. Indeed, since several of the houses in Gordon Place were being extensively renovated at the time, most of the usual parking spaces were taken up with builders' skips. So there were fewer cars to be identified. This was useful for anyone like John Mahon looking for people who might be taking an untoward interest in his comings and goings. It was professional instinct that you kept an eye open at all times for anyone watching you.

On the Monday there were two men in the Mercedes. One, a black, was dressed in a sports-jacket and wore his shirt open at the neck. The other, with a clipped moustache and shorn head, wore a running outfit. The passenger window was slightly open. When Mahon returned home he could hear the car's hi-fi playing a tape of Jessye Norman singing Mahler.

There were some of the usual cars parked nearby. A Volvo with a rusted luggage rack belonging to an antique dealer who did business in Kensington Church Street; an old MG owned by an actress whose face he'd seen on BBC TV but whose name he'd never bothered to find out, and a stockbroker's Rolls Bentley. He'd seen a mugshot of the stockbroker in the business pages of the *Sunday Times*. The man's wife took three children to school every day in the Rolls.

He memorised the number-plate of the Mercedes and went into his flat to collect his laundry. When he came outside again the Mercedes was there with Jessye Norman still in full throat.

Mahon glanced briefly at the two men's faces. The white man with the moustache looked him up and down. The eyes were restless. Mahon thought he was probably gay. When Mahon nodded at him the man returned a smile of recognition. It was most obviously a smile which said I've noticed you before. That was on the Monday.

On the Wednesday morning when he left his flat at a few minutes past eight, he noticed a taxi-cab parked a short distance from the corner of Pitt Street. The driver was eating a sandwich. Mahon noticed there was a passenger in the back.

Within the hour he was at Latchmere. He made a hullabaloo in the word-processing unit about typos in the final draft of his Poland report and insisted the corrections be seen to by lunchtime. He told the woman duty officer he was leaving to attend a CIA briefing on Nicaragua in the cinema at Century House.

But instead of going to the briefing he went to London District Surveillance, found a spare computer and tapped out his own name.

The name and address came up on the screen.

He tapped in another command to see if LD Surveillance had anyone on his tail. It didn't.

The conclusion was straightforward. If someone had a watch on him, it wasn't one of his own people. Or, if it was, then whoever had given the instruction had gone through some other system and taken an informal route to gain authorisation.

He now explored the standard route to gain access to the duties of the standard surveillance teams. He turned up the Soviet Embassy residences in Holland Park; the Czech house in Reigate; the Hungarians in Cheltenham. All of which suggested most of the London District teams were at full stretch outside their usual area.

By now he'd turned LD Surveillance inside out.

They weren't on his back. So who was?

When he returned home that night there was no sign of the Mercedes, the taxi, its driver, or the four faces who had now entered his life. But next day they were back in yet another guise.

This time there were two women in a silver Honda. One, in her thirties, had tidy fair hair, no make-up and wore a white sweater. Her companion was plump. She wore a heavy blue overcoat. He would not have immediately made the connection with the others had it not been for the sound of Jessye Norman singing Mahler. The coincidence led him to the conclusion he was definitely under surveillance. In itself that could be dealt with. It also led him to the decision to get the *Nightshade* file to a safe place.

'Yes,' Kirsty said over the telephone. 'Yes.' She was surprised to hear him. 'Come over as soon as you can. I'm decorating my bedroom.'

'Again?'

'Why not? It's a beautiful pink. Rather the colour of plaster, you know, when it's raw. Rather Italian. You can help me paint.'

'Without wanting to be too selfish,' he told her, 'I'd like your help. I've had a disaster.'

She sounded genuinely concerned. 'What's happened?'

'My fridge-freezer's packed up. The food's melting.'

'Bring it over here. You can use mine. I'll make space. How much is there?'

'Mostly junk food. Frozen chips. Some big bags. Peas. Chicken bits.'

'Have they melted completely?'

'Not completely.'

'Then they'll be safe. Do you want me to come and collect you?'

'No. I'll come over in about an hour.'

A friendly Kenyan Asian was happy to sell him what he needed. Within twenty minutes he was back in his flat with a small suitcase containing the frozen food.

He moved to the back of the flat so that even someone outside crouching down on the pavement couldn't see him. He divided the file into three sections. He wrapped each section in

111

polythene and sealed it with sellotape. He broke open a large bag of frozen peas and tipped some of them out. He then slipped the file sections into the bag and resealed it. He stuffed all the frozen food, a miscellaneous selection of ice-cream, strawberries and burgers into the black rubbish bin liner on top of the doctored peas.

Once he'd packed an overnight bag he sat down by his desk, lifted the telephone and stretched up to look up out of the window through the bars.

The two women in their Honda had positioned themselves skilfully.

He was well in view. So was the Honda's registration number. He dialled the police.

'I'd like to report a suspicious car.'

The duty operator asked his name and address.

'Anthony Dean.' He gave the number of next door in Gordon Place.

'What is it you want to report, Mr Dean?'

'There are two women who have been sitting parked outside my flat for a long time.'

'Can you give me a description?'

Mahon described the women, the car and where exactly it was parked. He gave its registration number.

'And what's made you suspicious?'

'They look to me to be watching this house or possibly the one next door. The residents are largely elderly people. There have been a number of suspected break-ins in recent weeks.' Which was true. 'Some of us in the area have teamed up to keep an informal neighbourhood watch.' Which wasn't true. 'If you don't mind I'd suggest some officers come and take a look at the car. But I'd be grateful if you'd keep my identity confidential. If I'm wrong it might cause some embarrassment.'

The duty operator said he appreciated the request. 'We won't trouble you, Mr Dean. Thank you for your help.'

He made one more telephone call and asked for a taxi to come immediately to an address in Pitt Street. They had one in the area. It could be there in a matter of minutes. They asked for his telephone number. He was careful to give them a real one, another neighbour's. For both the women watchers and police might spot the name of the cab firm and trace his journey.

When he heard the police siren he opened the front door, polythene rubbish bag in one hand, overnight suitcase in the other. He suddenly realised he was the one the police might suspect of burglary, and indeed they did so. He had walked into his own trap.

One white Rover patrol car blocked the top of Gordon Place. Another blocked the end of it. Caught in the middle were two elderly ladies and a man with a military bearing leading a King Charles spaniel on a lead, Mahon and the two women in the Honda.

The police moved in on the Honda, and one officer strolled towards him.

'You live here?'

'Yes, I do, officer.'

The police officer pointed at Mahon's case and the polythene bag: 'What have you got in there?'

'In this,' Mahon said, holding up the overnight bag, 'I've got some going away things. Sponge-bags. Shirts. Change of clothes and so on.'

'In that?'

'In this I've got frozen food.'

'Let's have a look.'

Mahon saw the police still surrounding the Honda. He hoped they were asking a great many awkward questions. Hurriedly he opened up the polythene bag. The police officer lifted out the sacks of chips, peas and burgers.

'I'm afraid my freezer's let me down.'

'They can be right bastards,' the policeman said. 'Mind you don't get food poisoning. My brother had it from melted fridge food. It's bloody dire.'

'I take your point,' said Mahon.

The policeman looked over the road at the Honda. 'Have you seen that car here before?'

'No,' Mahon told him. 'I don't think I have. This is a busy little street. In fact it wouldn't half be a bad idea if it was made one-way.'

'Thanks for your help,' the policeman muttered, walking away.

Mahon passed within a few feet of the Honda and his eyes caught those of the woman with the white sweater. Jessye Norman was no longer singing the Mahler.

The taxi was waiting in Pitt Street and Mahon asked to be driven to the post office in Shepherd's Bush Green.

For the time being he had thrown the watchers off the scent. He hoped the police were giving the women a rough time of it. He paid off the taxi outside the post office and watched it drive off. Then he walked the short distance to Frithville Gardens.

By the time he got to Kirsty's doorstep he felt confident there was no one on his track.

She was very happy to see him.

They loaded up the frozen bags into her freezer.

'If I were you I wouldn't try eating any of it,' he told her. 'You can get some bad food poisoning from half-melted stuff. And I can't remember how much of it I've had for how long.'

'Don't worry,' she said. 'I won't touch it. I don't believe in frozen food. I once read a story about some woman who found a little finger in a bag of chips. It put me off for life.'

She closed the freezer door firmly.

'I'm going to have a bath,' she grinned. 'A bubble bath. You can have one too.' She put her arms around his neck and kissed him. 'With me. We've got all day.'

'What about painting your bedroom?'

'I've suddenly thought of something better to do in there.' She kissed him once again. 'Aren't you thinking the same thing?'

He laughed. But she could tell his laughter disguised his preoccupation. She watched him go to the window and look out into the street. 'What's on your mind?' She paused. 'Don't worry about the food. It'll be all right. And if it isn't, well, it doesn't matter, does it?' Again she paused. 'If you like we can eat the whole lot,' she said, 'unless your *Nightshade* search is concentrating your mind to the exclusion of all else. It's really troubling you a lot, isn't it? Or is it Poland?'

'You understand?'

'One day, I hope,' she said, 'there'll be a time when bloody Poland and the whole of Eastern Europe will be left to look after itself.'

'I'd be out of a job.'

'I know. But sooner or later the British taxpayer won't be able to worry about Poland. And Bulgaria. And Romania. And all those other dreary little places. You know why? Because they won't be bloody well able to afford to worry about them. As a matter of fact I doubt that one person in a thousand could actually put a finger on a map and get within a thousand miles of bloody Poland anyway.' She took his hand. 'Forget it.'

'And I'm not discussing *Nightshade*,' he told her.

It was in the bath among the greenish bubbles that he asked her whether she'd mind if he stayed at her flat for a few days. He said he wanted a change of scene.

'Can I come over whenever I want?' she asked.

'It's your flat.'

'So it is!' she said. She ran her hands under the water between his legs and squeezed him.

'You won't tell anyone I'm here?' he asked.

'I'll tell the whole world.' Her hands let go of him. 'Just you wait.'

She stood up in the bath and brushed the bubbles off her body. Some of them landed on his face and shoulders. 'Get dry and come to bed.'

He looked up at her huge smile. He had never seen her quite so happy. It made him nervous.

20

When Yoram Katz offered to drive him to Kennedy, Finucane knew at once it meant bad news.

'They've lost him,' Katz said, one hand on the wheel, the other lighting a cigarette. 'Linger's going to tell you the details at the airport.'

'What happened?'

'He disappeared.'

'How?'

'Some story about police involvement.'

'In London?'

'In London,' Katz said. 'Mahon walked out of his apartment at exactly the same time the police were questioning the duty surveillance team.'

'I don't believe it.'

'It's true. According to Linger.'

'Do the police know what's happening?'

'I don't think so,' said Katz, fiddling with the car's air-conditioning. Stale air blew into Finucane's face. 'It wouldn't have happened in the old days, Lou, would it?'

'I'd like to think so.'

'I think,' Katz said, calmly, 'that's why Linger wants you back in London. She's now taking it very seriously.'

She met them at the British Airways desk. After Finucane had checked in they found a place to sit away from the crowd. There was very little time for talk. In fact Linger had few details to offer about Mahon's disappearance.

'He might not even have known he was being tailed,' Katz said.

'He'll know,' Linger said with the harshness of someone whose inefficiency has been exposed. 'We'll take him off the streets.'

'What for?' Finucane asked, quietly.

'To question him.'

'It's not as simple as that,' Finucane said.

'It has to be,' she told him sharply.

'Taking an SIS officer off the streets? Not only is that not simple, it's illegal.'

'The British won't know,' Linger said.

'Who's taking him in?' Finucane asked her. 'The embassy people won't allow it. They'll never agree.'

'They won't have to.'

'You're not going through the usual channels?' Finucane asked. He seemed to know what she was about to say. He was already shaking his head.

She said, 'We want your informal co-operation.'

'What do you think you mean by that? "Informal co-operation." Are you asking a retired FBI Special Agent to take him? You don't mean "informal co-operation". You mean *illegal* co-operation.'

'Is that a question or a statement?'

'I don't care which it is. You don't involve me.'

She smiled at him with excessive sweetness. 'You involved us. You were right. You did well. But you involved yourself at the same time. We can't go back. Neither can you.'

Finucane glanced at his watch. Time was running out: 'What do you have in mind, Miss Linger?'

'You'll have to use your own contacts to get him in.'

'My people are dispersed. I haven't seen a single one of them for over two years.'

'So?'

'I don't know where they are.'

'Then you'll have to find them.'

'I don't even know where the hell Mahon is.'

She raised her eyebrows in a poor imitation of innocence. She adopted the tone of voice she might use to charm some delinquent child. 'You can use your *original* contact. The one who told you about it in the first place. You don't have to give any names. Just make the right connections, that's all.'

Finucane thought of Lindsay. He didn't want her drawn into it. Her career was over. But Lindsay was caught, and so was he. Worst of all he realised the trap was of his own making. Linger had been careful; so had Yoram. Neither of them had asked for names. And he had not volunteered them. You didn't have to name your contacts if it meant putting them in unnecessary jeopardy. 'I can't promise anything,' he said.

'I haven't asked you to promise anything,' Linger told him. 'I'm telling you that you're already involved. In so many words you're volunteering.'

'If I refuse?'

She paused and once again looked at him with a gaze of wounded innocence. 'There are people who don't like you, Mr Finucane. You have a reputation for being a hard man. It can bite back at you. You've made some enemies down the years. They could still make your life a misery, even in retirement.'

Finucane looked at Katz hoping for support. He didn't get it. He looked at his watch. His flight had still not been called. Miss Linger seemed to have all the time in the world. She reminded him of his ex-wife's way with threats and complaints. She used to say, 'You'll always be married to the Bureau. You never genuinely married me anyway.' Or, when she was very drunk, 'You've put so many people's lives at risk, Lou. One day they'll bite back at you. You see. So many people hate you. And you don't even know it.' He never bothered to reply. He knew it all anyway. What was true couldn't faze him. So it hadn't seemed to matter. He used to protest a little. Finally, he gave up bothering. And she gave up bothering him. He found the answer in indifference to her and when he did so he discovered it was also the best time to leave her. She found her answer in the booze. That solved one problem.

The flight to Heathrow was being called. It didn't let him off the hook.

Finucane turned on her angrily: 'You don't have to threaten me, Miss Linger.'

Katz intervened: 'It's important, Lou.'

'I told you that, Yoram. The question is where is this taking us?'

Linger was laughing. 'You'll be met at Heathrow,' she said. 'London's been briefed. We're all very grateful.'

'Thanks,' said Finucane. 'Thanks a lot.'

He walked away to board the plan to London. He found a telephone in the lounge and put through a call to Lindsay.

He told her there had been developments. It would be a while before he would be back home.

118

21

Mahon waited until nightfall to return to the flat in Gordon Place.

He had decided he had to assess the threat, confront it, see if it was one. He felt almost superstitious about the confront-ation. It had to be done; like avoiding the cracks in the pavement. If he did he'd be all right.

He reasoned with himself, that the police would have obligingly scared off the watchers. He had enough faith in the police to believe they'd have started to ask some fairly awkward questions of the two women in the Honda. He resisted the temptation to telephone the police to ask if they had discovered who the women were.

Heavy rain and the rush-hour crowds absorbed him. He was relieved to be just another damp and faceless traveller on the short underground journey to Notting Hill Gate. It seemed almost like home again. The same young Irish violinist busking Bach with a look of saintliness in his hollow eyes. The puffy blazing red face of a wino holding up cracked hands for a few pence, two cider bottles wedged between his knees.

He walked up the steps and joined the crowds by the traffic-lights. His mind turned over the possible identities of the watchers. Were they part of a surveillance unit carrying out a routine check on him? What pattern of his behaviour had been charted out for them to watch; what picture were they completing? Or could they be part of Henry Newiston's possible suspicion of his wife's infidelity?

He had no answer. He had a choice of several different routes to Gordon Place from Notting Hill Gate. Instinctively he chose the most obvious and walked straight down Kensington Church Street. Twice he crossed the road to allow himself the casual look around at the traffic and any figure keeping cover. There was only the shuffling crowd of pedestrians bound for home, a pair of grumpy waiters hurrying for the evening shift, two nuns, habits covered in cheap macks, their faces white.

He turned right, still not completely certain he was on his own, making a slight variation to the direct route home, into Holland Street, past the shop offering heavy books on art, past the photographic salon of Baron. Children's faces grinned at him, behind them was a row of photos of Prince Charles from little boy to husband and father. It reminded him of an insurance advert showing man's journey into age and liability.

Past the pub on the corner, he turned right. Anxiously he skirted the ladder propped against the scaffolding of the house just this side of his flat. He reached in his pockets for his keys before climbing the steps to his front door.

There was only one doorbell. Each resident had a bell code. One ring for *Mrs JDB*, two for *Liddon*, three for *Okjikwa* and so on. His own bell wasn't marked with a name. His handwriting said 6. He gave six rings and waited.

No movement in the basement.

He waited and looked up and down the street. No familiar faces. No Mercedes. No Honda.

The absences reassured him. He'd avoided the pavement cracks and the ladder. Now a black workman was removing a plank wired to the rungs. A radio was turned on inside the building and played Joe Jackson.

He let himself into the house.

His mail lay in a neat pile on the battered pine table on top of the free glossy magazines *Property* and *Gentleman*. A buff envelope contained his bank statement. There was last week's copy of the *Spectator*. A letter from an estate agent asked him if he was thinking of selling his flat. 'There is much interest in properties within the boundaries of the Royal Borough of Kensington and Chelsea from the Middle East and Hong Kong.' A handwritten postscript suggested he might care to contact the Honourable Someone-or-other. He took the mail with him to the end of the hall and turned down the staircase to the basement.

Outside his door he remembered that he hadn't taken the time-worn precaution: sticking a fragment of sticky tape across the door as a check to enable him to tell on his return whether or not he'd had a visitor.

Much later he remembered the moment he'd noticed the omission and cursed his own forgetfulness. But it's always the simplest precautions one fails to take. In that, as in so many other things, he'd tell himself, the hunted and the hunter have much in common.

He turned the key in the lock and took three steps into the room. He felt a brief moment of relief. He had returned home. He'd thrown them off the scent. The air was stale. But it was still his air, his own place, and it was safe.

Instinct made him turn sharply. Just his head.

The faces of the two men were grotesquely flattened by stockings. Perhaps it was the sudden horror, the surge of nausea which gave him the exaggerated impression of the men's heights and widths. They stood, for a moment, quite still; perhaps they were as anxious as he was. He saw their suits. It was odd, he later remembered thinking, that they both wore ties and white shirts. They looked strangely respectable in contrast to the speed of the violence they let loose.

The knee came up between his legs. He felt his whole body turn sideways. *Property* and *Gentleman* and *Spectator* flopped to the floor. His letters floated, zig-zagging, and seemed to land slowly with weird courtesy, almost neatly, on the carpet.

The clenched fist – later he thought it must have been something heavy wrapped in cloth, – hit the back of his head and drove his jaw and mouth against his chest.

His stinging tongue and swollen lips later showed the force of the blow to the back of his neck.

There was a long sound of some china falling to the floor. The white of a broken cup blinded him. He heard all his breath leave his lungs in a long sigh like compressed air leaving the brake system of a gigantic road vehicle.

Eleanor Grochal immediately broke down when she answered the door to Mehta. She turned her head away from him and brought the back of her hand to her mouth. She seemed to say, 'I'm sorry.'

In the event, Mehta said it for her:

'I'm so sorry. Perhaps I may come in?' He saw grief and anger in her face.

'Yes,' she said in a small voice.

She was hunched up in an old mackintosh. There was a small fire in the drawing-room grate. Even so it was so cold that Mehta didn't take his coat off. 'Please do let me say,' he began. 'On behalf of us all how very sorry I am.' He made a reasonably successful attempt to hide his awkwardness. 'We can take some comfort from the fact the suffering was not prolonged.'

'What on earth makes you think that?'

He tried to ignore the reprimand. He tried another apology to let himself down lightly. 'I'm sorry.'

Unexpectedly, she laughed at him. 'Don't say that Geoffrey died in his sleep.'

'I gather – '

'Yes. Quite right. You gather he did.'

Mehta went on, determined to get through the wall of bitterness. 'I've been asked to come to see if there's anything, anything at all, that we can do to help. Funeral arrangements and so on? Dealing with the solicitors, perhaps? The Service always helps on these occasions.'

They were still standing, facing each other, across the cold drawing-room.

'I've no doubt Geoffrey anticipated that,' Eleanor Grochal said. 'He made all the arrangements himself. You didn't work with him, did you? So you won't perhaps appreciate what a very thorough man he was.'

'He had a great reputation for efficiency.'

'Then it won't surprise you that he's spared you the bother of wasting anymore taxpayer's money. There's no need for the Service's welfare department to assist me.' The attack turned suddenly to gentle reflection. 'In our day it was known as the Married Families Section. They got in touch with me after Felix died.'

'I did not have the privilege of knowing your husband personally.'

'Few did,' she said.

Mehta abandoned the formal excuse for his visit to the house in Orford. He had made some cursory preparations for polite chat on the way up from London. He thought perhaps he could say how magnificent the twelfth-century castle was; that perhaps Eleanor would like to take a walk with him to look at it. 'Castle walls hold so many secrets,' he'd said to himself this side of Ipswich. He liked to steer the subject's mind on to an associated train of thought before easing out a secret detail. He had never much liked the idea that you cracked the subject first like the leg of a lobster to dig for meat. That was an image Chayter had once offered to a seminar. Everyone else had thought it most appropriate. It held no appeal for Mehta's neat and realistic mind.

She seemed to have known he hadn't come just to offer the condolences of the Service. She had telephoned the Service; and she had been the one who told *them* that Geoffrey had deteriorated so suddenly that he had never regained consciousness before he died.

It was customary to make a routine enquiry when a Service officer died. On this occasion Mehta had seen it as a mere formality. It had only been his sense of courtesy which persuaded him, in passing, to ask the ward sister if Mr Hackett had received many visitors. No, she had said, he had no other visitors other than Mrs Grochal. Other than a colleague whom she assumed to be connected with Mr Hackett's professional life.

A Mr Freedman.

And Mr Freedman had brought roses for the unconscious Hackett.

Now, facing Eleanor Grochal, Mehta spoke to her very gently. 'You're quite sure he had no other visitors?'

She bit her lip and nodded.

'Not a Mr Freedman?'

'I don't know who you're talking about. We knew no one called Freedman. It hardly matters now, does it?'

Mehta found the lie easy enough to tell: 'No. It doesn't matter at all.'

He wanted to be gone. Fast and clean. He felt he had to make the polite conversation he had rehearsed. He didn't bother with the castle and historical blather. The easiest way out was to offer kindness.

'If there's anything at all I can do, please – do telephone me at any time you wish. Don't consider it inconvenient. This'll be a bad time for you. I understand. But you can take strength from the affection of friends. One needs shelter. The Service is a large umbrella.'

She followed him to the door.

Before leaving he offered her his hand and she held it tightly. Then she began once more to weep.

It was still raining when Mehta walked to his car. He walked fast and almost slipped over altogether on the track when he reached the gatepost. He wanted to get away as soon as possible. To speak to John Chayter alone. To get his ears only. He had begun already to suspect, very strongly, that Geoffrey Hackett's end had been accelerated; that, without putting too fine a point on it, the old man had been murdered. Why and by whom he had no idea at all. The one hope lay in discovering the identity of Mr Freedman. He had never heard of anyone called Freedman.

Perhaps the computer at Century House would yield the identity of Geoffrey Hackett's visitor.

Dilip Mehta drove back to London very fast indeed.

22

It was Chayter's turn to be sceptical.

'Geoffrey's cancer was first diagnosed three years ago,' he told Mehta. 'He had a reprieve for a time. Some surgery. By coincidence the pattern of the deterioration was rather the same as my father's. Toward the end he went downhill very fast. It was just as well, really. He was in a lot of pain. Poor old Geoffrey must have been as well.'

Mehta, who had asked for five minutes of the Director's time before that afternoon's Executive Meeting, tried once more to persuade Chayter that his suspicion was well grounded. Mehta was the realist; the records man, scrupulous observer of the niceties of getting things down on paper. He had been known to wield his elegantly phrased memoranda to great effect. He believed that nothing should ever be 'off-the-record'. Not for nothing had the Security Commission's investigation of three years before singled Dilip Mehta out for special praise.

Chayter was careful to hear him out. He gave little sign, but he felt Mehta's suspicion about Hackett's death to be verging on the melodramatic. No matter that both of them were already five minutes late for the Executive Meeting across the corridor.

'After all, Geoffrey went back a long way,' Chayter said. 'It's perfectly likely that some old friend or colleague turned up out of the blue.'

'Don't you think the visitor would have telephoned the sister?' Mehta asked. 'It'd have been a matter of common courtesy.'

'He may very well have had his reasons,' Chayter said.

'What do you think they'd have been?'

'I can't tell. Embarrassment perhaps. He may have had his

own reasons for not wanting to get in touch with the sister.' Chayter got to his feet and picked up his Director's file. A typewritten agenda was pinned to its cover. 'I'd be perfectly happy for you to look into it further, Dilip, if it bothers you.'

'It does.'

'All right,' Chayter said.

By the door he added, 'Let's not treat it as a priority, Dilip. Not at present, if that's in order with you. But do come and talk it over with me again. Whenever you want.'

Mehta said he would.

Then Chayter said, 'I'd keep it to yourself. It'd be better at present if we don't make it a subject for general speculation outside this room, don't you agree?'

Mehta nodded and followed the Director out of his office, across the corridor and into the Committee Room.

The routine meeting lasted just over an hour. Most of it was taken up with discussion of a finance paper offered to the Executive by Boden-Smith who talked at considerable length. Occasionally she gave Chayter irritated glances. She disliked the Director's habit of doodling elaborately constructed country houses whilst she was talking.

As the meeting ended Chayter asked Henry Newiston to stay behind.

'I want to put something to you very frankly,' Chayter began.

'Whatever you wish.'

'My mind's fairly concentrated at the moment on the business of appointing the right Deputy Director.'

'I can imagine,' Newiston said with a tone of sympathy.

Chayter continued to doodle. He was building a portico on the front of the house. 'In a sense the material is so good that it's going to be hard to avoid disappointing someone. You, Dilip, Linda. In order to ameliorate the matter I've decided to take a slightly unconventional step. I think Dick White used to adopt much the same tack with appointments. I have it in mind to ask all of you what your view is of the other candidates. I want to know how you'd assess the chances of the others.'

'It'd be a hard task. Maurice Oldfield recommended himself. No bad idea.'

'Exactly. It isn't a bad test though, wouldn't you say?'

'I'd be prepared to go along with it.'

'I thought you would be,' Chayter said, affectionately.

'I appreciate you asking.'

'You and I go back a long way together. We have a shared history, personally and professionally, that's probably greater than anyone else's. That's why I wanted to ask you first.'

'Thanks,' said Newiston. 'I quite understand your point of view. I'd hate to think, whatever the choice turns out to be, that our relationship might change.'

'Not on my part,' Chayter said.

'Same here.'

Chayter shaded in the pillars of his portico. 'And there's another candidate. The outsider. Mahon.'

'He's very good. It'd go down well with the juniors.'

'In so far as he's an outsider, I'd quite welcome your initial view of him.'

He stopped doodling and crossed his hands on the surface of the table.

Newiston said: 'I suppose that until fairly recently I'd have said that he's conspicuously self-sufficient and that that's a bonus in his favour. On the other hand, he's taken the Polish business very much to heart. I'd say he's been oddly subjective about the whole thing.'

'Upset?'

'In a way.'

'But he lost two agents. They were his first, weren't they?'

'Yes, they were.'

'You're saying you think he over-reacted?'

'Possibly.'

'The draft report is good. In fact, it's very good. That's the monument to the failure, if you like. It'll be remembered rather longer than the loss of two Poles, wouldn't you say?'

'Yes. Even so, I'd say his reaction wasn't entirely mature.'

The doodling started up again. This time Chayter was filling in a stick-man pushing a wheelbarrow. 'Apart from the qualities of his report there's the fact that we haven't seen too much of him here recently.'

'I think that's normal,' Newiston said. 'He's "in interval".'

'I know. But for a man who so clearly lives and breathes the Service and this place, for someone whose chief characteristic, at any rate one of them, is to be at his desk far beyond the

127

necessary hours, it's pretty odd that he hasn't in fact been here since he submitted his draft.'

'Once or twice.'

'Only once or twice. Still odd, isn't it?' Chayter said.

'I could put it to him if you wish.'

Chayter was doodling some trees now. More urgently. Hatching them with powerful stabbing marks. The effect was like a quick drawing of Van Gogh's. 'The difficulty is, Henry, that our friend Mahon has disappeared.'

Newiston didn't react.

'I've tried to find him,' Chayter continued. 'He's not on leave. I sent someone round to his flat in Kensington. He wasn't there at the weekend. He doesn't answer his call number.'

'Are you quite sure he's gone?' Newiston asked incredulously.

'I can only judge by the signs of absence. I want a second opinion. Treat it as a matter of priority, Henry.'

The signs of absence were there to see; or, strictly speaking, as Henry Newiston felt, not there to see. He went to Mahon's office and turned through the pages of his appointments diary. There were hardly any entries. Mahon was in the habit, as Newiston could tell, of crossing out each day with a single diagonal line. Either the habit had ceased a week ago or he had simply not bothered to score out the days. Other dates had been blocked off with the word Poland in a circle. He searched the drawers of the desk and came up with nothing. He asked the Duty Security Officer for the number to Mahon's safe and searched that too. Everything was arranged tidily. There were no signs at all that anything had been removed in a hurry.

His concern showed itself to Kirsty the same evening.

He didn't at once say what was on his mind. When he found her unusually attentive after an unexpectedly good dinner and when she said casually that he seemed unusually worried, he came out with it.

'Our friend Mahon has temporarily done a bunk.'

'Why?' she said.

'Search me.'

'How dreadful,' Kirsty said.

Newiston watched her. She seemed more shocked than he'd have thought she might be at the news.

'Thin air,' said Newiston.

'Well, I hope you find him,' Kirsty said.

'We're looking very hard.'

'Who's "we"?'

'As a matter of fact, I am "we". So far. There's no need for a full-scale alert. Yet.'

'I'm very sorry,' Kirsty said.

'I don't suppose you've any idea where he is?'

She failed to contain her astonishment. 'What on earth makes you think I'd know where he is?'

'Only a joke,' Newiston said. 'Sorry. Didn't mean to upset you.'

'You haven't upset me,' she said sharply.

She left him alone to watch television and went to the kitchen.

Loading the dishwasher she dropped a glass into it. The glass shattered and in retrieving the broken fragments she cut her hand. The cut was at the base of her right thumb. She walked past the drawing-room and then turned back to open the door.

'I've cut my hand,' she said.

'Is it serious?' He turned round and looked at her.

'I haven't any elastoplast,' she said.

'You want me to get some?'

'No. I'll just go down the road. They're open till eleven. I won't be long.'

She took her coat and hurried to the shop. She made it five minutes before it closed. But as the Kenyan Asian woman had handed her the small pack of Band-Aid she realised she had forgotten to bring any money with her.

'Can I pay you tomorrow?'

The Kenyan Asian woman said she could.

She left the shop in a great hurry. By now she was on the verge of panic. She found herself opening the door to the shop once again. The bell clanged. 'Thank you very much,' she blurted out and slammed the door shut.

The first telephone kiosk was out of order and it took her more than five minutes to walk and half run to the next one.

She dialled the number in Frithville Gardens.

There was no reply.

She dialled again. Once more nobody answered. So she dialled Mahon's number in Gordon Place.

She had to warn him. And of all people it was Henry who was on his track.

Henry had already gone to bed when she returned home and she was thankful for it. She wanted time to be alone, to think. She immediately decided she would go early the next day to Frithville Gardens.

In the kitchen she ran herself a glass of water and turned to lean against the sink to drink it. It was then she noticed, in the centre of the table, no less than three small boxes of Band-Aid elastoplasts. They stood in a neat pile and on the top was her purse.

It was Henry's way of saying to her that he had been deceived by her. His way of making her uneasy.

The little gesture gave her a sleepless night.

The first available time Chayter had to see Newiston next day was shortly before lunchtime. He cancelled his lunch appointment and heard Henry Newiston out.

The check through the departments, all of them, yielded a suggestion that Mahon had recently been a regular visitor to Nelson Unit. Henry Newiston said Mahon had gone to Nelson that very morning.

'Does Hanratty confirm the visits?'

'He's on leave.'

'What about his log?'

'Yes, it's all there. Here.'

Newiston pushed a single photocopy across Chayter's desk. Chayter read it. 'Looking into history?'

'So it seems.'

'What for do you imagine?'

'Who knows?'

'Mugging up for an interview?' Chayter said with a smile. 'But I can't believe he thinks we'll ask him about history, do you?'

'I doubt it.'

'What do you think he was up to there?'

Newiston left his small discovery, the one that counted, until last:

'I don't know,' he said. 'But there are three files which it seems he removed.'

'To do with what?'

'Anglo-American liaison.'

'From when?'

'1941.'

'What would he want with them?' Chayter said. 'They're as good as dead. I'm concerned about what's alive.' He walked to the side of his desk and aimlessly fingered through the sheets of paper in his in-tray. 'The odd thing about Mahon is that I honestly don't know who his friends are.' He stared at a memorandum from the Foreign Secretary. He seemed to be reading it upside down. 'Who does he see outside the Service?'

'I honestly don't know,' Newiston admitted.

'I'm not sure I know what his interests are,' Chayter said. 'Do you?'

'No.'

'You'd better begin at the beginning, Henry. You'd better put his recent life together for us. As fast as possible in the circumstances.' He was turning the Foreign Secretary's memorandum around. 'The one thing we do not want, at any price, right now, is a full-scale alert. So you'd better just check there's no possibility he might have gone across.'

'There are no signs of it,' Newiston said.

Chayter suddenly looked at him as though the remark was profoundly idiotic. 'There aren't many signs nowadays, Henry,' he said angrily. 'Times have changed. You'd better go and find him, Henry. He's your man, isn't he?'

Newiston felt the Director's eyes on him the whole way to the door.

As a parting shot, Chayter said very quietly. 'This one you can handle on your own. If you need my help ask for it. But don't ask for anyone else's. Not yet, Henry. Not yet. I think it'll be advisable to put it about that Mahon is on a fortnight's leave.'

'On whose authority?'

'Mine,' said Chayter.

Newiston had the door slightly open when Chayter added finally: 'I don't want the matter discussed with anyone else at all.'

'Understood.'

Five minutes later Chayter called Dilip Mehta into his office and told him exactly the same thing: 'I don't want you talking about this to anyone, Dilip.'

'I quite understand,' Mehta said.

'Go and talk to Hanratty,' Chayter told him.

23

The faces of the two fat women in the lounge of Cromer's Hotel de Paris stared with hostility at the Indian by the reception desk. You may be elegant, the faces said, but you don't belong here. One after the other the fat women lifted their glasses of Cinzano. The fattest woman fished out a slice of lemon and dropped it in the ashtray. The two sets of watery eyes watched Dilip Mehta and seemed to say don't you dare come any nearer.

The receptionist told him that Mr Hanratty had gone for a walk along the beach. He would be back for lunch. 'Who shall I say asked for him, sir?'

'A friend,' Mehta said. 'Please don't let me trouble you any more. I'll go and find him myself.'

'He went out with a book,' the receptionist said.

'Then I don't expect he's gone far, do you?'

'Not in this weather.'

Mehta walked across the lounge to where the doors opened on to a small verandah overlooking the promenade.

'Close it after you,' said one of the fat women, the ash falling from her cigarette on to her lap.

Mehta gave a polite smile and walked out into the freezing wind.

There was no sign of him by the pier. A mechanical parrot shrieked out 'My name's Polly. Polly is my name. My name's Polly. Polly is my name.' It gave a sudden whining moan and fell silent. The amusement arcade was boarded up. Mehta walked onto the pier. A girl ambled past him carrying an empty shrimping net. Three men dressed up like arctic explorers from an illustration in a child's book of heroic feats stood grimly by the rail. Their fishing-rods were tied to the boards. Mehta stopped by the entrance to the pier's theatre. It too was closed. But a printed poster said that later in the year evening entertainments would be offered by Frank Ifield and Bobby Crush. He peered into the building that housed the Cromer lifeboat. There was no one there except a man with a wrinkled face stooped over a table with tea towels and lifeboat souvenirs for sale.

He dropped a fifty-pence piece into the plastic lifeboat gift box and heard again on the wind, 'My name's Polly. Polly is my name . . . '

Turning, gazing across the expanse of pale sand to the small waves breaking white, he saw a figure, walking slowly towards the pier. He walked back the way he'd come and made his way down on to the beach plodding out across the sand.

'Hanratty?'

The figure turned. 'I've seen you before somewhere, haven't I?'

'Mehta.'

'Ah yes, I never forget a name,' Hanratty said. 'Faces, sometimes. Names, never.'

'Can I buy you lunch?'

'What a very nice thought, Mr Mehta. I didn't know you took your leaves in Cromer. I thought I was the only one.'

'I am not on leave, your record's intact. I want to talk some business with you.'

'There's jugged hare on the menu. I'm very partial to rabbit and hare, especially hare. Best at lunch. At night it gives you dreams.'

The hare wasn't at all bad and Hanratty, having asked permission, ordered up two helpings. 'Sea air always gives you a seafarer's appetite, Mr Mehta. I'm reading the Hinsley volumes, you know. *British Intelligence in the Second World War.* I had hoped for an acknowledgement in one of them. But it wasn't to be.' He turned to the waitress. 'Can we have a refill of the redcurrant jelly, my dear?'

'I want you to think back,' Mehta said. 'Over recent weeks. To all personnel who've been at Nelson.'

'It's been the off-peak season,' Hanratty said, sadly.

'Then it should be easy for you to remember names.'

Hanratty laughed. He liked to think people remembered his *bons mots* and in case you didn't he invariably repeated them. 'Faces, sometimes. Names, never.'

'Mr Mahon?'

'What about Mr Mahon?'

'What was he looking for at Nelson?'

'It's all in my log, Mr Mehta,' Hanratty said, defensively.

'Well, yes and no. It is and it isn't.'

Hanratty thanked the waitress for the second pot of redcurrant jelly. 'Home-made,' he informed Mehta. 'Try it.'

Mehta declined.

Talking with his mouth full, Hanratty grew splutteringly expansive: 'Mr Mahon was curious to know something of his pedigree. His father was a serving officer during the war. Lost his life in Madrid. I imagine that Mr Mahon has reached that age when a man wants to know where he comes from, where he's going. Like the title of that painting by Gauguin. *Where Have We Come From?* and so forth.'

'What would Mr Mahon have discovered in his file?'

'It's not *his* file. His father's file. His biography. Personal.'

'But what would he have found in it?'

'Not very much,' Hanratty said. 'They've long since been weeded.' He looked around the dining-room. The waitress stood by the door to the kitchen. The two fat women were gulping apple pie and ice-cream. Hanratty seemed to be calculating whether he could be overheard and must have concluded that the muzak provided satisfactory cover. He warmed to his theme. 'I assumed, in so far as Mahon's father was connected to early Anglo-American liaison, it must have had a bearing on the new negotiations of the alliance. Some of the material Mahon requested had already been looked at by the Americans. They sent some people over from Washington.'

'When?'

'Perhaps it was four or five years ago. Whenever the Royal wedding was. I had to hire a television set for them to watch it. They were very impressed. One of them bought a mug with Lady Diana's face on it. Odd to think it's probably being used this very minute in Langley, wouldn't you say. Coffee with pudding? They provide me with an After Eight mint. I expect they'll find you one too if we ask nicely.' He called to the waitress. 'Apple pie. Coffee with. Two mints if you will?'

Mehta persisted with his questions: 'If you wanted to find out the background to those files who would you talk to?'

135

'I'm only an archivist, Mr Mehta. A keeper. That's what I'd be called if I were on the staff of a great museum. Sometimes one settles for second-best.'

'Put your mind to it, please.'

The apple pie concentrated Hanratty on his answer: 'I'd have talked to Mr Hackett. He's the only one from that generation. Him and Dickie Wigart. Now they've gone the whole lot's died too, hasn't it? You might try Eleanor Grochal. I never took to her a great deal. Not, I'd say, what you'd call a warm woman, was she? Mind you, her husband wasn't either. By the way, can we look forward to a memorial service for Mr Hackett at All Saints, Margaret Street?'

'There isn't going to be one,' Mehta said.

'Why not? There's always a memorial service.'

'Not always. In this case Mr Hackett left specific instructions that no memorial service be held.'

'What a pity. It's an excuse for me to get up to town. I have an account at the Army & Navy Stores in Victoria. If I were you I'd try Dr Grochal.'

Hanratty spilled some of his coffee into his saucer. He was elaborately wiping the saucer and bottom of the cup dry when he suddenly asked: 'Why don't you put all your questions to Mr Mahon himself? Why come all the way out here to see me?'

'You're the man at Archives,' Mehta said. 'You're the first port of call. The keeper. Mr Mahon's abroad on leave for a few weeks. One is simply running a routine check. A paper to the Foreign Secretary. Anniversaries are all the rage, aren't they? We haven't got long to go till it's been fifty years since the start of World War Two, have we?'

'Quite long enough,' said Hanratty. 'Won't you have a brandy?'

'No thanks,' said Mehta. 'You have one yourself. Lunch is on me.'

'In that case, I'll have two,' said Hanratty. 'I'm very flattered you've come all this way to buy me lunch, Mr Mehta. It's the very first time I've ever been bought an official luncheon.'

'Just to make quite sure it isn't the last, please guarantee you'll make no mention of my visit to anyone at all, Mr Hanratty.'

'Two brandies and I'm all yours, Mr Mehta.'

136

There was, thought Mehta, to himself, something deeply unwholesome about the archivist. He couldn't quite put his finger on what it was.

Henry was at home trying to get a fix on Mahon's whereabouts. There was astonishingly little to go on. His quarry's bank came up with details of perfectly usual spending during the last few weeks. There was not a trace of anything unusual in the man's credit card accounts. Discreet enquiries to Mahon's doctor showed him to be in sound health if that's what not a single consultation in the last eighteen months meant. The duty man in Surveillance found nothing untoward during his albeit rather hurried visit to Mahon's address. The elderly neighbours said they hadn't noticed him coming or going very much in recent days. One said he was 'very much a man who keeps himself to himself.' The police in the area had no information. There was a mention of someone nearby having reported two people behaving suspiciously in the street in which Mahon lived. The police attached no importance to it. The two persons had been flat-hunting in the area. The police said they'd come back to them if they came up with anything. So far they hadn't called back. Slowly, Henry began to think the search might turn into something larger: no less than the pursuit of a colleague whose approach to any one of London's communist embassies might have been accepted. However, there wasn't a shred of evidence to suggest Mahon might have been even remotely contemplating anything so dramatic.

The clock on his study desk said eleven-thirty. He decided to pack it in for the night. He tidied his papers, locked them into his briefcase and turned out the study lights. He stood completely still in the darkness. It was an old habit he'd developed as an undergraduate after he'd finished a long and wearisome evening's work alone. He had always loved the darkness and, like those who said they did their best thinking in the bath, reckoned some of his best thoughts came to him at such times.

Standing quite still with only the faintest light showing at the edges of the study curtains he thought of Kirsty's transformation. As he loved the darkness, so he loved explanations. When he found himself denied them he felt a

137

curious pang of rejection. There had been a time in his marriage when he'd felt a profound sense of relief in telling Kirsty such things about himself. But when she gradually changed and built up her barriers of resentment against him it seemed to deny the old intimacies. He now kept himself to himself. Like Mahon does, he thought. He tried to think himself into Mahon's mind. It was a hopeless task. He turned back again to Kirsty. She seemed, he thought to himself, to have regressed. She was once again the skittish and volatile Kirsty. She smiled again just as she had when they'd first been lovers. There were signs that seemed to show a new Kirsty. Granted there were still complaints. Yet they were fewer and less strident. She had confronted the dinner for the Chayters as though she genuinely enjoyed it.

He knew the transformation had nothing to do with him.

If she was having an affair with someone she'd have come out with it by now. She laid great store, so she claimed, upon authenticity. He could imagine her saying, 'There's something I want to tell you. For your sake. I'm telling you because you needn't be concerned. I'm seeing a lot of So-and-so. As a matter of fact, we're lovers. In body. Not in mind. It takes the pressure off you.' He could see her smiling with pride. She always claimed to be acting, first and foremost, in someone else's interests, especially his interests. She'd said as much to him when he'd asked if she minded marrying someone in the Secret Service. 'Mind marrying a *spy*? Why should I? I'll never know *what* you're doing but I'll always know *why* you're doing it. It seems a perfectly honourable occupation to me. There's something of the spy in all of us when it comes to it. And the salary's all right, isn't it? Perks. Travel. School fees paid. Whacking pension. I don't object, Henry. You go and play your games. I'll clap when you win.'

But now she didn't seem to be on the sidelines. She had begun to engage in her own little deceptions. The farce over the Band-Aid. The regular leaving the house. For what? To telephone the lover? She never went to see anyone in particular. Except the Finucane woman. Was Kirsty using her for cover? Where did they meet? A hotel? That flat she'd been left. It couldn't be the flat. It was rented out to the woman from the BBC.

Deciding he wouldn't bother to take the thing any further he

138.

made for the door. It was then he heard the sound of someone on the doorstep. He stood in the darkness leaning against his study door and waited.

The key turned in the lock.

Hal? Surely not. The house rule was that he always telephoned if he was coming home unexpectedly.

Kirsty? She was upstairs.

He'd got it wrong. The door opened and there she was silhouetted against the yellow street-light.

He edged back a little into the study and watched, fascinated, as she gently closed the door, silently. There was a dull clicking as she double-locked the door. Then she walked slowly and deliberately in his direction. She stopped. Took off her shoes. Then she crept on. Once she was in arm's length he reached out and tapped her shoulder.

She let out a small scream.

'What the hell are you doing?'

'I'm going up to bed,' he said. 'More to the point what the hell are you doing?' He wanted to laugh. It was all so childish. 'I thought you'd gone to bed ages ago.'

'Well you were wrong, Henry.'

He was surprised by her calm. She was almost gentle towards him.

She said, 'Why don't we both go to bed? It's late, isn't it? Past bedtime, I think. Don't you?'

She stooped down and put on her shoes.

'Where have you been, Kirsty?'

'I don't expect you to believe it. I've actually been out for a breath of fresh air. I think we ought to get a dog or something.'

'A dog?'

'It'd make it easier for me to walk alone late at night.'

'You're scared?'

'No. Just that it'd look sort of more purposeful, if you see what I mean. A woman. Late at night. On her own. Taking a dog for a walk. It'd see off the kerb-crawlers.' She paused. 'There's no point us standing here in the dark, is there?' She switched on the lights.

Perhaps it was the sudden glare which shocked him into making the accusation. Whatever prompted him it came out with a sharper edge than he'd intended. 'Have you got a lover?'

'What?'

He could see she was very frightened.

'What d'you mean?'

'What I say.'

'Don't be absurd.'

'Is it?'

'Completely, Henry. Completely.'

There was no going back. He tried to make a joke out of it. 'You're always vanishing at night. The walks. Where do you go? And God alone knows what you do during the day.'

She backed away from him, frowning at him. 'I don't ask you what you do, where you go, why, or anything. So don't ask me. That's the arrangement. Let's stick to it.'

'Who could it be, Kirsty? Must be someone in the Service. You're not completely stupid, I hope.'

'You said it. I didn't.'

'Mahon. Don't tell me you're having a fling with Mahon.'

'Don't be ridiculous.'

'If you are I'd be very grateful if you can tell him I'd like to speak to him. I'm not the only one who'd like to, by the way.' He tried to smile at her. 'Come on. I was only joking. Let's go to bed. I'm sorry.'

She faced him, her hands on her hips. 'Sorry? I should fucking well think you are.' She was breathing very fast indeed. She mimicked him: ' "I'm sorry. Let's go to bed." Well don't let me stop you.'

With that she turned, walked back to the door, fumbled for her keys and let herself out.

The door slammed and Henry realised his clumsy joke had pointed him towards the truth.

Lindsay was woken by the telephone ringing by her bedside. She hoped it would be Lou. He might be coming home tonight after all.

It was a terrible line and she didn't at once recognise Kirsty's voice.

'Are you on your own, Lindsay?'

'Yes.'

'I need your help.'

'You know what time it is?'

'Yes. I'm sorry. Please. I desperately need to talk to you.'

'Go ahead.'

'Not over the telephone. I can't talk for long. Not now. He might come out looking for me.'

'Who?'

'Henry.'

'What's the matter with him?'

'*Please*. Lindsay. I'm going to find a cab somewhere. I'm going to Frithville Gardens. Meet me there, please.'

'Can't it wait till the morning?'

'No. Believe me.'

'Okay, I'll see you there.'

Lindsay replaced the receiver and gave a long sigh.

It was a quarter to one in the morning when Lindsay reached Frithville Gardens. The wind was wicked. She wished she'd worn a heavier coat. She cursed herself for not realising that Kirsty would take far longer to arrive than herself. She first of all opened the gate. Its creak was lost on the wind. The house was in darkness. The lid to the old rubbish bin rattled. She went back to the low wall and waited for her under the street-light.

Kirsty arrived flustered, incoherent, fumbling in her bag saying she couldn't find her keys. When she found them she dithered on the doorstep.

'Here, give them to me,' Lindsay said. She took the keys and unlocked the door.

Once they were inside and had reached the kitchen, Kirsty broke down and unburdened herself. She told it confusedly. 'I can't understand why he's gone,' she said, dwelling on her last encounter with Mahon. 'He was here. He wanted to stay here. So no one knew where he'd be. I was to tell no one. That's what he said.'

She stared at the wall. 'But he's gone now, hasn't he?' she continued. 'It doesn't matter me telling you, Lindsay, now. He isn't here any more.'

'Did you admit what's going on to Henry?' Lindsay asked.

Kirsty shook her head.

'But you're quite sure he knows?'

'Yes.' Now she gave into her anger. 'How could he have found out? He must have had someone watching me. Watching this place.'

'Or watching your lover?'

'That too.'

'You're really sure he knows about the affair?'

'I know. He always delivers his accusations as though he's joking at me. It's a sort of mocking. It's his main weapon of defence. I've been through it all before.'

'He may do nothing about it.'

'Henry? Do nothing? That's not the way he works. He'll do something, you see. Whatever it is he does it will be unexpected. That's his tactic. He is ruthless with his enemies. And that's what I am now. Henry's enemy.'

Lindsay asked her to remember everything Mahon had said last time Kirsty had seen him.

'We talked about silly things. You know how it is. I don't remember what he said in bed. We don't talk much in bed. Not about anything of much consequence. He never once gave me a clue what was going on or that he'd disappear.'

'Not even a hint?'

'Nothing.'

She was staring at Lindsay. 'You can't find out where he is, can you? Find out if he's all right. You see, that's all I want to know – that he's all right.'

'You love him, don't you?'

'Yes.'

'Did you tell him?'

'No.'

'Why not?'

'I don't know. Perhaps I felt it wouldn't be fair. Now I wish I'd told him. Now that his people are looking for him . . . I don't know, it might have made things easier for him. If he knows that there's someone, just one person, who he can trust. I could have helped him.'

'Perhaps you did help him.'

'No, I don't think I did.' She laughed bitterly. 'All I did was store a whole lot of half-melted frozen food for him. It wasn't even as though I ever did any of his mending or washing or anything like that. Just froze his food.'

'What are you going to do?'

'I don't know. Stay here.'

'Not going home?'

'No.'

'I can take you home if you like.'

'No.'

'Or you can stay with me if you want. Lou's away. I'm on my own for a bit.'

'No.'

Later, Lindsay would have occasion to wish she had persisted with the invitation. The only reason she had to forgive herself for failing to push it was what Kirsty said next:

'When he came here he was very preoccupied. He was happy, yes. But his mind was elsewhere. Perhaps he wanted to tell me he was going to disappear. Looking back . . . I don't like to think about it . . .'

'What's that?'

'That he might have gone over to the Soviets. But no, I know he hasn't. He has no need to. He's in no difficulty of the sort that'd push him that far. I *know* that.' She paused and then began to weep again. 'Oh where is he?' She was silent for a while. The she said, 'Now, I'm alone. It's probably for the best.'

'The only thing I can say that's helpful,' Lindsay offered, 'is not to rush at anything. Take some more time to think it over. They'll find Mahon. And if Henry does know about the affair between you then it's something he'll have to live with. You'll sort it out somehow. Maybe you'll make a new life with him.'

'I don't think I've got enough strength for all that,' Kirsty said. 'I've had enough.'

She looked utterly defeated.

You need a rest,' Lindsay said. 'Why not go to bed for a while? I'll make you some tea and bring you a hot-water bottle. You'd like that?'

'Yes,' Kirsty said. 'Thanks.'

Lindsay went to the kitchen. She found a packet of tea and set it on the kitchen table. She filled the kettle and set it to boil up.

She found an almost empty carton of milk in the fridge and placed it on the table next to the tea. For a while she stared at the fridge. She went back to it and opened and closed the door. She opened the door to the freezer compartment below. It had four drawers to it made of transparent grey plastic. They were stuffed full of foodstuff. She pulled the top drawer and lifted out a white plastic bag. The label said Garden Peas. She took it to the kitchen sink and opened it. The hard frozen peas spilled out. She saw the pack of frozen paper, a wad of xeroxes. She set them carefully on the draining-board. The kettle was heating and whining eerily.

She turned.

Kirsty stood in the doorway.

'It wasn't only frozen food, he brought,' Lindsay said. 'Here. Take a look.'

She laid out the frozen paper. It lay in a glistening pile, hard and dry. 'This is what he's left you with.'

Kirsty looked at the pile of paper.

'They're xeroxes of wartime papers.'

'Why did he bring them here, for God's sake?'

'You tell me,' Lindsay said.

'Why didn't he tell me?'

'Obviously he didn't want you to know,' Lindsay said. 'Doesn't want anyone to know.'

'I think I ought to put them back, Lindsay. It's not our business.'

'I don't know that I would put them back,' Lindsay said. 'It may be better for your sake, his sake too, that they're kept somewhere else, don't you think?'

'I don't know.'

'I think it'll be best if we move them.'

'Where to?'

They left the frozen paper on the draining-board and made the tea.

Kirsty fingered the paper. 'All this is what he was talking to me about.'

'Right.'

'But, why – why did he leave them here like this?'

'That's for him to explain. So long as they're here you're likely to be compromised.'

'I couldn't be more compromised than I am already.'

'Oh, I don't know about that,' Lindsay said with a wry smile. 'It'll be best I keep hold of them for the time being. They'll be safer at my place, don't you think?'

'I don't know what to think. I suppose they will.'

'You take yourself to bed with your tea and your hot-water bottle,' Lindsay said. She found a plastic carrier-bag beneath the sink and packed the frozen papers inside some old newspaper. 'I'm going home now, Kirsty. Try and get some sleep. Call me if you want.'

'I'll call you in the morning,' Kirsty said. 'I'm sorry I've involved you in all this. It's a mess.'

'Don't worry. You'll get out of it.'

She left quickly, letting herself out of the house. Her mind was on the problem of finding a cab so early in the morning to take her back to Kensington. The last tube had long since gone.

Before leaving the flat she had tucked the carrier-bag inside her overcoat. Now she could feel it, very cold, against her breasts.

To the man in the car opposite the flat it must have seemed that Lindsay was clutching herself against the cold night air.

He had been careful to park away from the street-light and Lindsay did not notice him. Once she had turned into the Uxbridge Road out of sight the man left his car and crossed the street.

His gloved hands took care opening the gate. It didn't creak. And he walked carefully up the path choosing his way. The dustbin lid rattling in the wind covered his footfall. He waited in the dark shadows beneath the porch until the light in Kirsty's bedroom went out.

Soon after that, he took a single key from his pocket, put it into the lock and turned it.

He stepped quickly into the house and closed the door.

He locked it from inside and walked in silence to the stairs.

24

It was a day for making history in the Secret Intelligence Service: the time had come to select the Deputy Director. So a few of the Wise and the Good had come together to exercise secret patronage on behalf of the nation. The meeting at Century House got off to an odd start when it fell to Chayter to announce a revision to the timetable. His calm authority belied his inner turmoil:

'We are going to see Mr Mehta this morning instead of Mr Mahon,' he said. His brisk announcement hid the reason for the change. For the fact was no one knew where the candidate Mahon had gone. 'Mr Mahon will attend later.' In so far as the timetable was what was called 'open-ended' no one objected. After all, it was an honour to have been called to make the selection and the Wise and the Good assumed the Service knew what it was doing. By definition, it had its reasons and sometimes didn't have to give them.

Chayter eyed the Chairman of the Board who seemed to wait for ever to make some comment upon the alteration. The Chairman was small and thin with sandy hair at that unpleasant stage before it turns entirely white. He was a member of the Cabinet Office with the title of Co-ordinator of Security and Intelligence. It was a title he relished largely because he had proposed it to the Prime Minister himself. You could always tell the self-titled mandarins. They were the ones with the longest titles. This one appealed to the Prime Minister who liked the convenience of tradition and regarded the cobbling-up of titles as a talent to be valued. The Prime Minister had personally fished out the Co-ordinator from the highest ranks of the Civil Service. He was the sort of Englishman who'd walked with the Wise and the Good since his nursery days: a man of contrived decency who'd learned to avoid blame since the cradle. The face wore the grin of a waxwork. Only the small reflections in the lenses of his half-moon glasses held a spark of life:

'I don't think the Board need have any objection, Director.'

So far so good, Chayter thought, with some relief.

'Mr Mehta this morning,' the Chairman continued. 'Mr Newiston this afternoon. Miss Boden-Smith tomorrow morning, Mr Mahon . . .'

'Shall we say tomorrow afternoon?' Chayter offered.

'Agreed,' said the Chairman in the tone of the headmaster who's just fixed the timetable for the benefit of the junior staff. 'Mehta to open.'

'Always the sound opener,' said Dearte, the life peer and Master of Dilip Mehta's Cambridge College.

Chayter watched the woman seated opposite him across the table. Dr Margaret Spencer was the Hampstead psychiatrist the Service most of all preferred. Along with Dearte she was the only lay member of the Board. Jamieson, Director of Personnel at the Government Communications Headquarters, Cheltenham, completed the number.

Any one of them, felt Chayter, might sense his own disturbed frame of mind, that he for one was now more apprehensive than any of the candidates waiting for examination.

The electric clock above the door to the Executive Room said one minute past ten when Mehta entered. He walked, slightly stooped, towards the high-backed leather chair that faced the table at which the Board was sitting. The chair was of the kind favoured by designers who assembled the sets for arcane general knowledge quizzes on television. He looked briefly at the Board lined up behind the rank of government issue glasses and water jugs.

Chayter hoped the testing of Dilip Mehta wouldn't be his test too.

'Do sit, Mehta,' the Chairman said.

The Indian sat upright and relaxed in the leather chair. Chayter saw him look quickly up at the painting on the wall behind the Board members. It was a tentative neo-impressionist oil of Carlton Gardens in the rain, said to have been the work of a previous Director of SIS, Sir Michael Rennie.

'I think you know everyone,' the Chairman said. 'And I have little doubt you know the procedure. In the first instance I should stress the Board is answerable to the Prime Minister. The appointment of Deputy Director is, all things being equal, in the patronage of the Prime Minister which explains why I am acting as Chairman. We can regard the proceedings as informal in the general sense though formal in the particular, d'you follow?'

Mehta gave a slight nod.

'We are looking inward as much as outward,' the Chairman droned on. 'This morning affords us the opportunity to make a fair assessment and, I hope you'll agree, it also allows you the chance to assess us. At the end of the day, we can be in no doubt that fair play has been done though, I am bound to say. . .' he paused and gave a girlish smirk, 'the proceedings are secret. Therefore one cannot say anyone will be afforded the chance to say they *saw* the prosecution of fair play.'

Mehta followed the example of the Board and laughed politely.

'I am a neutral Chairman. Each candidate will be afforded the identical preamble.' He nudged aside the lead pencil provided by Century House's Administration Section. From inside the jacket of his three-piece suit he produced a silver propelling pencil of his own. The smirk left his face. He was like a conjuror at a toff's children's party. Full of things in his pockets. The next item to come out was the thin gold watch at the end of the chain that dangled across the front of his waistcoat. 'Tell us about yourself, Mehta.'

Chayter found himself admiring Mehta's calm and his practised fluency. He watched Mehta look straight into the eyes of a different member of the Board at the end of every sentence: 'I have three brief points to make,' Mehta said. 'About myself, about the other candidates, and about the present state of the Service.'

He told them his record in dealing with Egypt's GIA in Cairo 'spoke for itself'. Yes, Chayter thought – this is Dilip, the builder of bridges. Dilip had courted Mitterand so that a new measure of trust had grown up between London and the DGSE in Paris. He was congratulating himself. The Board would, he said, be aware that he had formed an especially close friendship with King Hussein. Never, he claimed, had the

148

bond between the Hashemite Kingdom and Great Britain been on so firm a footing.

'Similarly, I have directed operations against Qadhafi. There is now a powerful string of agents sympathetic to Great Britain in Tripoli, Benghazi and Tobruk.'

He took great pride in the North African and Mediterranean successes most of all because they had brought Washington closer to London. He had served in Washington and had received congratulations from the White House.

'I offer the record as proof of a first-hand relationship with these centres because I believe it to be an overriding qualification for appointment to Deputy.'

'Also for that of Director?' the Chairman said, without taking his eyes from the end of his propelling pencil. 'To, as it were, duplicate the Director.'

'To support the Director,' Mehta countered.

Chayter felt a moment's reassurance. He remained expressionless none the less and watched the Chairman's half-moon glasses slide down the thin nose. The little eyes looked to Jamieson giving the man from GCHQ his turn to pitch in.

'Would you talk about yoursef?' Jamieson asked. 'About more personal aspects? What would you say your advantages are?'

'I have a contented family life.'

'But no children?' the Chairman interrupted.

'My wife and I have decided not to have children.'

'Why?' asked the psychiatrist.

'It's a private matter.'

'Precisely,' the Chairman said. 'Hardly a matter of public interest, wouldn't you say? Children.'

'You don't want children for emotional reasons?' the psychiatrist asked.

'It's on medical grounds,' Mehta said. 'I am perfectly prepared to offer the Board a chance to see a doctor's report on my wife. Her gynaecologist will provide one.'

'I don't want to see it,' said the Chairman. He turned to the psychiatrist. 'Do you?'

She looked at Mehta and shook her head, jangling her oriental ear-rings.

Dearte, red-faced, with a slight speech impediment that

turned his 'r's into 'w's cleared his throat loudly: 'There seems to be very little time in your life for interests outside the Service. There's your wife, of course. The family in New Delhi. But really very little room otherwise for anything else. Who are your friends?'

'They are mostly officers and colleagues in the Service. We have many American friends.'

'From the old days in Washington?'

'Yes. We see our friends when they come to London. Our American friends.'

'You lay the greatest store on the Anglo-American intelligence alliance?' Jamieson asked.

'It goes without saying.'

'Nothing goes without saying,' said the Chairman. 'It's a surprising cliché from a man like you, Mehta.'

'I hope I made myself clear.'

'Not entirely,' said the Chairman. 'You were asked by my friend here to speak of your advantages. But there's one undeniable fact we really cannot overlook. You're Indian.'

Mehta stared back coldly.

'What do you have to say about that?'

'I'd have thought it fairly obvious.'

'You know what I'm driving at?'

'Not entirely.'

'You know as well as I do that in the absence of the Director it'll fall to you to deal directly with Downing Street?'

'With you.'

'And sometimes the Prime Minister.'

'I realise that.'

'And with my staff.'

'Yes.'

'And you'll also be dealing with our American friends.'

'I've already said, in my judgement, I have the required experience and qualifications to do so.'

So far still so good, Chayter felt.

'I heard what you said. It may not, however, seem so to you, but it will to innumerable others that an Indian like yourself elevated to such a high position of responsibility in the *British* Secret Intelligence Service will lay us all open to charges.'

'Charges of what?'

'Eccentricity.'

'In that case,' Mehta countered, 'I freely admit to being Indian. But I'd like to say that if others level such charges then, with respect, the eccentricity is theirs. Not mine.'

The Chairman wasn't letting him go. 'What would you say if we were to appoint a Pakistani to the post?'

'I would assume you had made the appointment on the basis of merit after the same sort of careful consideration you're showing my candidature.'

'A Pakistani?'

'Why not? Isn't that the responsibility of the Board?'

'I'm asking you, Mehta.'

'I've given you my reply.'

'And I've offended you?'

'Not at all. I'm used to it.'

'Then you see what I'm driving at. The ground is well tested. I know you'll understand why it is that men in high positions of professional responsibility in this country's institutions still say, perfectly reasonably, that they wouldn't want their daughters to marry an Indian or a man of different colour.'

'I'd like to think the British have grown up enough to have discarded that sort of prejudice.'

'Oh, Mehta, so would I. So would I. But do you honestly believe they have?'

'You're in a better position to judge than I. I think the hypothetical question you've put is a false one. The question you ought to be asking isn't about your daughter or anyone else's. It's about you. Would *you* marry an Indian girl you loved? Would *you* object to others sneering at you if you did? I wonder.'

'I have offended you, haven't I?'

'I have no intention of preventing you from offering offence if that's what your position requires of you.'

'What my position requires, Mehta, is my responsibility to define – after proper consultation with the Prime Minister. . .' He turned over the papers in front of him. 'Don't think I've been unduly forthright towards you on an issue you *can't* help. Namely, the colour of your skin. What we're interested in is what you *can* help. Your ability, your professional expertise, your qualities of leadership, integrity and spark. Agreed?'

Mehta nodded.

'On the other hand,' the Chairman continued. 'You

certainly haven't spared the cutting-edge when it comes to criticising the other candidates.'

'I was asked to give my honest views on them.'

'I know that. But you weren't asked to compose some elegantly written condemnation of them. We all have to live with each other.'

'Those we choose to live with.'

'That's your opinion.'

'I wrote exactly what I felt to be the truth,' Mehta said.

'So we see. So we see.'

'I also said I would comment on what I wrote.'

There was a mistimed silence.

'Commitment – ' Mehta began.

'Go ahead,' the Chairman said, interrupting him.

'Commitment to the secret life, in the general sense, is what I believe supports my candidacy. I don't hold with the view that the Deputy who's unmarried is automatically given a greater freedom to devote him or herself, as the case may be, to the tasks in hand.'

'What about Maurice Oldfield? He was a great Director and a Deputy Director before that. He was a personal friend of mine. He wasn't married, was he?'

'He was an exceptional case.'

'Precisely so.'

'But his style is twenty years out of date. The mumbo-jumbo, the sloppy poetry invented for milkmen, butchers, mechanics, postmen, all that jargon so typical of the old men's era. It's all passed. It's dead and gone. Do you suppose Maurice Oldfield took his skin disease to a psychiatrist? Oughtn't he to have been psycho-analysed? If not, why not? He was a bachelor.'

'We're not discussing dead officers, Mehta.'

Mehta looked at Jamieson. 'Aside from such issues, if that's what they are, the desk work matters. We are no longer like travelling salesmen. That's best left to the Foreign Service itself. What's required of us is a stability of mind and intellect. We no longer risk our lives in dangerous field operations. The risk now lies in making incorrect assessments. It's often been said within these four walls that real risks can be assessed in advance and precautions taken to obviate them – '

The Chairman interrupted: 'You know who said almost exactly those words, Mehta?'

'They've often been said, haven't they?'

'I don't doubt it.'

'The person who said those words added, "It is the almost meaningless incident that often puts one to mortal hazard." You know who said that?'

'I have heard it said.'

The Chairman failed to disguise his fury. 'I'll tell you who not only said that but wrote it down – Kim Philby. It hardly behoves you to quote his bloody silly nonsense in here, at interview.'

'I make no apology, sir. I think he was quite correct.'

'Noted.'

The Chairman's chest gave out an asthmatic whistle.

Chayter took up the questioning: 'And what about the Service itself, Dilip? Where do you see us going now?'

'I think greater financing of the South American Department is required. The same goes for Mexico and the Caribbean and Central Africa. I'd continue to lay stress, perhaps even greater stress, on the United States.'

'Why?'

'We've often discussed it. The vacuum of political leadership. The general view in Washington that we don't treat American policies as seriously as we should. The general issues suggest that there well may be a nasty turning point in the Anglo-American intelligence alliance. Nothing, absolutely nothing, should be allowed to threaten it.'

'I don't think anyone will disagree with that,' said the Chairman checking his watch against the clock above the door. 'Finally, the Board requires to know what you would do, given the responsibility, about a colleague whose treachery, no less, you had no doubt about.'

Chayter, absorbed by the questioning, saw Mehta hesitate before replying, giving the impression he was composing his reply with care.

'What rank would he be?'

'Middle,' said the Chairman.

'Depending on his or her position – '

'It's a man,' the Chairman interrupted.

153

'Depending on who he was I, personally, would opt for allowing him to believe he had compromised himself on some other matter altogether. I'd leave him in play for as long as possible but always believing himself to be under grave threat.'

'How would you allow him to be compromised?' asked the psychiatrist.

'Probably on personal grounds,' Mehta said. 'On grounds, for example, of a sexual nature perhaps.'

'Suppose there weren't any?' asked the Chairman.

Mehta looked at the members of the Board. 'There usually are some to be found somewhere.'

'True of all institutions?' asked the Chairman.

'I'm not saying that,' Mehta replied. 'But I would never deny the general and most likely possibility of their existence, would you?'

'I'm asking you, Mr Mehta.'

'I've given you my answer.'

'Very well,' said the Chairman.

The Board was silent.

'Any other questions?'

There were none from the Board.

'You, Mehta. Any questions?'

'None, sir.'

'Thank you for coming to see us. That's all.'

Before leaving Chayter gave Mehta an approving smile. Thank you, he wanted to say, for the diversion. One day he might thank Dilip for his barring of the woodshed door to the searchings of the Wise and the Good.

After the door had closed the Chairman put his hands flat on the table and sat back:

'Well? What do you think of the guru?'

Chayter started: 'He's one of the very finest intelligence officers in the West.'

'Prickly,' said the Chairman.

'Fine mind,' said Dearte.

'He seems to be centred,' said the psychiatrist.

'I didn't expect to hear Kim Philby being quoted with such approval,' said Jamieson.

'Well, well, everything that's been said about Mehta could have been said of Kim,' the Chairman announced. 'Except that presumably Mehta isn't an alcoholic, not a womaniser, speaks without stuttering all the time, and isn't, as far as we know, a communist.'

'All of which is in his favour.' said Dearte.

'All of which you could say about ninety-five per cent of the population of the United Kingdom,' the Chairman replied.

'I wish I could share your optimism,' the psychiatrist added.

'I gave him a rough ride,' said the Chairman. 'Because my inclination is that he'll turn out to be the best of the bunch. One always kicks one's favourite dogs the hardest. My only qualm is over his rather wet suggestion about what he'd do with a traitor. But I suppose he's cunning.'

Chayter waited for Catering to bring the trays of sandwiches and wine before leaving them to talk amongst themselves.

Hurrying back to his office he cursed the Board. He had protested against the appointment of the Chairman to no avail. The man was anything but neutral. Never trust self-declared neutrals: they're either cowards or liars. This one was a self-appointed time-server.

He found, not entirely to his surprise, that Mehta agreed with him.

'Treat you badly, did they?' Newiston asked.

'Only the Chairman. He doesn't let the others speak.'

Newiston was unusually jolly: 'Crucify the opposition, did you?'

'I expect the same from you,' Mehta said. Then he remembered he'd not been asked about Mahon as a candidate.

That was, indirectly, the reason why Chayter had called them both into his office.

'I'll have to give them some indication as to why Mahon's failed to turn up.'

They knew what he meant.

It was, they all three knew, the hardest decision, almost bar none, that a Director had to make: namely, at exactly which moment did you admit to yourself that one of your people had gone. Once you'd admitted it you could begin the full-scale search. The pain was acute. For if the other side announced they'd got him first you were caught with your pants down.

'Could he possibly have gone across?' Chayter asked.

'I doubt it,' Newiston said. 'There'd be some sign.'

'Tell Henry about your visit to Grochal,' Chayter said.

Mehta once again told the story of his visit to Hackett's sister in Orford. He told of the visit to the hospital, the talk with the ward sister; of the visit to the dying man paid by the man named Freedman.

'Do you know anyone called Freedman?' Chayter asked.

'No one,' Newiston said. 'Are you suggesting Hackett's departure has something to do with Mahon?'

'They were friends,' said Chayter. 'Of a sort.'

'Of a sort,' said Newiston. 'No more or less than any of the rest of us.'

'You seem doubtful,' Chayter said.

'Me? Not at all. I just hope I don't get asked this afternoon about the bloody mess Mahon's created.'

'There's no reason why you should, Henry,' said Chayter, irritated by the apparent lack of seriousness.

'You'll be pleased to hear they didn't ask me,' muttered Mehta.

They'll ask me, Chayter thought to himself. Sooner or later they'll bloody well ask me. And if it gets out before I know where the man's gone – if someone else, someone in London, Washington; or, God help us all, in Moscow, announces it first? He knew exactly where the blame would be directed. Whose resignation would be called for. Who'd be taking early retirement, for personal reasons, to some job with a bank in the City. The future for the retirement of those disgraced was always better defined, more carefully prearranged, than for those who retired with advancement to the Grand Cross of the Order of St Michael and St George. So far, as Lizzie had commented in the New Year last time around, he hadn't even got the Order. 'You'll never get more initials after your name than before it if you don't do *something* soon.' It had seemed quite funny then. Now there was no joke in it.

He gazed out from the window across Lambeth.

'Were you asked about Mahon?' Newiston said to Mehta. 'Not a word.'

How do I play it? Chayter thought. He wanted them to hunt Mahon as if their lives depended upon it. But he wanted them to hunt separately. To remain answerable solely to himself. So he turned his back on the view from the window:

156

'I want you to find the bugger. If you don't we'll have to postpone the appointment of Deputy. That affects you, Linda, me, the Service.'

'You'll carry on with the interviews?' Newiston asked.

'Carry bloody on. Yes. As though nothing at all has happened. Just as though one of the candidates most definitely hasn't bloody vanished.'

'I did wonder why they didn't ask me about him,' Mehta said.

'Luck, Dilip. But as far as I'm concerned the luck's running out.'

Chayter said it in a contradictory way, with a relaxed charm in his voice. It hid the fact that he had decided to keep his own counsel. He was thinking ahead. He wondered whether the other two were doing likewise; whether perhaps they had confided in anyone else about Mahon's disappearance. After all, Mahon was a candidate for the post they wanted; an outsider, but still a candidate. Suppose the Board were to be split? Suppose Mehta and Newiston secured equal votes and the casting one was left to the Chairman? It would mean both of them would have excited fairly impassioned opposition from at least two members of the Board. That would let either Boden-Smith or Mahon in. And Chayter, at this moment, had little hope for the success of Boden-Smith if she won. You could have a female monarch, a female Prime Minister – but a female Director of the Service was more akin to having a female Archbishop of Canterbury. Like the poor old Archbishop, the Director was in touch with more that was invisible than visible. It was still a man's job. And the feminist lobby hadn't yet been heard to protest against the male dominance of the Service. Perhaps the lobby didn't give a toss anyway. So it might fall on Mahon. But Mahon had disappeared.

Therefore, just before returning to lunch with the Board, Chayter decided to keep his two subordinates as much apart as he could afford. For if Mahon didn't turn up and a Deputy was appointed and if his head was on the block – then the newly appointed Deputy would certainly replace him.

If you don't do something soon.

This wasn't the time. Yet the temptation to talk about it was almost overwhelming.

Perhaps because his mind had been prompted by Dilip

Mehta's uncharacteristic and perhaps involuntary reference to Philby and the passing mention of Oldfield, Chayter recalled one of Oldfield's favourite stores. 'If someone dumps you in the shit remember that he or she isn't inevitably an enemy of yours. Likewise, if someone pulls you out of the shit, it doesn't follow that he or she is your friend. But, one way or another, once out of the shit, don't talk about it.' It was said to be a story of Russian origin.

Chayter's version was simply not to acknowledge that you were in the shit at all until you were drowning. That fate he was hell-bent on avoiding.

'Good luck this afternoon,' he said to Newiston. 'Remember we're all on the same side.'

'You don't expect anyone to believe that, do you, Director?'

It was the last occasion all three of them shared common cause for laughter.

'I take full responsibility for what happened in Poland,' Newiston told the Board. It was an impressive display of sincerity. 'There are special risks attached to disinformation. We went into it with our eyes open. I calculated the risk worth taking. I don't depart from that view in spite of what eventually happened.'

'I think we've understood that,' said the Chairman. 'I don't think we need weep too many tears for the Poles. No offence to anyone here present, I hope. Even the Prime Minister has said, more than once, that they've got the Pope. In that respect Warsaw may not be said to be lacking in supplies of advice from on earth or elsewhere.'

Dearte wanted to discuss history. 'Your father was a distinguished officer in the Service. What do you think you learned from his example?'

'Professionally or personally?'

'Both.'

'Professionally, he educated me in the necessity for firm and structured organisation of couter-espionage. He was able, more than anyone else, to draw upon his experience in Section V. The main difficulty he and his colleagues faced was the connection with MI5 as it then was. He always felt that proper organisation would have dispensed with so much of the panic that characterised communications during the war. MI5

158

wanted the complete intelligence picture. My father always insisted it should confine its efforts to counter-espionage at home, on the domestic front. The rivalry led to a hopeless fever of inter-departmental rivalry. The end result of this confusion was that SIS concentrated too little upon counter-espionage abroad. It was being stretched to gain military intelligence. It was hard for anyone to argue against the case for gaining military secrets fast. There was a war on. The military intelligence was what was required.'

'My father's move was, therefore, to appoint specialists to stations overseas. He was able to run his specialists without day to day reference to MI5. In this way he short-circuited the bureaucracy in London. And I believe that his actions very greatly contributed to the eventual establishment of the Anglo-American intelligence alliance. What I learned from him, above all, was the abiding importance of the alliance. It had to be built firmly on trust. I believe, as he did, that when the trust is broken so too is the special relationship between the allies. The preservation of that is, to my mind, our most important task. When it's weakened so is the Service weakened.

'As Deputy, I believe I can offer a guarantee that it will be strengthened. I trust Washington and I am certain, if it's not too immodest a declaration, that Washington trusts me. Furthermore, I feel sure Washington will trust me more than any of the other candidates.'

Newiston's *apologia* impressed all of the Board except the psychiatrist. 'I'd be very interested to know what it is you think you learned from your father personally.'

Sensing he was winning, Newiston talked with enthusiasm about his father: 'I learned to keep my own counsel, to exist alone, that to be of value and service to others it's first of all necessary to be one's own man. To be independent. To capture in life, as it were, the solitary high ground.'

'Does your wife share your view?'

'Entirely.'

'Is it an issue you talk about often together?'

'Frequently.'

'How frequently?'

'We have a very full life together. Of course, like any married couple, we have our differences. But we have always

159

believed in being available to each other to talk them over in depth. If this sounds too cosy, let me say that we've always thought we should, as they say, pitch our tents slightly apart to preserve respect for each other as individuals.'

'Would you say it's a close relationship?'

'Very.'

'And how does your son fit in?'

'Closely. Very closely. He enjoys the sense of confidence the united family unit offers.'

'But you sent him away to school?'

'Not any school. To Eton. I think Eton's a special case, don't you?'

'Perhaps you'd tell me why?'

'I went there too. Like father like son. We weren't just packing him off to any old Doodleboy's Hall. Head, heart and hand – all at Eton are taken into consideration and valued. I believe in excellence. I learned that from my father.'

'Did you love your father?'

'Very much.'

'Your mother?'

Newiston shifted in the leather chair. 'From afar, I'd say. She was an exceptionally beautiful and delightful woman. She was also very ambitious for me. I suppose that has much to do with my being an only son. She was also a manipulative woman. She would get her own way with people without them being entirely aware that was what she was doing. One had the sense that she got her way by persuading others that *they* would be happiest if *they* allowed her to have her way. The system seemed to work to her benefit very satisfactorily.'

'But you didn't love her?'

'I have always thought love, by definition, is a word that's indefinable. One is always suspicious of anyone who says "I love this-or-that." It's the stuff of soap operas and women's fiction.'

'What about – instead of "I love this-or-that" – "I love you"?'

Newiston twined his fingers together. 'I stick by my point of view. Love is the most debased word in the language. It's used more often with meaning unattached to it than any other in the English language. How often do you say or write "Love" without thinking what it means?'

160

'Oh, I think one says many things without pausing to reflect, don't you?' said the psychiatrist.

'I don't disagree with you.'

'Are you quite sure?'

'Entirely.'

'Me too,' the Chairman interrupted, hoping to end this avenue of questioning.

But the psychiatrist hadn't finished: 'Would you say you're what's sometimes called a workaholic?'

'I've never said so.'

'Would you say so now?'

'I believe other people say it about me. But I regard it as something of a compliment. My father was dedicated to his duty and the Service. He was dedicated to the well-being of his colleagues and the Service *qua* Service. I've no doubt he thought of little else. And he was very successful.'

'Never got his knighthood,' rumbled the Chairman.

'That's correct. But I think it would be inappropriate for me to comment on the omission.'

All except the psychiatrist laughed. She was staring at Newiston very hard.

Newiston looked away from her. 'The one person who objected most strongly to what she felt to be an insult was my mother.'

'Every Englishwoman would like to be called a Lady,' said the Chairman. He turned to Jamieson for approval and got a solemn nod.

'Was she very bitter about it?' the psychiatrist asked.

'Yes, she was. Very.'

'Do you think she knew why he never got his knighthood?'

'No, I don't.'

'You think she asked your father?'

'I've no doubt she did. She was the one who wanted him to get it. And I think the Chairman has suggested very cogently what the reason was. But if my father knew why he didn't get it then he most likely never told my mother.'

'Did he tell you?'

'Not in so many words.'

'What did he say about it?'

'He said it may well have been because the Honours

Committee weren't able to be informed about the complete picture of his career. Much of it was too sensitive even for the Wise and the Good.'

Dearte broke in: 'Is that right, Chairman? Surely, the Honours Committee wouldn't have to know much?'

'I think that's right,' said the Chairman. 'It came up in the early 1960s, I think, didn't it? On the other hand there may have been something, some detail, some petty or even personal rivalry which persuaded a member of the Committee to advise against it. The minutes aren't available. Sooner or later anyone who's half-way an achiever gets recommended. The Committee doesn't recommend in so much as it blackballs.' He paused. 'I knew your father.'

'I know.'

'A very fine man. Let me say, off the record, that as far as I know, there was absolutely nothing whatsoever in his private or personal or indeed in his professional life which would have led him to be blackballed. He was greatly liked. A man of profound integrity.'

'Thank you,' Newiston said.

'Would you like your son, Hal, to follow in your footsteps and join the Service?'

'I've never been a father who dictates a life plan to his offspring. But if he said he wanted to make a career in the Service I would not prevent him from doing so.'

'You'd be delighted?'

'Why not?'

'And I think you take after your own father quite a lot, don't you?'

Newiston laughed. 'Workaholic?'

'Amongst other things.'

'I regard that as a compliment.'

The members of the Board smiled at him.

'Finally, Mr Newiston, what would you do if, assuming it was your responsibility to take executive action, you found a middle-ranking colleague was a traitor?'

'I'd take it upon myself to deal with him,' Newiston said at once. 'Quietly, with discretion. I'd get him out with a minimum of fuss. I have often considered treachery of the sort I imagine you have in mind to be infectious. Even if I'm wrong it's a catastrophe which infects and destroys morale and soon

162

enough loyalty. It eats at the centre. And we know what happens when the centre cannot hold.'

'That's a first-rate answer,' said the Chairman who by now didn't seem to mind that everyone including the candidate was in no doubt at all who it was he preferred.

Back in his office Chayter found a sealed envelope on his desk marked DIRECTOR: IMMEDIATE & EYES ONLY. He opened it, cursing to himself. Come on home, Mahon, change your mind. Come on in. We understand you, Mr Mahon. Sit down and tell us all about it. Tell Daddy. We're just one big happy family. Are you trying to bring us all down with you? Gone political, have you? Trying to make a point? Getting a licence to pick up the odd fifteen quid a gig talking to spotty student union gatherings up and down the nation on crap like *Individual Rights & the Rights of All*? Stupid ignorant bastards.

He felt in his pocket for extra-wide waxed dental floss.

He stared at the IMMEDIATE & EYES ONLY. The United Nations? A signal from our man at the UN saying the Soviets had applied for increased office space. And who was on the list amongst the fifteen new Soviets? The three unholy women sharks. Shendrikova, Telichkina and Savelieva.

The dental floss cut a lower gum. 'The Chairman, Mahon; the Chairman is going to ask where you've been.' He spat a small amount of blood into the washbasin in the corner. 'He'll be asking if you're treacherous, Mahon. Why not come in and say you aren't?'

Tell us what you're up to he thought; I will find you out. Come in, I want to see your face. We'll see you're all right. You could still persuade the Board. Wherever you've been we'll close the zip on your trouble. No need to expose yourself.

He recognised the signs of his anger. Newiston and Mehta would be playing the search safe. They'd know if Mahon's disappearance got back to Downing Street the Board would be disbanded. They wouldn't make an appointment during stormy weather. They'd forbid it. Draw up the hatches with an inquiry.

The signs of his anger prompted him to take action himself.

He spoke the Russian names like oaths. Galina, Inna and fecund Tatiana, beloved supplier of cocaine to the Brit with the sales contracts worth multi-millions to the Defence Department. Galina with the legs of a male tennis player.

If you come back, Mahon, I'll feed you to the sharks. I'll make you bleed and chuck you in the Manhattan tank with them. They'll eat you alive and very slowly.

Meanwhile, there'd be no Brahms with Lizzie at the Festival Hall tonight. She could take the au pair instead.

He pressed the buttons on his telephone to raise the duty clerk in Personnel.

'I want the home address of Hanratty.'

25

Hanratty's was a God-forsaken neighbourhood.

Poor sod had found himself a flat overlooking Wandsworth Prison. Must have thought, Chayter reckoned, that we'd put Archives together with the rest of us at Century House. The family under one roof. From here Hanratty would have thought he could get to work on that awful lady's bicycle in his fluorescent safety waistcoat quite easily. Hanratty must have been living in the past to overrate the importance of Archives quite so carelessly. It must be a miserable journey from here to Nelson at Heathrow.

He rang the bell to the terraced house a second time. The street stank of vinegar and fish and chips.

Poor sod could at least feel good about leaving this hell-hole every morning.

The wind carried the echo of an electric bell from somewhere inside the prison walls.

'Who d'you want?'

A round West Indian woman's face stared up at him through the basement's railings. 'You want Tina? She's free.'

'Mr Hanratty.'

'Him? He's on the top. Ring the Ground Floor. They'll let you in.' She smiled briefly. 'I thought you were a friend of Tina's.'

He pressed the bell to the ground-floor flat. 'Sorry, I'm not.'

When he looked back down the steps to the basement he saw the fat woman disappear inside. One of the windows in the door was boarded up.

From behind the front door an old voice shouted: 'Who is it?'

'Hanratty, please.'

'No, you're not. He's upstairs.'

To think a man in Hanratty's position lived amongst these people –

'Open the door please.'

When it opened it seemed at first there was no one there.

'Mr Hanratty is upstairs. You a friend of his, are you? He doesn't see people.'

The voice came from a wheelchair in the shadows. 'I expect you're wondering how I unlock the door? Look down there. They moved the lock for me. The girls downstairs did that last Christmas.'

'How very thoughtful of them,' Chayter said hurrying to the stairs.

'Takes all sorts,' said the figure in the wheelchair.

'I've always thought so myself.'

He climbed the stairs fast in the dark to the top floor.

When he found the door at the end of the passage with an enamel sign saying BOSS he assumed it was Hanratty's place. From inside the BOSS's flat came women's laughter, a chorus of shrieking delight, some howls of pain from a man. Hanratty was choosing to watch some strange sort of television.

When the keeper of Archives opened the door, he greeted Chayter with a look of shock.

'Come in, sir,' Hanratty said. 'This is a nice surprise. Or is it bad news?'

'That's what I want you to tell me.'

Four cats stood on the back of the collapsed sofa by the window. One arched its back. The animal must have sensed the Director didn't like cats. Perhaps Hanratty had told it so.

'Sorry to interrupt your televion.'

Video cassettes lay on top of the colour magazine of last Sunday's *News of the World*. Chayter read a video title upside down: *Water Sports*.

'A friend gave me that for my birthday,' Hanratty said.

'He has original taste.'

'A she, a she,' the archivist protested. 'Her little joke.'

'The tart in the basement?'

'No. I don't approve of all that. But you can't get away from it, sir, not around here, you know. What with the prison and the unemployed.'

'Always the Conservative, Hanratty, aren't you?'

'Not since mother died, sir.'

The keeper of Archives was very nervous. 'Would you like a drink?'

'No, thank you. What I do want to know, what I want you to think very hard about as a matter of some urgency, is exactly why Mr Mahon has been spending so much time out at Nelson.'

'He hasn't been back recently. I've been on leave.'

'I know. Cromer. Think back, Hanratty.'

'It's all logged.'

'I'm sure it is. What was he looking for?'

'He got what he was looking for, sir.'

'I've seen a copy of your log, Hanratty.'

'You have?'

'Yes.'

'Everything is in order.'

'No. It isn't.'

'If there is anything I can do – '

'What was he *looking for*?'

'The records of his father's life and service. His war service.'

'Such as what?'

'The wartime telegrams from Lisbon, Tangier and Madrid. His father died in Madrid.'

'I know.'

'I would imagine there was a lot of material from the Service as well as MI5.'

'What precisely d'you imagine?'

'It's hard to say. There were the wartime operations in Portugal. No one, I imagine wanted to offend Salazar. He favoured the Nazis in my view. Isn't it common knowledge?'

'Stick to it, Hanratty. Tell me what bears on Mahon.'

'It all does, sir, if what Mr Mahon wants is a picture of his father.'

'Did he say exactly why he wanted what you call this "picture"?'

'Not in so many words. I assumed he had his reasons. I don't ask. I can only make up my mind from questions people ask and not from any questions I might ask, if you follow me. I've never asked about Portugal but I assume it was being monitored from Spain. Why not? Perhaps it was the other way around. And Mahon's father, as I've said, was in Madrid.'

'But what is Mahon searching for in the Madrid history?'

Hanratty lifted the most predatory of the cats and held it against his floppy stomach: 'I think he was looking for what wasn't there. He was trying to find out, still is, I imagine, what had gone. You know that SIS archives were way back held in Central Registry near Glenalmond. That's where they held the source-books. It was William Woodfield who ran Glenalmond in those days. He must have been a fine archivist. We still have the original card-indexes. But you can be sure the Iberian Section source-books went long ago. They looked through them at the time of Philby. I remember because it meant we were so short-staffed at Queen Anne's Gate. People were scooting around all over the country. All I am saying is that Mr Mahon is searching for a needle in a haystack. Well, to be exact, he's looking for where the needle lay. But it's not for me to offer him, or anyone else, advice.'

'Offer me some, Hanratty. Think yourself into Mr Mahon's shoes. His father was killed in Madrid. One of what, fifty, a hundred wartime people of any consequence in the Service who got killed. At least half of them disappeared without trace. Of, say, half the rest, there were all too many whose deaths weren't fully explained. That's understandable. Suppose you were in Mahon's situation. Where would you go?'

The cat purred against Hanratty's stomach.

'I'd take the route he's taken, I think. If I had the time I'd look at the Soviet source-books. That'd be with your permission supposing I didn't mind you knowing what I was doing. I'd turn out all the Iberian material. What's left of it. I'd look at the American source-books. But all the while I'd know it was a hopeless search. I've said. Like where the needle was in the haystack. Impossible.'

'Anywhere else?'

'I would have gone back to the people on the ground at the time. But when Mr Wigart died the main living source died with him. And now Mr Hackett's gone too there's no one. You could try his sister. She could help you with Bletchley. Then again, if she can't, you might like to approach GCHQ Archives . . .' Hanratty gave his chief a look of mischief. 'I hear that GCHQ causes us quite a bit of trouble. They're the *prima donnas* nowadays, aren't they? Beloved of the PM, the virgins the unions want to ravage? We ought to have their archives, sir. We do things better.'

'I'd never thought of you as an empire builder, Hanratty.'

The archivist enjoyed the comment. 'One never knows what one will find in other people's archives. I like to think one's not too jaded to be surprised once again.'

Even with *Water Sports*, Chayter thought. 'And what about all that Wigart and Hackett knew about Madrid?' he asked the connoisseur of video porn. 'You think they knew a great deal more than we've got on our files?'

Hanratty looked surprised by the question. The answer was so obvious. And such a question – coming from the Director . . . 'Of course,' Hanratty said. 'But they weren't allowed to write their memoirs, were they? That's the privilege we afford to traitors who've got away with it, like Kim.' The cat struggled to free itself from his master's embrace.

'Go on then, Burgess,' Hanratty told the overweight pet. 'Go find Blunt! Lovely animals, aren't they? My little family of moggies. Burgess and Blunt and Blake and Bettaney. All the B's. Traitors four.' He brushed the cat's hairs from his shirt front. 'If I were Mahon I think I'd have tried to get into the Bletchley archives. But I could spare him the trouble. The early stuff's all been destroyed. They shredded the lot when there was the union trouble.'

Hanratty perched on the edge of the collapsed sofa. Bettaney jumped on to his lap. 'You know, Mr Chayter, I've already been through most of this with Mr Mehta. I've told him everything I could. Like I've told you, sir. You yourself might make something of *Nightshade*. I can have a courier dispatch it in the morning first thing.'

'That won't be necessary.' Chayter told him. 'You see, I requested the *Nightshade* file earlier this evening.'

'Not from me, sir, you didn't.'

'Correct. I sent in my own people from Century House.'

'What did you conclude, sir?'

'I didn't get the chance to draw any conclusion. You see, the file's not there.'

'Not there?'

'Not there, Hanratty.'

'Yes, sir. There can be no question. Your staff, with respect, they wouldn't know where to look. One person on his own couldn't find it.'

'I sent six people. They turned the place inside out. They're trained in that sort of thing.'

'They went through Nelson?'

'Everything.'

'I don't believe you, sir.'

Chayter took a small glossy magazine from his pocket and handed it to the keeper. 'They found this in the bottom drawer of your desk.' It was a particularly refined piece of unpleasant German pornography.

The cat Bettaney must have understood his master's fear. Or perhaps it was the sudden tightening of Hanratty's grip that made the animal squeal. 'It must have been stolen, sir.'

'Exactly.' Chayter was standing. 'There are two things you're going to do to save your neck, Hanratty. The first is to get rid of all this squalid stuff.' He kicked the porno video across the floor. The cats tore around in panic. 'The second thing you'll do is to say absolutely nothing whatsoever about the disappearance of the file. Do you understand?'

Hanratty whispered his agreement.

'Nothing. Because if you do, I'll personally instruct the Director of Public Prosecutions and the police and the Service and anyone else I can think of to put you away in solitary for as long as it pleases me. You understand?'

He understood.

'In the morning you will find, on your desk, a formal note saying you personally arranged for the *Nightshade* file to be dispatched to me at Century. You will sign it and return it to me by twelve noon.'

'I'm sorry about this, sir.'

'So am I,' said Chayter, walking to the window.

Hanratty watched his chief draw aside the curtain. He had drawn aside the old curtains and was lifting up the length of imitation lace. Twice Chayter raised his hand. 'Some police officers are coming in now. They'll move you to another address and give you instructions. Ostensibly they're going to arrest the tart in the basement, her maid and anyone else they find. When that's done it'll be your turn to leave.'

'Not Mr Jenkinson. He's an invalid.'

'He's being taken to a hospital for the time being. All your mail is being dealt with by us.'

'You're having me arrested?'

'On the contrary, you're going to be looked after. But, God help you if you so much as breathe a word about my visit to you now or that file. I promise you, you'll never be a free man again.'

A plain clothes officer from the Special Branch was in the doorway. 'Put this over your head, Hanratty.'

He was holding a blanket.

'Right over your head. Come on. Out you come.'

Chayter sat in the back seat of his car watching the departures. The tart and her maid went without a murmur. Only Mr Jenkinson protested. He wasn't being allowed to take his wheelchair. He was crying out it had been a gift from the Salvation Army. There would be protests about it. A large black police officer carried him in his arms and laid him down across the back seat of an unmarked police car. 'I'm not Jenkinson.' Mr Jenkinson shouted. 'It's a mistake – !' The car door slammed and the protests stopped.

The last officer out was a woman. She was carrying the four cats with the traitors' names. She dropped them on the street. They huddled together. Then the fattest of them slunk towards the gutter and began to pee.

Chayter reckoned it was Burgess.

'Time to go,' he told his driver.

Time too, Chayter thought, for Mahon to come back.

He sat in the back of the car with a fixed stare ahead and each time the speeding car passed others going in the opposite direction he closed his eyes against the glare.

Now, the decision had to be made: whether or not to tell the Prime Minister. Should he ask for an immediate and secret meeting? But to pass the news on could only look like an admission of incompetence and defeat. The blame, ultimately, would focus on himself. He had never believed in making admissions and apologies.

He searched for any way at all he could get himself off the hook. Suppose, he agonised, it's too late anyway? He found himself haunted by the spectre of a more public and dreadful humiliation.

171

26

To the outside world the flat was the London base of an American re-insurance concern with headquarters in Miami. The executives came and went from the modern block overlooking Regent's Park. If the wind was in the right direction you could sometimes hear the eerie night noises from the animals in the Zoo nearby. Insomniacs were well-advised to install double glazing. The owners of the flat had done just that along with an electronic security and video surveillance system fit for a pop star or Arab prince. The executives showed unfailing courtesy to the doorman. There was nothing the little old soldier wouldn't do for the Americans who gave him a crate of Scotch at Christmas and on his birthday which was on July the Fourth. It was a safe-place used by the Central Intelligence Agency, one of the few not covered by the fulsome and protective skirts of the British Secret Intelligence Service and MI5. Decorated piecemeal by Harrods with highly polished reproduction furniture, the heaviest of crimson velvet curtains and thickest of Wilton carpet, it was ready for swift disposal when the day came.

The Americans, Mahon decided, could have brought him to a less comfortable secret retreat to recover from the battering they'd administered. It was a place to suit everyone's tastes or no one's. On the low marble table in the drawing-room was a pile of fat books: anthologies of *The World's Great Photography*: books you didn't have to read at all. Some of them, tat for relaxation, were still covered in their transparent wrappers. They brought to mind the file wrapped similarly in Kirsty's freezer the other side of London.

The questions and answers went round in circles for three days.

Mr Finucane was polite. Mr Mahon was polite. They vied with each other to show just how deeply they were committed to the search for truth. More than once they had almost said to each other, with mutual sympathy, that they were both on the same side.

Mahon would say: 'It wasn't standard practice to beat me up.'

'I wouldn't have gone so far,' said Finucane.

'Then why did you?'

'I did not, Mr Mahon. My job's to ask you questions.'

'I appreciate that. But I've made it clear I'm in no position to offer you the answers. Please believe me, it's not that I'd be reluctant to do so if I knew them. Understand I don't know the answers. There's nothing more to say.'

Whereas Mahon was obviously apprehensive, Finucane was almost embarrassed. The American liked his adversary and vice versa. Neither sought to make an enemy of the other.

Mahon had proved perfectly agreeable to talking about his father's past. He had never entertained a single thought of animosity towards the Americans. Neither had his father. On the contrary. His father, as the record showed – if indeed the Americans had anything resembling a full record of his father's life – had been a good friend of the United States. Like father like son. Mr Finucane must understand he was in no position to reveal all the details of his father's career.

More than once Mahon requested that he be allowed to produce some form of written statement. Finucane denied their discussions were being clandestinely recorded. Mahon was sure they were. The recorded version could easily be tampered with at a later date. It was a reasonable suggestion which would have allowed Mahon more time for reflection. It would also serve to reduce some of the sharpness of the verbal cut and thrust. He would also gain time. The Americans couldn't, after all, realistically keep him for ever and he was sure a man like Finucane wouldn't sanction further violence.

The American proceeded with a scrupulous care. Gradually, Mahon realised, interrogator and subject were drawn closer together. It was an inevitable process. As it stretched out across the hours Mahon noticed the American becoming even more circumspect. He recognised that Finucane knew a great deal more about him than he was revealing. Mahon adopted the best strategy of defence. He told his interrogator he wanted to be as helpful as possible. He only lost his temper when the American hinted his personal life might not be everything it was cracked up to be.

'There are rumours you're having an affair with the wife of one of your colleagues.'

'Really?'

'It could damage you.'

'Since when have the American intelligence services had any interest in the private morals of United Kingdom intelligence officers?'

'Since before you were born.'

Who had the old American been talking to?

The only way to combat the courtesy was to waste time. So Mahon gave him little details of misinformation. He also apologised for his memory. That's why he'd preferred to offer the written statement about his father. The American would have to offer more than courtesy to crack the nut.

Soon enough he did.

'You know, Mr Mahon, that we know what's in the *Nightshade* file.'

'I can't comment. If I were to comment at all you know I'd be in breach of the Official Secrets Act.'

'We know the whole story.'

'I doubt it.'

'Believe me.'

'If I were to believe you then you'd have to let me walk out of here now wouldn't you? Because there'd be no reason for you to be questioning me about this file you talk of, or my father, or what you call rumours to do with the extra-marital carry-ons of my friends and colleagues' wives, or anything else. So the burden of proof, Mr Finucane, rests with you. It'll be easy to free yourself of it. Let me leave and then I'll know what you're saying is true.'

It looked like stalemate.

That was until near midnight.

Finucane took the telephone call in the next room occupied by two of the security guards.

He had no doubt time was running out. They could not hold

174

Mahon much longer. He had to tell Linger he was getting nowhere.

She didn't like what he told her.

Moreover she had news for him. 'We were told three hours ago that material purporting to be secret intelligence bearing on the Anglo-American intelligence alliance is liable to be circulated to the British Press. We've been told by Century House it's phoney.'

It was staring Finucane in the face. The bluff. He'd lay his shirt on the file having been destroyed or stolen. The British would claim it as a clumsy Soviet forgery. The shit was floating near the fan. He told Linger: 'There's going to be mud on my face, on your face, and on a lot of people's faces who won't thank me. And they won't thank you.'

Her voice turned even colder: 'Then you get the truth out of Mr Mahon. There's going to be no shit in my mouth.' The line went dead.

He returned to the drawing-room and tried a different tack:

'Do you think Dickie Wigart was the victim of a calculated murder?'

'I don't know.'

'It has never, not even once, crossed your mind he might have been?'

'What makes you ask?'

'In the circumstances we have to consider every possibility.'

'You think,' Mahon asked, 'it's a probability?'

'I'd like to know what you think? For example, who do you think might stand to gain by Wigart's death?'

'Why don't you tell me, Mr Finucane?'

It was stalemate. So Finucane conjured up the ghost of Hackett:

'His friend, old Hackett – who'd gain by murdering him?'

If Mahon had a view he didn't enlarge on it.

'You tell me.'

Finucane's silence was interrupted by the guard once more calling him out to the telephone.

This time Linger was very brief.

She told him the interrogation team was being strengthened and he'd be spending tonight at a different address. That was all she said.

When Finucane replaced the receiver and turned round he saw two new faces in the doorway.

They were new yet older and more experienced faces. It didn't escape Finucane's notice that both were military personnel in civilian clothes. He saw they'd made little attempt to hide their hand-guns beneath their coats.

The larger of the two men said, 'We're going out of London, Mr Finucane. The car's waiting in the street.'

The man looked the jumpy type.

Finucane hoped he had the safety-catch in place.

There was no reply to Lindsay's calls to Frithville Gardens. Surely, by now, she told herself again and again, Kirsty would have reached her somehow.

Now, the file had quite literally thawed out and she was appalled by what she'd read. She felt she too had been duped and trapped.

By turn fearful and angry she tried to reach Lou. She telephone the Embassy.

This time the duty officer was curt to the point of rudeness: 'He's unavailable to callers.'

She told herself that no news was bad news. Worst of all she felt utterly cut off from the two people who might be able to tell her she was wrong.

Mahon had no idea what time it was when it started.

He recalled the face of the man who'd given him the coffee. It had tasted sweet and strangely bitter. Then they'd watched a video of *Some Like It Hot*. The faces turned into screaming masks. He realised he was hallucinating. The floor above him seemed to be collapsing. The steam blast against Marilyn's ankles was never ending. He saw his face merge with hers distorted by mirrors in a Laughter House. She was screaming and he opened his mouth to scream too but could only produce a hideous whine.

Somebody raised his hands out in front of him. His legs were drawn wide apart and, slowly, hands lifted his feet and placed each one into separate trays of water. His hands were guided to the wall. He could only prevent himself from falling by balancing with his finger-tips. They had left him alone in the darkness grotesquely suspended like a fly stretched and tied by the spider's web.

Finucane's excessive courtesy had failed. So they'd brought in specialists of a different kind, skilled in the administration of an altogether different form of excess. The game consisted in his being disoriented, left to torture himself. He had been through this type of nightmare in training up in Hereford with the Special Air Service. Now he would find out if he could could stand up as well to the real thing.

27

Next morning it was Boden-Smith's turn to face the Board. She talked fluently and at length about the importance of the Anglo-American sharing of intelligence. Her view was that Parliament, especially Labour Members, underestimated its value. She met with no disagreement. There was no immediate solution to the continuing criticism of the Service's excessive secrecy. 'I'd rather we erred on that side of the fence,' she concluded. 'There's a lot to be said for our not being permitted to answer to Members of Parliament, many of whom entertain philosophies that aren't, in any case, supportive of the Western intelligence war.' Her remarks were made with an air of belligerence. She wanted to be a fighter, a competitor and was obviously less passive than the other candidates. Indeed, she had gone so far as to praise all of them. Once again it was the Chairman who put the boot in and he waited until the end of the interview to launch into her:

'The one abiding weakness in your case is the fact that you're a woman.'

'I regard that as an advantage.'

'Don't interrupt me.'

Her neck reddened.

The Chairman stepped up his attack: 'You have the respect of your colleagues. The Inspectorate hold you in high regard. More than one of its members have told me as much. You have outstanding administrative abilities. But you can't claim to have the respect afforded to male colleagues. It's something we have to be mindful of. I know all the arguments for promoting women in the Service. I've heard them a thousand times. It's all very fine when things are going well and a woman's in charge. At such times it's as if a man were running things. But it's when things turn sour that a woman can't turn to others in the same way as a man can without appearing vulnerable.'

'With respect – I couldn't disagree more.'

'That's the difficulty, Miss Boden-Smith. We are looking for someone to forge agreement, someone pliable. We can't find room for someone whose chief characteristic is obstinacy. That's not what we're looking for in a Deputy Director. We can't shut our eyes and pretend you're a man.'

'I'm not pretending for a moment that you should do so,' she barked at him.

'Then what do you suggest we do to overcome your natural disadvantage?'

'Look at my record.'

'We have done.'

'I stand by it.'

'Naturally,' said the Chairman, looking down the table. The psychiatrist nodded. She had some questions.

'You have no objections to me asking some personal questions?'

'No objections at all,' said Boden-Smith.

'I cannot betray personal confidences,' the psychiatrist began, quietly. 'On the other hand your name has more than once come up in consultations some of your colleagues have had with me.'

'It has?' Boden-Smith said with surprise.

'It has been put to me that for quite some time you have been engaged in an affair with a married colleague.'

Boden-Smith turned pale.

'Is that so?' the Chairman asked her.

'I don't think it's any way relevant.'

'Simply tell us whether it's true or not.'

'Certainly not.'

'Why?'

'Because I'm not going to demean myself, the Service or indeed this Board by being party to malicious gossip. Indeed, I think you – ' She was staring at the psychiatrist ' – you will do well to apologise for asking the question.'

The psychiatrist slightly inclined her head. She stared wistfully at Boden-Smith who'd by now turned deathly white.

The Chairman broke the embarrassed silence. 'Is this affair over?'

'No comment.'

'Don't be so absurd, Miss Boden-Smith. It really doesn't matter one bit if this matter's closed. Heaven alone knows, we're all perfectly adult.'

'No, it isn't, as you put it, adult to raise matters of this sort.'

'You deny it then?'

'Look – the very fact of putting the question suggests there's some mud to be chucked in my face. Clearly, you – ' again she was glaring at the psychiatrist, 'you believe I've been pursuing a relationship of the kind you describe. Otherwise you'd never have asked the question in the first place, would you? Now you've brought out the question the mud's stuck. So why don't you say you have a real reason to believe that whatever your patient told you is a fantasy, completely false, in short – a lie.'

'I don't think the worse of you for it,' the psychiatrist said, with a tone of boredom.

'I couldn't care less what you think of me in that respect. Since when have shrinks been the arbiters of morals? I don't expect you to think the better or worse of me. But if you honestly believe there's a part of my personal life which may affect my candidacy one way or another then I'd advise you to bring it out into the open.' She was even more belligerent than she had been in her dismissal of the Labour Members of Parliament.

The Chairman was growing impatient: 'Why don't you just say "No" and have done with it? Have you, or have you not been engaged in an adulterous affair with a colleague – who, incidentally, I assume to be male?'

'Male,' said the psychiatrist.'

'Well?' the Chairman asked.

But Boden-Smith hadn't finished with the psychiatrist. 'I believe you have been deliberately put up to asking the question. For some reason that escapes me, you think credence should be given to some bit of idle gossip you've learned from a patient undergoing analysis. Why should the Board believe what someone obviously of unsound or temporarily unsound mind has to say? Is that the basis of an efficient and truthful assessment? I am not a patient of yours or anyone else's. I have no guarantee that whatever I say is not going to be placed on the record.'

'It needn't be,' the Chairman said.

'Then why on earth are you persisting with this line of questioning?'

'Because it's of consequence.'

'To whom?'

'To you.'

Boden-Smith turned back to the psychiatrist. 'Then why don't you tell us who told you? Let's have a name. Names. Who am I supposed to have been sleeping with? Come on. Tell us.'

'There is no need to mention names.'

'I think there is.'

The Chairman looked at the psychiatrist again. 'Do you want to withdraw the question?'

'No.'

'In that case, I will withdraw it,' said the Chairman. 'Satisfied?'

'Thank you very much indeed, sir.'

'I have one more question to ask you,' the Chairman said. It was the question about the middle-ranking traitor.

'What would you do about him?' said the Chairman.

'I would allow the law to take its course.'

'Assuming you were certain of the evidence?'

'Of course, and I would, in such circumstances, make entirely sure I was certain. After all, the consequences of such a man or, indeed, woman being found innocent after such proceedings would, to say the least, be unpleasant.'

'Oh, I agree,' said the Chairman. 'I agree entirely.'

'And I would assume,' Boden Smith concluded, 'that we would be secure in the protection of the law.'

'In what particular respect?' the Chairman asked.

'I would require the life sentence to be handed down.'

'By "life" you mean "life"?'

'Yes,' said Boden Smith. 'And preferably solitary confinement into the bargain.'

'There's nothing else I want to ask,' the Chairman said, with a sigh. 'Anyone else?' He waited. 'Thank you, Miss Boden-Smith. We can call it a day.'

Linda Boden-Smith got out of the leather chair and straightened her blouse.

When she turned and walked towards the door, Chayter noticed her blouse was soaked through with sweat.

'We have half an hour to discuss our recommendation. The only point I'd like to make about all three candidates concerns Boden-Smith. The last question was withdrawn. It should on no account, one way or another, influence your views.'

The discussion was amicable. Not entirely to Chayter's surprise there proved to be no need to put the decision to a vote.

Mehta was written out because, as Jamieson put it, he lacked what he called *gravitas*. Everyone agreed with that and Dearte's view about Boden-Smith was based on a similar line of thought. She could do the job. She had a fine mind. But SIS found itself, he said, in rather the same position as the Church. 'Women are, as it were, ideal members of the congregation. They're not yet ready for close contact with the altar.'

Which left Henry Newiston as leading candidate.

'Before we finish, what do we do, Director, about Mr Mahon? Do you want him left in the running? I assume you do.'

'I'm in your hands, sir,' Chayter said.

'We'll be guided by you.'

'In that case, I'd like to postpone making a decision for a week.'

'So we're all agreed it's between Newiston and Mahon?' the Chairman asked.

They were all agreed.

'Good. Then let us know when you want us to return.'

The psychiatrist hung back, making sure she was the last to leave.

'Mr Chayter,' she said matter-of-factly, 'I don't want you to think I was flying a kite.'

'About Linda?'

'What did you think of her reaction?'

'Roughly everything I'd have expected. The only thing that surprised me was the Chairman's mildness towards her.'

'I find myself out of tune with his attitudes,' said the psychiatrist.

'With his old-fashionedness?'

'No. Out of tune with his unspoken belief that you must all compete against each other. If I were to be asked what's wrong with your Service I'd say that it's your failure to share your secrets.'

'That's always been a problem.'

'It always will be. The pity is you don't recognise it.'

'You may be right,' Chayter said.

But he counted himself the exception to the psychiatrist's view.

He said, 'I'm grateful for your thoughts.' And he led her to the door.

28

Things had changed at the Regent's Park address. They showed the marks of a heavier hand. Plain clothes men in the foyer young enough, Finucane reckoned, to be his sons. The shining faces were twitchy. They were no more than spot-bothered teenagers. Finucane couldn't help sucking his teeth at the sight of the hands fingering their chests. They weren't used to wearing hand-guns. There were others in the apartment. Double yesterday's numbers. These were perimeter-fence guards from the Air Force bases with weathered young faces and not an embassy complexion amongst them. The new men made no effort to disguise the fact they were fully armed. They wore their guns like fancy dress.

If there was one thing Finucane didn't like it was the discovery that his operation had been interefered with from on high. It made him angry and anxious. The whole atmosphere suggested there was someone acting out of fear. Too many personnel meant panic.

He immediately asked to see Mahon. They said No. The doctors were in there with him. 'They don't want to be disturbed.'

One of the new guards told him he was wanted on the telephone. He insisted that he first had to see Mahon. 'The phone, Mr Finucane. It's urgent.'

A voice said, 'It's New York.' He realised it would be Linger.

He took the telephone and cut her short. 'You listen to me, Miss Linger. Mistake number one – taking me off him last night. Mistake number two – taking me to some God-forsaken Air Force dormitory. No phone. Nothing. Three – doctors. What the hell for? He doesn't need doctors. You tell me what this is. CIA in a panic? Come on. Who said the military had to be involved? You didn't ask me. Am I in charge of this thing? Or not?'

She let the tirade blow itself out. 'We've got somewhere,' she began. 'If you want details of the sanction you'll have to wait.' She was at her most school-marmish. 'You have no authority to request details.'

'What the hell are you talking about?'

'You did fine,' she interrupted. She was massaging him. The voice was thick with flattery. 'You did fine, okay. I asked for a second opinion. You're answerable to me. That's confirmed.'

'I am retired.'

'And you're answerable to me.'

'I am not.'

'Mr Finucane. Please. Let's not quarrel.'

'I am not quarrelling. I am telling you the right way. The right way of going about this is not, repeat not, to bring in a whole division of military, Air Force, God alone knows *what* personnel waltzing around with guns. You and I came to no arrangement on logistics. You're the one who's over-reacting. The whole God-damn thing stinks of over-reaction. I'm not even allowed to see Mahon!'

'You will be. When the doctors have finished.'

'Finished *what*?'

'Making their report.'

'To whom?'

'To me.'

'To *you*? I'm the one who's interrogating him.'

'You've finished that,' she said. 'You have leg-work.'

'*What*?'

'We know where the files are. He's admitted the where-abouts. You're going to bring them in.'

'Wait a *minute*, Miss Linger.'

'No,' she snapped. 'You listen to me – '

The quarrel grew more violent still. 'Who did he tell? You tell me.'

'The parameters of your duty don't embrace that inform-ation . . .'

'For Christ's sake – ' the CIA jargon infuriated him. He was being used. No more than a pawn in the game. He was retired. They weren't going to move him around their board any longer. 'I want to speak to the people who have the answer from him. *If they have it.* You tell them to speak to me. I'm not going on unless I know exactly what he admitted. On that basis I'll decide my further involvement. Who did you have question him? How was he questioned? Who are these people?'

'They participated on my specific authorisation. Don't you take that badly, Mr Finucane. I'm responsible.'

'Damn right. You're responsible!' He could see what it meant. She had called in the specialists. How far had they gone with him? The presence of the doctors across the passage disturbed him more than ever. 'If they've damaged him you'll have hell to pay.'

'No one's damaged him, Mr Finucane. It took very little time.'

I bet, he thought.

'We have a car waiting for you,' she was saying. 'Our people know where to take you. We want you to bring the files in. You'll be taken to the Embassy with them. I've sent a man to meet you and take them. Then you'll be through.' She paused. 'It's your operation, isn't it? You began it. We want you to finish it. That's neat. The best way.'

He slammed down the telephone.

Star of India and ylang-ylang body oils filled the bathroom with their heady scents. Towels lay where they'd been thrown around the bathroom. Finucane stepped on them reaching for the top to the lavatory cistern. It was jammed against the ballcock protruding like the stern of a sunken warship abandoned by the tide.

The apartment in Frithville Gardens looked exactly what it was: a smashed-up love-nest. He searched each room and knew that he was following someone else's search. He left footsteps in the talc. The hall stank of violets.

'Fifty years of the lease to run,' the embassy man droned behind him with his attention to the niceties of real estate values. 'Lounge, bedroom, kitchen, bathroom. Lease holder Mrs K.G.F. Newiston wife of H.L. Newiston. Mahon says his mistress.'

'I know,' Finucane rounded on him.

They were back in the kitchen. The freezer door was open.

'This is where he says we'll find the files – ' He pulled out the freezer shelves.

He stepped back and trod on some soggy potato chips. Trying to pick one of the chips from the sole of his shoe he over-balanced and had to reach out for Finucane to stop himself falling over. 'That's what he said,' he told Finucane.

'You heard him?'

'Not personally.'

'Me neither. And they're not here, are they? You think he'd tell the truth?'

'They gave him the treatment.'

Finucane leaned against the sink. 'They what?'

'You know, sir. They put him through it. Disorientation. He wasn't lying.'

'Wait a minute. They did *what*?'

'Used the new approach.'

The embassy man described the methods. Straps. Feet in the water. The hood. Finger-tips against the wall. When he'd finished he said with a frightened laugh, 'Always works.'

'It does? Then where are the files? You tell me.'

The man from the Embassy had no answer.

I'd have done the same, thought Finucane: told them everything – *almost* everything and held the salient details back. Told them I was screwing about with my superior's wife; confessed the whole little deceit. Names. Addresses. Times. Told them what they wanted. But held back the one piece of the puzzle they needed above all others. Made it look as if it really mattered: all that fornication. Man to man. He could hear Mahon spilling it out. Then they'd have taken the pressure off. Turned on the lights and told him there wasn't a mark on his body. Time for a deep sleep. And knocked him out with a slammer jab. Since time began, he smiled to himself, torture's been a clumsy business. There's always a way around it. He felt relieved the specialists brought in by Linger had failed. Mahon had survived the products of their bent imaginations and Finucane was pleased.

Mattresses, pillows, duvet and satin bed-sheets lay scattered on the bedroom floor. His shoes crunched broken lightbulb glass. It must have been one hell of a fight.

Transfixed, he stood by the curtains without moving.

He lifted them to one side. Now he could see the stream of blood. The splashes. Crusts of blood and hairs had stuck to the unpainted surface.

He'd seen it all before. The scene that always made the stomach heave. Blood spatters. He looked into the young face of the man from the Embassy and could tell the young eyes had never before seen anything like this.

He looked hard at the signs of the horror, trying to relive for himself what had gone on. He tried, vainly, to imagine whose blood he was staring at. There was, of course, no answer.

The short-wave radio crackled from the embassy man's belt.

'We have to leave,' the man said.

He was shouting at the young man: 'Get the hell out of here. Keep your sticky fingers off your fucking guns.'

They looked at Finucane like frightened schoolchildren.

He pulled up a chair to Mahon's bedside. The guards left the two of them alone.

'Bastards.'

'Don't talk if it hurts.'

'It doesn't.'

'It wouldn't. They're trained to let you hurt yourself. I'm telling you what happened, Mr Mahon. You did everything you told them. You took the files to Frithville Gardens. You took them to Mrs Newiston's place.'

'She didn't know. She isn't involved. It's nothing to do with her.'

'Maybe it is. You can help her. You can help yourself. Me too. Help me, please. What happened?'

So Mahon told him slowly through his drowsiness, bit by bit, what had happened.

Finucane knew he was telling him the truth.

'I arranged it. Kirsty must have found them.'

Finucane thought of the brown dried blood streaks. 'Or someone else found them?'

'I don't know.'

'Who?' Finucane asked. 'Who else knew?'

'Believe me, I don't know.'

Finucane believed him. 'Who did Kirsty tell about her affair with you? The husband know?'

'I'm certain he didn't.'

'Why?'

'Because he would have come out with it. To my face. I know him as well as anyone. He'd have hit me with it like a hammer. That's his way.'

'Not used it against you? If you're a threat to him?'

'Me? A threat?'

'You tell me.'

Mahon closed his eyes. 'I don't know. If you believe me let me tell you something else, Mr Finucane. Kirsty won't betray me.'

'She won't?'

'She loves me.'

'She tell you that?'

'She didn't have to. I know.'

'Let me tell you something, Mr Mahon. That apartment's been turned inside out. It's a battlefield. Someone's head was beaten against the wall. Time and time again. There was a lot of blood.'

He took his handkerchief from his pocket and unwrapped it. 'I found these on the wall. Stuck to it. On the floor. The carpet.' He unfolded the handkerchief still more. 'These are a woman's hairs. These I took from a pillow in the bedroom. These from a towel in the bathroom. And I think you know whose they are, don't you?'

He watched Mahon staring at the hairs.

'Kirsty's,' Finucane said.

'I'm afraid you're right.'

'I know I'm right. And she's not there. I have to tell you from my experience I doubt she left that apartment of her own accord.'

'What happened?'

Finucane was on his feet. 'We'll find out. Now we're looking for the files and her too. I don't know exactly what they did to you last night. I wasn't here. There's one thing you can be thankful to us for. You probably have an alibi.'

Mahon rubbed the bruises beneath his eyes. 'You'd better call in the police.'

'Not yet. I'm going to ask that you leave here with me, okay? Get yourself dressed. The people here may try and stop us. But

I suggest you take the gamble. It's in everyone's interests, right now.'

'They have my clothes.'

'I'll get them.'

29

Lindsay had a night of terrible dreams. The worst nightmare wasn't what most people called a *real* nightmare. Its plot was true. But Lou's face kept on breaking in and the voices belonged to embassy people refusing to let her speak to him. She tried to scream to get Lou's attention and heard her own voice coming out like a whisper. Then Lou vanished and her secret took over and she couldn't shut it out.

Her father had told her that he was leaving her mother. 'I want to tell you that, in the park, you know, I've been receiving stolen goods. You know – ' That was her father's voice. He'd always said 'you know' when he was about to tell her something she did not know. 'A woman's necklace. Not much. Enough. And then, you know, these guys come by and I pass it on. And I get, maybe fifty, sometimes a hundred. Commission.' He said the word commission as though it in some way made things sound the more respectable.

She loved him for being able to tell her all this. He was a petty criminal. He'd been completely honest about his dishonesty. He was a rare exception amongst fathers. He trusted her with his weakness. So she thought: It's a big deal when father tells his little girl that he's on the wrong side of the tracks.

'Know why I take on this sort of work, Lindy?' (It had always been Lindy not Lindsay. She'd reverted to her real name the day she'd enrolled at college.) 'I'll tell you. Because I can't finance the booze for your mother, you know. It's expensive. It's English gin. You wouldn't understand.'

Lindy had told him she understood.

'Trust me?'

'Trust you, Dad.'

'Okay. So this is what I'm going to do.'

He put his arm around her. 'We're going away. We'll tell your mother. We have to leave this town awhile. Okay?'

'Where to, Dad?'

'Madison. I'm going to tell your mother.'

He kept on saying it as if he was trying to gather courage he didn't have.

'Okay, Dad. You tell mother.'

'You won't say anything?'

'No.'

'Promise?'

'Promise.'

He kissed her cheeks and turned out the lights in the bedroom.

That had been the night her mother had taken the gin and the gasoline to the park. It was the same park where her father handed over the stolen goods. Her mother sat down on a bench and poured the gasoline over her clothes.

Then she set fire to it.

She woke cold and with her hair completely wet. She'd sweated it out.

Afterwards she must have fallen asleep. She'd turned the pillow over.

Then she dreamed she was attached to the edge of some high building knowing she could step off the window-ledge to safety. She realised she couldn't move. She stared down, hundreds of feet below, to the streets of a city she didn't recognise and began to scream.

She woke up at one-thirty in the morning desperately wanting Lou back. Where was Kirsty? She must get hold of Lou to tell him she had the files. She must tell him and no one else. Lou had always accepted he might be killed. Maybe a gunshot, a knife blade in and up behind the ribcage. You can count the ways of violent death, he'd said, but you can't choose. She had once told him she had dreamed that they'd both die violently together at the same moment. Then, another time, she had dreamed he was her father. She afterwards regretted having told him that particular dream. But it had frightened her and had slipped out. She didn't pause to think it might hurt Lou to hear it. Anyway, it was a dream about her father as he'd been when her mother died. The gin. The gasoline. The nightmare always began the same way with her father's confession about the petty crimes. Nearly always the dream ended violently. This time it included the newspapers. They'd got it right. 'You can always trust the local papers,' her father used to tell her when he felt the moment right to give her a bit of worldly advice with which to face the future more easily.

'The local papers don't have so much news to handle. So it's harder for them to invent crap. And anyway most people in the neighbourhood'll know whether the stories are true or false for themselves.'

She fell asleep again and at once dreamed again of the newspaper headlines which came to mind like flashes in an old movie: PARK KEEPER'S WIFE SUICIDE INFERNO and WINO MAMA BLAZE DEATH.

She dreamed of the aunt who'd kept the cuttings. It was the first time the family had got its name in the press and the aunt kept the cuttings with the family photographs and the war medals of the brother who'd been killed in the Pacific.

When they found her mother her face had been burned off.

Lindsay had overheard the aunt telling someone the face reminded her of a rat's after the birds had been at it. Only it was dry and cindery. Lindsay had once seen an image like that in the training manual a kid at school had borrowed from her policeman father. It was before her mother's death. The girl said her father kept it along with copies of Kinsey on the top shelf of the bedroom wardrobe. The girls had examined it as if it were a movie magazine. The girl got caught smuggling out the Kinsey volumes and her father had her beaten for it.

She was dreaming vaguely of Kirsty and Mahon when an eerie beating against the windows woke her.

Terrified, she lay still staring at the window. Then she saw the length of wire disconnected from a TV aerial slapping the window. She felt it was taunting her. She couldn't spend the rest of the night in a half-sleep suffering the nightmares or lie awake listening to the beating of the wire against the glass.

She'd telephone the Embassy again.

The duty officer was cool with her: 'We can't give you a guarantee of it reaching him.'

'I'm his wife.'

'I know who you are, Mrs Finucane.'

'You have to believe me – it's important.'

'Okay. You put your phone back down. I'll see if I can't have someone call you. If you haven't heard anything in thirty minutes call me back, okay?'

Squatting on the bed she drew the bedclothes around her. It was very cold. She listened to the rain beating slantways against the bedroom window. She stared at the bedside clock. It said just after three in the morning.

Call back, please, she whispered. This time, when she shivered, it wasn't the nightmare, not the cold, but a fear she couldn't put from her mind no matter how hard she tried.

South from the Finucanes' apartment, across the river, the rain beat against the windows of Century House. The lights shone dimly through the windows from Chayter's office.

'The one thing we've overlooked,' Mehta said, 'is the most obvious. The one none of us dare face. The CIA want the intelligence alliance broken off. They want to go it alone. We're no more than a glorified radio station. We don't even have our own listening satellite launch facility.'

'They'd discuss it with us first.'

'Why should they?'

Chayter had no answer.

His silence prompted Mehta to come up with a new angle:

'They want the upper hand with the renegotiation of the treaty. Once they've got that the way's open to renegotiate the defence agreement altogether.'

'Without reference to NATO?'

'They start with us. They prove the feebleness of the treaty. That it's built on a quicksand, that it's been crippled from way back. Fire off the fact that we've never been trusted anyway. All the way back. Bettaney. Blunt. Philby. Maclean. Burgess. To the atom spies. Right back to *Nightshade*. Either because we could not command loyalty in our Service or because we were too loyal, either way we've never revealed the whole story. It's a system of cheating every secret service employs. But we've been rumbled. So they will use that to break the alliance off. It suits them now. And they can begin by publishing the *Nightshade* file. The thing'll be more poisonous in the hands of the United States Press and TV networks than even if it were already in Moscow.'

'What do you think, Dilip?' Chayter asked with a smile of fury.

'It adds up neatly,' Mehta said, without a trace of apology. 'We don't know where Mahon is.'

'Do you think Henry has found him?'

'Let's hope so. Henry has to stop Mahon now.'

'I wonder. I wonder.'

Chayter spoke to the wall. 'Where are you, Henry?' Without turning he continued: 'Tell me it again, Dilip. Let's see if we can find the missing bits. Just once more. Start at the start.'

Lindsay grabbed the telephone.

She heard the silence. The echoing woman's voice. Her own name.

'Mrs Finucane?'

'Yes.'

'We have received your enquiry. You have no need for concern. Your husband is completing government business. If you could exercise some patience.'

This was the familiar language of the government's approach to the bereaved. What was the voice saying?

'Who are you?'

'My name's Linger. This is not a secure line. You'll appreciate the situation.'

'You don't appreciate it. I need to see my husband.'

'We quite understand your feelings.'

'Do you?'

The appeal in her voice seemed to floor the caller. The voice dropped eerily. 'I'll tell your husband you called.'

'Wait a minute – '

The line was dead. She held the receiver in her hand and listened.

There was a new noise. It was coming from the bathroom.

She replaced the telephone receiver and pulled on her white T-Shirt. She walked slowly and quietly across the carpet in her bare feet.

Beyond the desk, the piles of books and reference cards, she turned to the bathroom door. Behind it she could hear another door beating in its frame like the slow flapping of a giant bird's wing. A dull, even thump muffled by the wind. The rain, like hail, rattled against the windows. Still, there was the beating of the door. She gripped the handle to the bathroom door. Beyond it she could imagine that ill-painted door opposite the bath. The one leading out onto the roof and its muddle of rusted fire escapes and sodden filthy brickwork.

Had she left the door to the roof unlocked? Had someone found a way of opening it from the outside?

She found herself stretching down the T-shirt across the front of her thighs. She shivered and tried to steady her shaking hands.

'Is anyone there?' she heard herself ask. Her first thought seemed to be for the unseen night visitor. 'Can I help you?' The request was ridiculously polite. She bit on her lower lip. Her mouth was dry.

'Whoever you are . . .' with that she found the nerve to open the door.

It was everything she dreaded.

The figure in the darkness. Unidentifiable. Standing still like a corpse. Man or woman? Drenched.

'Lou?'

It wasn't Lou. She saw the hand-gun. Then the other hand reaching quickly for her throat.

Her scream lifted to the wind and rain.

The slam of the door to the roof mingled with the first of her screams.

Dutifully, untangling the knots that were coincidences in the crazy ball of string, Mehta returned to the start of his elaborate speculation. It was a code of deception. The elements of deceit were, as he put it, held at the very edge of the funnel's exit.

'Smith said in Madrid that Wigart had begun what he called his affidavit about *Nightshade*. That he thought the old boy had completed it and *had* dispatched it to London before his death.'

Chayter remained sceptical. 'He didn't use the Embassy.'

'He didn't like the Embassy. He didn't like Smith. Smith didn't like him. So he sent it to us.'

'Through the mail? No. Not Wigart. Not his style.'

'It never got here as far as we know. But suppose it did? Suppose it was intercepted? Suppose it held the missing links in the story of Mahon's father? The links he couldn't find at Nelson. The ones even Hanratty doesn't know? Suppose Wigart wasn't just another sad old victim of some drunken mugger in Madrid – suppose he was murdered, that his death was the result of premeditated murder. It can't be written out.'

Mehta warmed to his theme. It was his own life he seemed to be talking about. 'There's Hackett too. Who was "Freedman"? Why would anyone want to spend an hour with Hackett on his death bed? The man was as good as dead, wasn't he? Drugged to the eyeballs.'

'Coincidence.'

'You think so. The cancer patient fully dosed with heroin to ease the pain. Apparently comatose but finding the odd interval of utter clarity. Diminishing intervals. But moments. You'd only need one to say something even at the very end.'

'You're saying Hackett told the visitor something before he died?'

'I'm saying either that or the opposite. I'm saying there's every possibility he did. Or that his visitor made bloody sure he didn't. And that he dispatched Hackett himself. It's possible. Can't you think of how you'd have done it?'

'How would you have done it, Dilip?'

'The same way as any doctor or sympathetic nurse would do it. Squirt in an overdose. Ease the pain. Forward death. Finish the pain. It's too easy.'

'Much too easy,' Chayter said. 'So easy you'd better get the duty sister out of her bed wherever she is. Now. Find me the name of the Chief Constable of Suffolk. I want him personally to go to the hospital and check every inch of dangerous drugs record. Tonight. And I want the duty sister brought here and Hackett's sister.'

It was only another south London dog barking its head off in the rain.

At first the rain dulled the noise. It was the sort of midnight row you were used to. The neighbours ignored it. Sure enough, before one a.m. they heard it stop. Most of them then fell asleep, relieved. If it hadn't been a night when the old woman was sitting up with the World Service on BBC, well, as she told a journalist next day, 'I'd never have heard the little dear start up again.'

Her abiding love of dogs and her sympathy for the hardships of canine life drew her to put on her dressing-gown and heavy shoes. Over the top she draped her late husband's army mackintosh. Taking the heavy torch her grandchildren had provided for emergencies in the night, she left her house guided on her mercy mission by the unearthly sound.

She rang the doorbell to her next-door neighbour's. She rang and rang. There was no reply.

The garden gate was firmly locked. The rain soaked her feet squelching inside the shoes. She'd half a mind to take her shoes off altogether. But this was a dog-loving neighbourhood and the dogs made the pavements filthy. Even the rain couldn't wipe the pavements clean of their little messes. So she plodded back home, through her own house, and out into the garden to where the weight of the roses had forced down the rotten wooden fence.

The dog howled on without ceasing.

'There, there. Now, now,' she began to intone. 'Come here.' She sucked her teeth forcing friendly squeaks from her lips.

Rose briars tugged at the old beige mackintosh. Struggling through the broken fence, pulling herself free towards the next door lawn, she shone the torch straight at the dog's face. The beam reflected back from its eyes. She knew fear in an animal's eyes.

The dog stiffened at the sight of the old woman plodding towards it.

'Worn out, are we?' the old woman said. 'There now. Everything's all right, isn't it?'

It wasn't. The torch beam picked out the elbow of the body in its shallow grave beneath the ceanothus.

The woman kicked the sodden earth aside. She took off her left shoe and dug. It wasn't long before she'd followed the elbow to the shoulder, the neck to the hair. Stark fear made her lift the head until she could turn it.

Now she realised what she had found. She no longer heard the dog's moaning. She couldn't remember later whether the dog had stopped or whether it hadn't. She didn't even notice the creature beat its retreat and vanish in the night. She shone the torch into the dead eyes. She remembered thinking how strangely they stared back up at her. Full of accusation they seemed to cry 'You're too late.'

'And I never did know her first name,' she told the journalist. 'They always kept themselves to themselves. People do nowadays. Pity, isn't it? If they didn't I think there'd be a lot less of this violence, don't you?'

'You've no idea what Mrs Newiston's first name is?'

'Was,' the old woman corrected him. 'We weren't on first-name terms. That's how things are now, isn't it?'

'What did you do next?'

'I called the police. You could ask them what her first name was. They'd know.'

'They aren't saying anything. What did you do then?'

'I looked around for the dog. It'd gone. Don't know whether it was a hound or a bitch. I went back the way I'd come.' She hed up her scratched forearms. 'That was the roses. I got in a tangle. I was trying to pull myself free when I was sick. I couldn't stop myself being sick. And I'm not a big eater.'

The journalist fell silent. So the old woman added finally, 'Then I made myself a strong cup of tea and stayed up all night. Couldn't sleep, you understand.'

The journalist said he understood. 'What time was all this?'

'It'd have been about three in the morning. Three. I heard the church bells chime. No, come to think of it that may have been on the wireless. I was listening to the World Service.'

She was still talking when the journalist thanked her and left, not a great deal the wiser, to see if the police would break their unusual silence.

Lou Finucane pulled an old trick.

'I'm calling the CIA. The phone? Okay with you, my friends?'

The guards were pleased to find the old guy in a better mood. They tried to accommodate him. One offered him a Budweiser. 'Good,' said Finucane and took a hefty mouthful.

'You want to be alone?' one of the guards asked. 'Your call?'

Finucane had all the time in the world. 'You stay right there. Learn to love your duty and you'll live a longer life.'

The guards laughed with him like he was a nice old father. 'Calling Langley?'

'New York,' said Finucane.

The guard wore a look of appeal: 'Ask who won the fight.'

'Sure,' said Finucane tapping in the digits of any old number in New York. He held his hand over the mouthpiece. 'Is this secure?'

'Sure,' a guard said.

'You have listeners on it?'

'Not on that one. It's fine. You're okay.'

'Good.' Finucane paused. 'Answer me, please,' he said. He waited. Then, 'This is Finucane.'

' . . . '

'How are you, Miss Linger?'

' . . . '

'Good. I want to clear with you that it's okay we go back to have one more look at the apartment.'

' . . . '

'Right, Frithville Gardens address. I want to take Mr Mahon with me.'

' . . . '

'I understand the danger of the situation. I'd advise we take a driver. You give me authority to take a hand-gun. That okay?'

' . . . '

'No. I don't think I'll need a rifle. But if you insist.' He cupped his hand over the telephone. 'Do you have a high-velocity rifle?'

The guard said they had two.

Finucane saw the chief of the guard detail in the doorway. He spoke up a little louder. 'I'm reluctant to go to Frithville Garrens unarmed. Okay, I'll ask the chief of detail.'

He looked into the chief of detail's face with feigned anxiety. 'Can you confirm protection if I go with Mahon to Frithville Gardens?'

The guard gave him a fix-anything-anytime nod of confirmation. 'We'll give you a back-up car.'

Finucane hadn't thought of that one. He didn't want a tail. But he couldn't risk raising the chief of detail's suspicions. The call had gone on long enough anyway. He prayed the man wouldn't ask to speak to Linger himself. He'd ditch that with brief flattery. 'Your people have given first-class co-operation.'

' . . . '

200

'You what?'

' . . . '

'You'll pass that on. Okay, I'll tell them. Thanks for everything. I'll call you directly I have anything further.'

'You want to move?' the chief of detail was asking.

'Now. Yes. I tell you how we'll do it, okay. I want the back-up car left in the street out of view. We'll use radio, okay. I need a hand-gun and a rifle. Miss Linger says we're to take a rifle. I want a hand-gun in case Mahon turns nasty.'

'You need any other people?'

'It's best on my own.'

'I appreciate that,' said the chief of detail ponderously. 'Let's set it up.'

Finucane wasn't quite out of it yet.

'What they tell you about the fight?'

'I forgot to ask. Want me to call back?'

'It's okay,' said the guard. 'You've got other things on your mind.'

He drew the chief of detail on one side. 'I'll brief the drivers outside. I don't want anybody around here knowing what we're doing, understand? We have one last chance to make this thing work. You're with me?'

'Sure.'

Finucane gripped the man's shoulder. 'Thanks. Let's find the weapons.'

' 'S okay. I'll bring them. And Mahon's clothes.'

He went to find Mahon.

'We're leaving,' he said.

'Now?'

'No need for questions. We're going.'

On a sudden impulse Finucane dialled his home number.

The out of order signal disturbed him.

30

To begin with Newiston watched Lindsay, sizing up her fear, slowly closing the narrow door until he'd shut out the wind and driving rain. Then he said quietly, 'Finucane isn't here, is he?'

'Yes,' she lied to him.

'I don't think he is,' Newiston said. 'He's not a man to let you be the one to find the intruder.' He lifted a towel from the rack beside the basin and began to dry his face.

She saw his hands were filthy dirty and his shoes caked with wet soil. He had the appearance of desperation; yet his manner was weirdly calm. 'We're going to have a look around together,' he told her.

'Lou isn't here.'

'That'll make things easier.'

'What is it you want?'

He dropped the towel back onto the rack. 'Turn around. We're going to find the files my wife gave you.'

'I don't know what you're talking about.'

He gave her the friendly look of a policeman admonishing a wayward child. 'I think you do. It's a very serious crime to receive government secrets. You'll be sent to prison for a long time. I've come here to make matters easier for you.'

'Then why didn't you phone before you came here? Why break in?'

'Because it'll be easier *for you* if no one knows I came here. Once you've handed me the files I'll go. You'll be off the hook.'

'You've made a mistake.'

'I have? Oh, no. I don't think so. The mistake's yours. Also my wife's.' He shrugged. 'She told you about her lover and the files he left at her flat. I'm sure you've kept them safely. Now it's only a matter of you handing them to me. That's all. It's simple. And it won't take a moment, will it?'

She thought: If you're bluffing, it's a convincing show.

'I promise you they're not here.'

'I do hope you're wrong,' he said politely. 'I hope you won't make me force you to hand them over.' He glanced quickly at the gun. 'I haven't brought this for my protection.'

'And not for mine either, I guess.'

'That's right, Mrs Finucane. Please don't force me to use it. If the circumstances arise I won't hesitate, I promise you that.'

'I promise you they're not here.'

'I don't want promises. I want facts. The fact of their whereabouts.'

'Then let me use the phone.'

'That's not possible. It's disconnected.'

'It's not.'

'Yes, I'm afraid it is.'

She stared at the telephone on the desk.

'Did you – ?' she asked.

'Yes,' he said. 'I did. We really can't take any risks.'

He smiled. And suddenly he was no longer the policeman but the wayward child. He wasn't bothered to disguise how pleased he was with himself. 'I don't have to tell you I haven't got time to stay here. If there were more time I wouldn't have to consider using force. Time's a luxury neither of us can afford.'

Now she could see the tension in his features. Was it fury he was winding up inside himself? Or restraint?

'My wife valued your friendship,' he said. 'She obviously needed a confidante. There are few wives who can cheat successfully without chatting over the sordid details with somebody or other.'

'I can't help you,' she told him. 'Why not go now? You can use the elevator this time. Go and talk it over with Kirsty. She's the one you should be talking to. Not me.'

She'd known men whose jealousy was so powerful it could induce nausea. She supposed it was his talk about Kirsty that had turned his face so ashen.

'Kirsty is dead.'

She stared at him. There was no feeling in his eyes. No grief in the face. His hands were perfectly steady. He held the hand-gun between finger and thumb raising and lowering it slowly as if he were fanning his face.

'When?'

'This evening.'

'But that's terrible.'

'She was murdered.'

'Who – ? It can't be right. Who would want to murder her?'

'I think you'd better give me the file, Mrs Finucane, don't you?'

'No, no. Listen to me. You tell me Kirsty's dead. Murdered. You come in here. You force your way in demanding files I don't have. How can you be so calm about everything? It's madness.'

Directly she heard herself say it she realised what must have happened. She didn't doubt a word of what he'd told her any longer. He stood there presumably knowing exactly what was racing through her mind, allowing despair and fear to break her down.

She blamed herself for the stupidity of her commitment to Kirsty's trivial affair. If only she had refused to have anything to do with it. She remembered Kirsty's intensity; how there had been no escape from it. She had only sought to help, to offer friendship. She had failed herself and it was like those awful dreams of childhood. She had no control over them. They were like those horrific images in the forensic textbook; the descriptions of her mother's incinerated face. The harder you tried to wipe them from memory the more they returned to haunt you. They had presented themselves like warnings of the hidden threat. Now it stared her in the face. There he stood; gun in hand, staring at her with the eyes of an animal behind bars in a zoo. Only the bars weren't there between them and the animal was standing calmly before the pounce. He had said everything without saying the one thing that she now had to face. Why wasn't he with the police answering their questions? Why hadn't he gone at once to Hal to be with *him* in his grief? Why not at home or some hospital? Why not *anywhere* but here?

The questions pointed to the one appalling conclusion. He was standing there, close enough for her to smell the dampness of his clothes, perfectly calm, holding the hand-gun. He had murdered Kirsty.

She wanted him to leave at once. To hell with the file. He could have it. Take it. Go.

But therein lay the worst horror. Because she had told him the truth: the files weren't there. She'd obeyed the old advice: keep a secret object on the move; never leave it in one place too long. She'd adopted Mahon's trick and been too clever for her own good.

She'd removed them from Lou's safe, parcelled them up and given them to the doorman. The files were in his safe. She remembered his jolly boast about the safe's time-lock. Only he knew the combination. More correctly, he shared the number with the man at the head office of the apartment block's managing agents. But Lindsay had no idea of his name. And the doorman lived in Southend. He didn't turn up for duty until eight o'clock.

'Can we sit down for a while, please?' she asked him. 'Can we talk this thing over? Please? And I'm very cold. I'd like to dress, okay? I don't mind you watching me.' She already felt she was his prisoner. 'If it makes you feel safer . . .' She heard her own voice. It must have sounded like her father's talking to her mother when she was on the edge of an alcoholic blind. It sounded gentle. But it never hid the fear. It was the silence and the calmness which frightened her so much and the sense she was utterly on her own. Where was Lou?

Her back towards him, she dressed slowly. She caught sight of him watching her in the reflection of the window. There was one lie left to tell him. If, she thought, I can tell it like this, with my back to him, I might convince him. Staring at his reflection in the glass, she said: 'Lou has what you want.'

'He has?'

'Yes.'

'Where is he?'

'I don't know.'

She saw him close in on her. He gripped her arm. 'Your husband – ?'

'Yes.'

'I don't believe you.'

'That's your problem.'

The grip tightened painfully. 'Then you'd better speak to him, don't you think? We can wait for him here together.'

With Mahon in the back of the saloon heading south of the river across Waterloo Bridge, Finucane was preoccupied with what he knew was true: Mahon isn't bluffing, he thought. He had possessed the file. He had been Kirsty's lover. There was just an outside chance that Kirsty had moved the file to her house. It would have been a stupid move, but Kirsty had shown a talent for reckless stupidity.

Which was why they were driving through the rain to south London.

There was a problem with the driver. He had his radio turned on. It was open to the apartment in Regent's Park and the Embassy. But neither had called the car. So far they were out of touch. Finucane hoped it would stay that way so he'd be left to get to the Newiston house without interference.

'Straight on,' Mahon told the driver. His voice was flat. If he was scared he wasn't showing it.

Finucane took over the instructions: 'When we reach the end of the street, stop. Give us five minutes. That's all. If we're not back then you call up Regent's Park and the chief of detail.'

'What do I tell him?' the driver asked.

'To get here fast.'

'Left at the traffic lights.'

A burglar alarm wailed from the undertakers at the corner.

The car stopped at the lights. A man wheeled a motor bike across the street in front of them.

The lights changed.

'Take it easy,' Finucane told the driver. He'd seen two policemen sheltering in the door of a betting shop. 'Okay, let's go.'

Mahon chanted the directions. 'Right and right again.' He turned to Finucane. 'And if we find nothing?'

'We think again.'

'Right here,' Mahon told the driver. 'Third on the left.'

It was Finucane who saw the police cars first. 'Slow,' he told the driver.

'The street's blocked off,' the driver said.

The car stopped and the back-up car stopped behind.

'Turn the lights off,' Finucane said.

He looked at Mahon and the two of them got out of the car.

Finucane looked at the driver. 'Tell your friend behind we'll be back in a few minutes. Give us five minutes. Don't move from here. And if we don't come back you know what to do?'

'Yes, sir.'

They walked towards the first of the patrol cars. Finucane looked at the young policeman with polite concern. There was less of the American in his accent now. 'Excuse me,' he began. 'Can you tell us where the nearest filling station is?'

The policeman was a joker: 'You need a drink?'

'We've run out of petrol.'

'You've got a half-mile walk. If they're awake. Where's your car?'

Finucane told him. The policeman gave directions to the nearest petrol station.

'Thanks,' said Finucane. 'What's going on?'

'Someone's found a body in a garden.'

'Not at number twenty-seven?' Finucane asked.

The policeman looked at him and shook his head. 'You know the street?'

'A friend of mine lives at twenty-seven.'

'We've found a woman at forty-three.'

'How dreadful.'

The policeman's reply was lost in the crackle of the radio.

There was no need for Finucane to look at Mahon: they both knew the number of the Newistons' house.

He looked back at the light of the police cars and hurried down the street to his own car.

He saw the driver walking towards him.

'Sir,' the man was saying. 'The Embassy's been calling.'

'What do they want?'

'A message from your wife.'

'*Wife?*'

'Would you contact her, sir, please.'

But hadn't the telephone been out of order?

The penny dropped.

The police driver was going at more than one hundred and ten miles an hour. The ward sister when she queried this was told not to flap.

How could she do otherwise? They were taking her to

London in the middle of the night, and they hadn't even told her why. The woman next to her in the rear had not introduced herself. When she protested to her she hadn't even fed her cat before leaving home, the old lady told her not to fret so much and fell silent.

She tried to sleep but couldn't.

It was just as bad when she was hurried like a criminal through the corridors of the modern building south of the Thames. They wouldn't tell her where she was. She found herself ushered into an office.

A man introduced himself as Chayter. 'Mr Mehta here will ask you some questions.'

She was on the edge of tears, wide-eyed with anxiety.

Mehta spoke to her slowly. He began by asking her to explain what precautions were taken to prevent the theft of pain-killing drugs on the cancer ward.

'We don't have what you call a cancer ward.'

'But on your ward. Morphine?'

It was all done with the greatest care. Instructions were followed scrupulously. The routines were clear-cut.

'But for some periods the cupboard or cupboards where you keep drugs are unsupervised.'

She was very frightened. 'There's always someone on duty. The supervision of such drugs is a very serious matter.'

'Even so, occasionally there's no one in the vicinity of the cupboards. They're allowed to go unwatched?'

'It's perfectly possible they're unwatched sometimes. We're understaffed like everybody else.'

'And perfectly feasible for a nurse to leave a tray of drugs for treatment with syringes and so forth unattended?'

'It could happen.'

It was Chayter's turn.

He handed her a photograph.

'Have you ever seen this man?'

The ward sister looked at the face in the photograph. She tilted her head doubtfully. 'I don't think so.'

'You remember Mr Hackett?'

'Yes, of course.'

'He had a visitor at your hospital on the day he died.'

'I believe he did.'

'You remember his name?'

208

'Not offhand.'

'A Mr Freedman?'

She studied the photograph once more, holding it away from her to reduce the glare of the light.

Chayter handed her two more photographs to inspect. 'Do you think that was the man?'

'His visitor?'

She felt Grochal's eyes watching her.

At length she said, 'He was very pleasant. I do remember.'

'Who do you think he was?'

'I couldn't say. One doesn't ask patients' visitors who they are. They're usually family.'

'Think back.'

'Didn't he say he was an old friend . . .'

'Did he say that?'

'Yes, I think he did. He asked to be left alone with Mr Hackett. That's right. I do believe he said he was an old colleague.'

'Did anything he said strike you as odd?'

'Not as far as I remember. You must know that sometimes visitors to terminally ill patients want to be left alone together. There are so many things, intimate things, which people want to say to each other in the last days. I do remember that he brought a bunch of white roses.'

'But the photographs. The face? Is that the man we know as Freedman?'

'I think that's the man who visited Mr Hackett.'

'You'd be prepared to swear to that?'

She looked around wildly. 'But *why* are you asking me? Do you know him?'

'Yes, we do.'

'Then why are you asking me? Please – tell me. Have I done something wrong?'

'No. On the contrary. Thank you very much. You can go home now. I do apologise for bringing you all this way in the middle of the night.'

'But what is it about?'

It was left to the police to explain about Mr Freedman.

He was, they said, being sought in connection with the murder of his wife and they wanted him to help them with their enquiries.

Until now Eleanor Grochal had behaved with admirable calm. Perhaps she thought they really were going to explain everything to her in greater detail. She already had most of the picture: Freedman, whoever he was, had tampered with the drugs cupboard in the hospital, and he had spent some time alone with Geoffrey shortly before his death. All that she understood. They had allowed her to hear the nurse's story. Now she wanted to know everything.

She felt owed an explanation. 'What happened to Geoffrey?' she asked with a look of reluctance.

Chayter raised his hand for silence. He was watching Mehta on the telephone, scribbling notes. 'The Embassy have told Finucane to go to this address,' Mehta was saying. He handed Chayter the piece of paper on which he'd written the address. 'The Americans have begun to move.'

'I'm going,' Chayter said.

Eleanor Grochal watched him stand up. 'May I know now?' she said.

'Wait,' Chayter told her, the photographs of the man Freedman still in his hand. 'I'm going on my own,' he said to Mehta. 'You talk to Dr Grochal.'

'I am very upset.' Eleanor Grochal said to them.

Chayter was at the door. 'Mr Mehta will explain matters to you.'

Mehta went to the door with him and said something Eleanor Grochal couldn't hear.

Once they were alone, Mehta turned to her: 'Your brother was murdered.'

She flinched and gave out a small moan of pain. It seemed, Mehta said when it was all over, that something inside her had already warned her to hear it. The moan seemed to be an acknowledgement of a truth she'd already perceived.

'Almost certainly by the same man who murdered Richard Wigart.'

'Dickie too?'

'I'm very sorry.'

'You've brought me here to tell me this?'

'Sooner or later you needed to know.'

'I think that's right,' she said, with a note of warning in her voice.

'I understand what you're feeling,' Mehta said.

210

'Do you?' she asked, her eyes full of tears.

Mehta had no reply to offer.

'You see,' she told him. 'Geoffrey's last months, even years, were clouded with despair. He wanted to confide about his past. He was weighed down and, so it seemed to me, the cancer of his body was in some way connected with the cancer of his mind. Do you understand what I am telling you, Mr Mehta?'

Perhaps Mehta did. He said, 'Did you know what was weighing on his mind?'

'No.'

'Is that true, Dr Grochal?'

'Yes, it is. It was to do with the past. And we always said that a secret told to one another was no more a secret. So we agreed we wouldn't talk about our professional pasts. I am sure you will come to sympathise with that view yourself, Mr Mehta.'

'You had no idea Geoffrey's life was in danger?'

'He was already dying, wasn't he? His death was inevitable. The doctors had predicted it. We share that in common with Geoffrey, the inevitability of death. What we don't share is the knowledge of the approximate moment.'

Mehta agreed. He didn't want to prolong the philosophical discussion. 'We have made arrangements for you to stay here tonight.'

'I'd prefer to leave now.'

'I'm afraid that won't be possible, Dr Grochal. Your staying here is in the interests of your own safety.'

'Why?'

'Because if we don't complete matters by the morning your life is in danger. I must ask you to believe me. We can't take the risk. There is far too much at stake.' He offered to help her from the chair. 'Our residential quarters are reasonably pleasant. The night steward will provide you with a hot drink and a toothbrush if you wish.'

He led her, weeping, from the room.

The duty steward was waiting outside in the corridor.

'Mr Mehta, the Director wants you to go with him after all.'

'Take charge of Dr Grochal.'

'Don't worry about me,' said Eleanor Grochal.

But Mehta was already hurrying down the corridor.

31

Sooner or later, Lindsay thought, he'll kill me.

Her efforts to get him talking had so far met with little success.

She watched him pace from window to window to peer out across the rooftops and sometimes down to the deserted streets. Then he'd turn sharply to foil any move she might be planning to make against him. Satisfied she didn't seem to present a threat he'd give her a look that said *be a good girl*.

She wondered whether to talk to him about Mahon. She supposed he had tried and failed to find him. She decided against mentioning him. She could see he was fighting to keep control of himself. Yet it was impossible for her to tell how close he might be to breaking down. She tried to read his mannerisms: clicking in his mouth, sucking of the dry lips, the nervous sniffing. Above all she tried not to let her own fear show. She thought it best to keep him calm by offering commiseration instead of challenge.

'What'll you do when all this is finished?' she asked him.

His reply surprised her: 'Feel sure I've done the right thing. When you know you've been true to yourself you can achieve anything. The main thing is to act correctly.'

'You'll begin your life again?'

He began an absent-minded search amongst the books on the desk and read out the author's names: 'Ford Maddox Ford. Elizabeth Bowen. James Hanley. James Hadley Chase. Angela Carter. Alan Ross. A.L. Barker. Aubrey Menen.'

He lifted up one of the books and let it drop to the floor:

'And Saul Bellow. What a strange collection you have made.'

She wanted to divert his attention: 'All we do is make collections for other people.'

'Can't they do it for themselves?' he asked sharply.

'We make it easier for them.'

'Anything,' he observed oddly, 'for an easy life.'

'And yours,' she said, softly. 'Will it be easier now?'

'No reason why not, don't you feel? We'll see. It's always a good thing to clear the air, wipe the slate clean. I am sure you know what I mean. A good feeling.'

'I understand,' Lindsay said, realising she did not. 'I mean, it must be hard to bear the remorse.'

'About my wife?'

'Yes.'

'I've always worked on the principle that there are some human beings who are destined to be victims. People bring things upon themselves, most especially the disloyal.'

'Do you really believe in that?'

He turned his back on her for a while and she couldn't see his reaction. She desperately wanted to keep him talking, to steer him away from whatever inner hell his mind had entered. His mood struck her as akin to the potential suicide's. She imagined he had probably considered his life as some twisting path leading inevitably to destruction. If he felt his own destruction was imminent then he'd see to it that others paid the price for it. And she felt certain she too was just one other on the list of victims he'd drawn up.

They both heard the sound of the car pull up in the street below.

'Don't move,' he told her.

He stared out of the window.

She could see his hands shaking violently. When he turned away from the window he said wildly: 'Two bloody laughing nurses. Not your husband.'

He looked at his watch.

'What's the time?' she asked.

'Time he came home.'

'He'll come. If he doesn't we'll find another way of getting what we want.'

The suggestion appeared to convince him she might even be persuaded to enter into his conspiracy.

He leaned against the wall staring at her. 'You should understand I'm not engaged in this solely for my own sake. Other people are involved as well, you know.'

He sounded to her like the convicted criminal grasping for any straw that would show the world he was an innocent victim. He was skulking like the paranoiac spy he was in the hostile world of his own invention. He was trapped by imaginings that offered him no respite from fear.

'I understand you,' she said, suddenly.

'That isn't difficult. Can you imagine what it's like to have a father of whom people say "That man was a murderer"? Do you know what that's like?'

'I don't know. I can only imagine.'

'My father was a loyal man. Like all of his generation he was misunderstood. Like history is misunderstood. All we can be sure of are the family patterns. Do you know why? Because they do repeat themselves. I wonder if you understand that?'

'Maybe.'

'Then let me tell you about our friend, Mahon. Some people would say he can't be blamed for following the pattern of his father's treachery. "Blood will out." There are plenty of people who'll subscribe to that one.'

'Do you?'

'Yes. In so far as I'm protecting my father's reputation.'

'And your own too?'

'My own too. Very much so.'

'So why do you hate Mahon so much?'

'Hate may be too strong a word. One can't blame him for trying to find out how and why his father died. I've always thought the death of one's father is as great a matter of interest as his life. More so if there are people sworn not to reveal the reasons for death. There again I've always thought those secrets attached to men's deaths are as many and often as potent as those attached to their lives.'

'Is that true of Mahon's father?'

'Judge for yourself. He was an idealist. The Service can't have room for idealists of any kind. We're servants. You don't employ servants on account of their ideals. They destroy the families they work for. Mahon's father had to go because he was about to betray the scheme of things for the free world. It wasn't murder.'

'Then what was it?'

'A despatch. My father *despatched* Mahon's father. He rendered service to his country. The secret's safe. Now that

Wigart and Hackett have gone too I'm the only one left alive who knows it.'

Apart from me, Lindsay thought, with savage regret. And I wish I didn't know. If she had read his mind rightly he wasn't asking her to join his paranoid conspiracy to keep the silence. Instead, he'd as much as told her, however indirectly, it would be necessary for him to kill her; and that she'd have to accept it. The only vestiges of sanity he had left were moving him to explain why he had to kill her.

In telling her, he had trapped himself into the single course of action left to him. Lou had once said how hard it is to think yourself into the mind of the murderer during those last moments before he commits the act. No one had ever told her quite how appalling is the sense of hopelessness the victim faces. Untrue, she thought, that the will to live is the strongest force of all. It's a lie. What they don't tell you is the seeping resignation that overtakes you when faced with the killer who's half sane. If only he were completely mad, she thought, I could appeal to some corner of his manic irrationality. It was the moments of his dreadful sanity that scared her.

'You'll have the files you want,' she told him. 'Be patient. They'll come. You see.'

'I know,' he said. 'It's all worked out.'

She was too scared to draw him any further. She no longer wanted to learn what it was he'd worked out. She only wanted Lou to come. At least, she felt, looking at Newiston by the window, we have that in common. She told herself to wait, resigned, and wondered if it was true what people said about drowning, that you saw the whole of your life in the last few seconds. Would it all come rushing back as a nightmare or something else?

Chayter took the shortest route to Kensington and parked a minute's walk from the Finucanes' mansion block apartment.

'I think I should come with you,' Mehta said.

'No. You wait here. Give me ten minutes from when I go. Ten minutes. Do not call the police unless I'm not back by then. If you do have to, then make sure they send plain clothes people. No fuss at all. No noise. Tell them to report to you personally. You take them to the address and stay with them. Ten minutes.'

Mehta watched his chief walk away in the rain until he was out of sight.

He settled down to check the car's radio-phone, to watch the bright green lights of the car clock ticking away and the rain coursing down the windscreen.

Ten minutes seemed to be passing unnaturally fast.

Finucane had a longer journey through the rain to Kensington.

He rehearsed his options:

'There are several ways of going in. The elevator up through the six floors. The stairs also through the six floors around the elevator. The fire-escape outside through the centre well of the building. You reach it through a small alley in Thackeray Street. The gate's kept unlocked. It has to be in case of emergency. It takes you up to the roof. There's a door to my place from the bathroom out onto the roof. It has a small lock. You could kick it down. But it'd create a noise. As to the rest of the geography there's a newer block across the street in Ansdell Street. You can't get access inside the building without waking the caretaker. But you can use the fire-escape at the back. On the roof you have a clear sight of my place and the roof.'

'What happens if they take the lift or the interior stairs out? Neither of us will get to them.'

'I know. We'll go up together. All I want is for Newiston to know he can't move out.'

'We still can't tell him where the files are. We don't know.'

'I'm telling him I do know.'

'But you don't.'

'He'll go along with me if I say he has to come out with Lindsay if I'm to take him to them.'

'You're completely sure she hasn't got them in your flat?'

'No. I don't know what she'll have done with them.'

'What do you think she'll have done with them?'

'Moved them about. She was trained to hide things. The best way of learning how to find anything is first of all to learn how to hide it. That goes for people as well as things. Didn't anyone ever tell you that?'

'No.'

'You're learning, Mahon.'

Finucane parked the car outside a convent in Kensington Square.

A dim blue light filtered through a stained-glass window. The nuns were at early prayers in the warm and dry.

'How long do we give it?' Mahon asked, stepping out into the driving rain.

'As long as it takes.'

They walked together to the corner of Ansdell Street. Finucane, holding the rifle under his coat, looked up.

There were lights on in his apartment.

The few small shops to their left on Thackeray Street were mostly in darkness. They passed the hairdresser's, an art gallery with a painting of a bunch of white tulips in the window, the Italian restaurant on the corner. Beyond that was the entrance to the mansion block.

They peered through the entrance doors across the dimly lit hall. At the far end of the hall was the lift and to one side the start of the carpeted stairs.

'He may be ready for me,' Finucane said. He unlocked the door. 'We say nothing when we get to the door. We'll go to the fifth floor by elevator. Then we'll activate it so it goes on up. Empty. He'll think we're using it. He may come out. We'll be on the stairs.'

Mahon followed Finucane across the hall. He saw him opening a box of switches. Then he saw, on the carpet in front of the lift, the signs that someone had very recently been there before them. There were wet patches where someone's shoes had brought in rain. He caught Finucane's attention. Finucane understood. He shrugged and then turned off the switches in the box.

They walked on through the darkness. Mayon took out his hand-gun, clicked back the safety-catch. The lift was on its way down. Its doors opened and they got in. Finucane pressed the button marked 5.

The lift climbed slowly.

At the fifth floor its doors slid open. Then shut.

They stood listening in the darkness.

The voices were distant but audible. Two men's voices. On edge. Trying and failing to keep the whispers low.

'It's Finucane I want to see.'

They recognised Newiston's voice.

217

'Put it away.'

That was Chayter.

It could have been 'Come in', or 'Come on', Newiston said.

What followed struck Mahon as vintage Chayter. *Always think yourself into the other man's shoes.* Conciliatory to the last. Let's hear you talk yourself out of this one, Mahon heard a voice telling him in his head.

A door slammed shut.

There was no more sound.

Finucane drew Mahon deeper into the darkness. His voice was scarcely audible:

'I'm going up onto the roof opposite. I want you to drive them out on to the roof of my place. Give me three minutes. Either way they have to come out. Either this way. Or onto the roof.'

'I follow you,' Mahon said.

He heard Finucane's feet racing down the stairs and started to count away the seconds.

32

'I couldn't be more pleased to see you,' Newiston told Chayter.

He stared at Lindsay.

'She's guilty as well.'

Chayter looked dumbfounded. He pointed at Newiston's hand-gun. 'I don't think there's any need for that, Henry. It's all over.'

'Over?' Newiston frowned. 'It's just beginning.'

'I understand what you've been through, Henry. Now it's all over. The crisis has passed.'

'We must resolve it,' Newiston insisted. He was wide-eyed. His hands were shaking.

'The best way is for you to let me take you home.'

'Why?'

'We can't spend the night here.'

Newiston stared back at Lindsay. 'She has the files.'

'We can talk it all over later, Henry.'

'No. No. I insist. For the sake of everyone concerned that here and now the files be handed over. Then the whole thing can be finished with.'

'Not quite. We've already lost Wigart, Hackett and your wife.'

'Yes. But you of all people know why.'

'Perhaps I understand.'

'I don't know that you do.'

The sweat was pouring down Newiston's face.

Lindsay interrupted. 'You've been very considerate to me, Henry.'

Her remark enraged Newiston. He was shouting: 'Put your hands on your heads. Walk away. Go on.' He reinforced his instructions with waves of his gun. 'Keep your distances between you.'

'Why not put it away,' said Chayter with an air of great disappointment. 'The police will be here in a few minutes.'

'Not unless you decide to do something childish.'

'Like what?'

'Calling them here.'

'But Dilip's outside.'

'Then call him in.'

'How do you suggest we do that?'

'It's up to you.'

'He's in a radio-car.'

'Then for God's sake bring him in.'

'No. I've already told him to call the police if I'm not down there with him again within ten minutes. You've already lost more than five minutes, Henry, waving that gun about. It isn't like you at all.'

It was Chayter's turn to keep up the chatter and he was taking it on as best he could.

God alone knows, Lindsay thought, from where he dredges up this comforting tone. At any minute she expected him to say: *'There's a good boy. Give it to Daddy.'* She didn't mind what he was saying or how he said it. She was overcome with relief that he'd turned up.

'You don't think I'm being unreasonable, do you?' Newiston said.

'Oh, I wouldn't say that. But put yourself in my shoes. One of my oldest friends has done away with Dickie and Geoffrey too. The old brigade wouldn't have harmed a fly. There's another point of view, I suppose, the kinder hypothesis. Namely, that you put old Geoffrey out of his pain and suffering. Yet, it was his right to arrange his own time of departure. Same for Dickie. Same for Kirsty. Same for all of us, Henry, wouldn't you say, when it comes to it? But there are mitigating circumstances. There always are.'

'I don't know what the hell you're talking about. This is a matter for congratulation.'

'You're none too well, Henry. It can be resolved.'

'Keep moving. Out through the bathroom.'

'Do let's talk it over first.'

'You're not interested in the complete picture.'

'You owe it to yourself to paint it for me. To all of us for that

220

matter. Wouldn't you say there's been enough pain? Don't put yourself down by making matters worse.'

Lindsay was aware of Chayter's unusual courage. He wasn't to be diverted from this interminable blather even facing the snout of the gun. He has balls, she found herself laughing to herself in the euphoria of relief. He was slowly wearing his man down with the outpouring. Any second she expected Newiston to give in, break down. She prayed he would.

'Geoffrey aside,' Chayter continued, 'there's the equally sad case of Dickie. I didn't carry a flame for the old queen. But he had a right to a better end, Henry. What was he – *mugged*. We're wondering. The pantomime police in Madrid think that's what happened. But I wonder. I do *wonder*, Henry. The wimp Smith. Bald, short-sighted, too fat and a member of MCC he may be. But he's a suspicious little sod. Quite right. We're paid to be suspicious. Some of us have sent a few people to early unmarked graves, haven't we? Men and women we've never even met. Faceless friends. No more than ciphers on the main-frame. You can tap in a killing on the keys of the computer, Henry. Few of us are so old-fashioned as to start waving guns about like those cultured young men who flash their willies in Kensington Park Gardens.'

The gun stabbed the air. 'Keep moving.'

'Not quite so fast,' said Chayter as though talking to a masseuse who was getting too enthusiastic. 'You know something terrible's happened to Kirsty. We do know, Henry.'

'Then do as I bloody say.'

'And Hal? What about Hal? With his whole life ahead of him. Think about Hal. Not much future for this country, is there? But it's his future. You can mortgage your own with this insanity of yours. But you mustn't mortgage his.' He lowered his voice. 'Give it some thought, Henry.' He seemed to have found a mark. 'Before it's too late. There's always a way out of anything. There is for you, believe me.'

Though for the life of me, Lindsay thought, I don't see it.

How long could Chayter keep it up for?

Newiston provided the answer: he wasn't giving his victims any more time. He slipped back into the earlier calm of mind and issued his instructions with the cool of a big-game poacher, mechanically. He stared at Chayter:

'On the usual ten-minute siege interval, stage one of

bringing me in on rod and line.' He seemed to be chanting what he thought must be running through Chayter's mind. 'That leaves us three minutes. Shall we allow an extra two for Dilip's naturally cautious inclination? Then there's the time it'll take for the police to get here. Shall we say ten minutes.' He sounded like an auctioneer fighting to raise the bidding. 'Shall we say fifteen?' He jabbed the gun at Lindsay. 'Open the door to the bathroom. And out on the roof. There's been enough talking now. Out you go.'

Lindsay edged backwards into the bathroom and reached down for the handle of the door to the roof.

'Hurry.'

She felt Chayter's hand on hers holding it tight and preventing her from turning the handle. She could feel the cold sweat on his palm. 'We can forget all this, Henry. What matters for us all is the future. The only benefit our world really has over any other is that we can destroy the historical record. None of this happened. You can walk out of here a free man. A period of rehabilitation. Pick up the pieces. There's precedent for all that. You know the record can be disposed of with the flick of a finger.'

Henry paused a moment, his eyes on Chayter. 'Nice try. Get that fucking door open.'

Chayter released his grip on Lindsay's hand.

'Move out,' Newiston said. 'Hands in sight.'

Chayter moved closer to Lindsay. 'I am sorry about this,' he said. Then he turned to Newiston and said, 'All right, Henry. You've won.'

Mahon stumbled over a polythene rubbish bag in the corridor and began to insert the keys to the flat. Metal scraped metal. The keys didn't fit. He imagined Finucane must have handed him the wrong set. The front door key fitted, he reassured himself. Why not these? He tried again until he realised what had happened. Other keys had been inserted in the locks from the other side. They'd been slightly turned. It was enough to prevent anyone from getting in unless you kicked the door down. He felt around the door-frame. It had been built to last. You'd need a massive sledge-hammer to get anywhere at all and probably a crow-bar too. For a few seconds he stood and listened and heard only the silence of the mansion block asleep, a humming in unseen wires and the thumping of his own blood in his head somewhere behind his ears. He cursed Finucane for not having considered how easy it was to paralyse the lock and door.

Peering into the darkness he saw the faintest glimmers of light from the mechanisms of the lift. There was no other light. He felt for the polythene bag with his foot, stepped over it and walked like a blind man with his arms outstretched along the last of the corridor. After a few long yards his free hand touched a door. At first he thought it was a cupboard. When he reached up his hands touched a curtain. Lifting it aside he saw the frosted glass and through it the lighter grey of the dawn sky, yellowish and acid. He followed the edge of the door down and found the handle. He pushed it, jerked it until finally it began to move and gave way sliding free.

He edged out, screwing up his eyes against the slanting rain.

Water poured off the roof cascading down to hit the ground far below his feet. He left the escape door open and walked onto the steel walkway.

Ahead the short flight of steps climbed to the roof-top and the sky. Making his way up them he removed the safety-catch from his hand-gun. He peered through the rain for sight of the door that led into the Finucanes' flat. Praying his luck would be in, that it might, like the escape door, be unlocked, he edged on. His prayers ended abruptly with the sight of the three figures across the roof. One had his back to him. The other two had their hands on their heads. The two figures facing him were walking backwards very slowly towards the low parapet of the roof.

Beyond that was the death-drop to the street below.

From his vantage point on the roof across the street Finucane also saw the three figures through the rain. He moved from the broad disused chimney stack. A broken wall-fitting tore his coat. A few more steps sideways and he was at the edge of the brick-housing of the water tanks.

From here he could see the two figures with their hands on their heads moving steadily across the roof to the low parapet. They continued to walk backwards slowly and towards him. There was a third figure which he could make out less clearly.

He guessed it was Newiston and realised he had calculated wrong.

He'd reckoned Newiston would stay inside and respond to Mahon.

He cursed Mahon for taking so long to get into the flat. He had keys. He had a gun. What the hell was delaying him now? Or had Newiston already gunned him down? He cursed the Englishman's caution. He must have tried to talk the bastard out of it. Who the hell was it with Lindsay?

Rain streamed across Newiston's face. He held the gun in both hands with his arms stretched out in front of him. He pointed it now at Lindsay now at Chayter. 'Keep on moving back.'

They did as he told them. The fact they were nearing the very edge of the roof with nothing between them and the street below was inescapably obvious. All that was in question was who he'd kill first. The gun was mostly aimed at Chayter.

'There is a little time left,' Newiston shouted above the wind. 'You know what I need. Finucane doesn't have them. Where are they?'

His shouting lacked conviction.

Lindsay heard Chayter saying, 'Tell him. It doesn't matter. Go on.'

'The caretaker has them.'

'Where?'

'In his office safe. It's time-locked. He's the only person who can open it. He'll be here at eight.'

'You hear that, Henry. Eight. Plenty of time. I'll see to the police. You can have them.' His voice was as clipped as Newiston's had been before. 'There's nothing that can't be negotiated. You know that. Nothing we can't cover up. God knows you of all people realise that. Put the gun away. Let's go inside.'

If Newiston heard it he wasn't giving a reply. It was easy for Lindsay to imagine what would happen next. She could amost physically feel the space behind her, the darkness, the vertical drop beyond. Or the sudden searing thud of the gun's rounds breaking open her head, her own death stare, the black and white pictures of the savaged corpses in the forensic textbook, only now the morbid portraits showed her face and not her mother's.

224

She was wishing he'd finish it when she realised that Chayter's last throw had been the saving of his own life. It seemed impossible there could be a further dimension to the horror. Yet here was the Englishman, bargaining for *his* life. He was the one who could offer Newiston immunity to save his skin, not hers. She was dispensable. It was Chayter who wanted Newiston alive. It didn't matter what happened to her. It'd turn out to have been just one of those accidents. The broken body smashed by the last fall from the roof. The post-mortem falsified with perfect British manners. Her post-mortem. *Whilst the balance of mind was disturbed.* Chayter had got what he wanted. She'd told him where the files were. Now he had Newiston where he wanted him. And she was the only one left with the full story of Newiston's sad little secret. Dispose of her and the end was simple. Looking quickly at Chayter she saw the triumph on his face.

As though to confirm her fear, Newiston shouted, 'And the woman?'

'Does it matter?' Chayter's indifference was less startling for being so predictable.

Newiston waved at Chayter to move aside. Lindsay started to follow him. She took two steps.

'Not you!' Newiston screamed at her. 'Move back. Go on. Back! It'll be easiest for all of us.'

Lindsay stared at Chayter; he looked through her – for him she was already dead.

The range shortened for Mahon.

For Finucane, his wife had moved the crucial distance he needed and given him the chance. There was no more need to wait. He had the shape of Newiston's face in his sights and he squeezed the trigger.

Mahon fixed his aim high on Newiston's back. He also fired.

One after the other, with only a fraction of an interval, the rounds slammed into Newiston. His body jerked backwards, a little upwards, then sideways. The flesh ripped from his face splashed Chayter in the eyes.

Lindsay saw Newiston's grotesque contortions. She saw him collapsing slowly. Chayter had thrown himself to the ground.

She thought the nightmare had ended when Newiston's gun

fired crazily. The round must have struck something metallic. Or so it sounded for it seemed to raise a never-ending whine on the wind across the roof-tops. Only afterwards, when the silence returned, did she turn around to where she had heard something like a crack from across the street. She felt Chayter beside her. He too was staring at the sky and then at the house opposite. But there was no one there.

It was Chayter's extraordinary courtesy she remembered next. 'Good morning, Mahon,' he said with the dreary good manners of an airline steward. 'Welcome aboard.'

She wanted to scream. Yet no sound would come.

They were groping around Newiston's corpse.

She saw that they had found his hand-gun. It looked now almost like the plaything of a child. The she heard her own screaming begin. It was the disembodied wailing of an animal inside her howling and moaning to be set free. 'No! No!'

She saw Chayter shaking his head. 'You've nothing to worry about now,' he said in that same foul and courteous voice.

Again, with that odd little gift of foreknowledge, the intuitive sense for what might follow next, she heard Chayter mimicking Newiston with the voice of the auctioneer: ' "*Shall we say ten minutes? Shall we say fifteen?*" ' Then, anger sweeping inside the shabby humour, he spat out: 'Why do the police always take so long to arrive?'

She also recalled much later that Lou had once said Chayter had a reputation as a mimic. It was one of those false talents, borrowed, cheap and cruel. 'Show me a mimic and I'll show you someone whose feeling is gained at the expense of others,' Lou had said.

She wanted to remind him of his own base bargaining, to scream at him, to make him show some sign of feeling for the tawdry little secret kingdom that he ruled. Instead, she felt her body shaking and found herself unable to utter a word. He was putting Newiston's gun inside his coat. The wailing of the police sirens in the distance was distorted by the wind.

Chayter was saying:

'They never bloody learn when they do arrive. Why can't the bastards resist making that bloody awful row?' He turned to Mahon. 'Who was it over there?'

If Mahon heard the question he appeared to be feigning deafness. Or perhaps he didn't want to say. Perhaps he thought, in the present circumstances, the question was extraordinarily irrelevant.

'As far as we're concerned,' Chayter said to her, 'nothing happened.'

Now she discovered her voice. 'Are you talking to me?'

'It's always the best way,' he said, casually.

She watched him walking away across the roof space with Mahon, discussing the way to deal with the police. They were silhouetted in the light of the bathroom door that led out to the roof.

She began to follow them inside until she saw the figure with the rifle coming through the escape door and realised who had been across on the other roof. Only then did she begin to weep and Lou cradling her did nothing to stop the flood of tears.

33

In the afternoon at Century House, Chayter began by telling his Executive: 'Our friends have made it perfectly clear they wouldn't wish to have an inquiry. On reflection, it's a gesture of hope. The oddest things in life can create a reconciliation. One oughtn't to discount untimely death as a factor in such things. One can't put a dead man on trial for murder.' The certainties tripped off his tongue.

'Which "*friends*" are you referring to specifically, Director?' asked Mehta, his voice heavy with an irony he might have hoped would seem like innocence.

'In Washington.'

'Ah, friends,' Mehta said. 'That's reassuring.'

'And really – absolutely no inquiry?' Boden-Smith asked.

'It was decided nothing could be achieved by holding one,' Chayter told her, leaning back in his chair as though his own satisfaction had exhausted him. 'Like any other institution the Foreign Service isn't entirely unfamiliar with the necessity of occasionally being open about suicide. The circumstances were, to say the least, unusual. But then circumstances are, by definition, unusual. Some things will have to change. For one, a new Appointments Board will have to be convened for the post of Deputy Director. But our Cabinet friend sees no reason to change the procedures. I may decide to do a little transplanting in Archive Records. That only affects Hanratty. One can always find a niche for the likes of Hanratty. It's time he had a change. I doubt he'll complain too much.'

'And,' asked Dilip Mehta, 'Mahon?'

'A written warning,' Chayter announced. 'A failure to observe the rules of access to Archive Records. He'll take Newiston's desk over. I don't think one ought to forget that he was instrumental in saving my life. It'd hardly be appropriate for me to point out exactly whose life he was instrumental in saving. There is the almost harder issue of what remains of the Newiston household; namely the son, Hal. The Etonian.'

'Does he know what's happened?' Boden-Smith chimed in, maternally.

'I told him,' Chayter said, abruptly. 'He took it remarkably well. Then I suppose with his background he would. I've always thought Etonians were better at dealing with bad news than good. If you're provided with the chance of starting at the top the only way open to you is down.'

'You told him everything?' Boden-Smith asked.

'Not quite everything. I thought it more sensitive to put the official record of his mother's death to him. *Person or Persons Unknown* covers a multitude of sins. There's no reason for the police to pursue the matter other than to satisfy the record. But I suppose the record's never satisfied. No one has fitted Henry's father into the puzzle entirely. And I do wonder whether poor old Geoffrey was burdened with suspicion, or did he know everything.' He paused for a moment before drawing his own conclusion. 'I'd go for his having been suspicious. Otherwise he'd have come straight out with it all. He knew he was dying. What had he to lose except to start the whole thing off.'

Mehta was not so sure. 'Newiston murdered Dickie. That was the real start.'

'Except it might have rested there had Geoffrey kept his own counsel.'

Mehta hadn't finished. 'Do we keep our own counsel as far as Finucane's concerned?'

'That's better left to Washington,' Chayter said. 'I don't foresee any great necessity for them to prosecute him, do you? As a matter of fact, I've told them I hope they won't. If it hadn't been for him I wouldn't be here now. They've asked for the files to be destroyed. I've seen to that myself. There's no further record. Put it another way, the record's been wiped clean.' He paused. 'You're at liberty to disagree with me.'

Presumably with their minds fixed on the next rounds of the Appointment Board's interviews, both Dilip Mehta and Linda Boden-Smith stayed silent.

It was left to Chayter to announce the final irony:

'I don't want objections to Newiston's memorial service.

That'll take place not because I have requested it but because the son has particularly asked for one. It'd be heartless to turn down the request.'

'You'll give the address?' Mehta asked.

'No. Hal Newiston has asked for someone else to give it. Someone who, as it were, goes as far back as his father did.'

'There are none of the old school left,' said Boden-Smith.

'Except Mahon.'

'You can't ask him,' said Mehta.

'I haven't asked him. The son has asked for him to say something. And I don't envy him the task, do you?'

34

The bomb, a week later, that shattered the windows of Selfridges, tore apart the offices of British Airways and American Express and led to the police closing off Oxford Street, also indirectly held up the start of the memorial service. It meant that the thin turn-out could be blamed, like so many things that spring, on Qadhafi's Libya in particular or terrorism in general.

The congregation seated itself throughout the church in St Margaret's Street. The hymn 'There is a green hill far away/ Beyond a city wall' was the more poignant for its not being sung at all. The congregation mouthed the words and watched Mahon walk up the aisle to the front of the church. The notes of the organ echoed and died. The priest was the only person to say *Amen*. Even this effort was smothered by the scream of police sirens from Portland Square.

Mahon hesitated a long time before he spoke. He seemed to be looking into the faces of every single person facing him.

He focused on the boy in the front seat, seated next to his Eton housemaster. The face that stared at Mahon was Kirsty's. Its mouth was fixed in that sad smile. But he was sitting up straight like his father used to; not with Kirsty's easy sprawl. His eyes looked back at Mahon's. They were open very wide. The wife of his housemaster was sobbing.

A few seats behind them sat Boden-Smith. She was wearing a black hat like an upturned flower-pot with a veil across her face.

Further down the church, next to his wife in a sari, sat Dilip Mehta. His hands clutched the hymn book to his chest.

Then, at the far end of the church, on the left, near the door, sat Chayter with his wife. Here the congregation was oddly large. Were there one or two dozen plain clothes men protecting the Director and his wife? It was hard to tell. There were still more of them in the shadows.

And at the end, on the other side, sat Lou and Lindsay Finucane.

'His mind of man, a secret makes,' Mahon began. 'I meet him with a start – He carries a circumference – In which I have no part.' He must have learned his short address by heart. He consulted no notes. 'Those who we remember this morning did indeed have what Emily Dickinson called circumference. For theirs was a circle we all embrace. And their circle embraced us too. Their lives, as we, their friends, know as well, were of course devoted to a way of life which few are invited to understand. It isn't those issues we are here to consider. Rather, we celebrate a future and that belongs to Hal Newiston.' He was staring down into Kirsty's eyes. 'Your gift is the knowledge of them. Our gift is the knowledge that with the help of friends you'll make your own way. But it's a way with no signposts. But when the street seems empty you can be sure there are friends who'll take your hand.'

He could see the knuckles, the finger nails digging into the boy's pale skin and the eyes staring up at him unblinking. He had nothing else to say so he walked back down the aisle. The leather of his new shoes creaked.

'The final hymn,' the priest boomed out. 'For Those in Peril on the Sea.'

The Finucanes found it an odd choice. Hard to think what the congregation had to do with the ocean now that Britannia no longer ruled it anyway.

Yet the decline of two offers from Chayter outside the church a short while later wasn't, come to think of it, odd at all.

Lou and Lindsay Finucane were with Chayter. They heard him thank Mahon for 'your appropriate words, and add, with a reverential tone, that Mahon had been recommended for the Order of the British Empire; and Mahon, there and then, actually turned it down. 'Think about it,' Chayter said. 'You'll come round to it.'

The Director turned to Hal and put his hand on the boy's shoulder. 'And, Hal, you know there's always a place for you with us. The open door.'

The young face stared across the street. Then he looked

straight into Chayter's eyes: 'Thanks a lot,' he said. 'But it's not my scene.'

Lindsay Finucane caught the look of recognition in Mahon's eyes.

Neither needed to tell the other that the boy's voice was identical to his mother's.

All the Director could add was what he'd said a few minutes before:

'Think about it. You'll come round to it.'

Hal gave his father's smile.

'I have,' he said. 'And, thanks all the same, the answer's no.'